TORN

J.A. OWENBY

Mama didn't want me. She reminded me of this on a consistent basis while growing up. And as hard as I tried, nothing would change her mind. Finally, I had to make a choice: her or me.

My heels clicked against the cold tile floor of the hospital and my heart fluttered as I searched the room numbers.

I rubbed my clammy hands against my jeans and spotted the ladies' restroom. Hurrying toward it and needing a minute before reaching her room. I pushed the door open and scanned the bathroom for anyone else. It was empty.

My purse landed with a thud on the bathroom counter. The twist of the faucet squeaked loudly as I turned the cold water on, splashed it on my cheeks, and wiped my face with a paper towel.

"Breathe," I muttered. "She can't hurt you anymore. You're grown."

My pep talk wasn't working. Fear was gnawing at my stomach.

I reached into my bag, grabbed my powder compact, and touched up my makeup. My green eyes shone brighter against the redness left from my tears. I ran a brush through my long, blond hair and dabbed a hint of gloss on my lips, more out of habit than need.

"Let's do this, Lacey. Suck it up," I said, talking to my reflection.

My chest tightened and then I released a slow, deep breath, heading out of the restroom and down the hall toward the ICU.

My hand trembled as I approached her room and reached for the door handle, having no idea what to expect. What would it be like, seeing her after all this time?

The door opened and closed behind me without a sound. I pulled the curtain aside and tried to comprehend what was in front of me.

The room was silent except for the rhythmic *whoosh* of the breathing machine. The ventilator had left its mark on Mama's face, and her upper lip was swollen and bruised.

As I pulled the chair closer to her and sat down, I half-expected her eyes to flutter open and her lips to whisper what a bitch I was. But she lay still.

My goodbyes had been said years ago, but this was different; this was final. There were no more second chances, or third. None, ever again.

I stood up and paced around the tiny room. I should have been holding her hand and begging her to wake up so we could forgive each other, but I couldn't. It didn't matter how many years we'd been apart—every time I thought about her I remembered how she had cost me everything. And not once did she ever utter the words *I'm sorry*. In her mind, it had all been my fault.

I leaned against the wall and tucked a piece of hair behind my ear. In spite of my resistance, tears pooled in my eyes.

"Are you happy now?" My voice quivered and only the sound of the ventilator responded to my question.

It amazed me how I could love her and hate her at the same time. I knew I was supposed to love and honor my parents, but how could I when she had almost cost me my life?

My mind raced with dark memories and then I realized that for the first time in my life I was minutes away from being free. Relief washed over me as the tears flowed down my cheeks. I pushed the memories away. With freedom just around the corner, I needed to say what I felt even if it was locked away deep in my heart.

I approached Mama and brushed her thin, brown hair away from her forehead. I stared at her, her image burning into every part of my mind. Her eyes were closed with no movement and there was no response to my touch. She'd already left—her body only remained breathing due to the machines.

"I've missed you, Mama," I whispered. "As much as I hate you, I love you more. I wish things had been different. I wanted you to love me so badly. Maybe now you finally will."

I kissed her forehead and stepped back, wondering if death would finish the job quickly. Knowing Mama, she would hold on as long as she could to capture everyone's attention for her grand finale. The doctor thought it wouldn't take any longer than a few hours for her body to stop breathing on its own. I hoped it would happen sooner.

A moment later, I left Mama's room and walked down the hall to the ICU waiting room. My older sister Krissy, the golden child, was leaning against the wall as she stared out the window.

"Krissy," I said, approaching her.

She turned toward me, her eyes rimmed with redness. We stared at each other for a few moments, and then I nodded.

"Lacey, are you sure? You don't need any more time?" Krissy asked.

"I'm sure."

She pushed herself off the wall, wiped her eyes, and turned away to find the doctor. It was time to disconnect the machine.

With my goodbyes said, I walked toward the exit to the hospital. I burst through the sliding doors and came to a quick stop as the fragrance of the spring rain filled my nose. The walkway was lined with bright green grass and an abundance of red and pink tulips. The last drops of rain slid off the tree leaves as I breathed it all in. It was breathtaking.

I was finally free.

2

TWENTY YEARS EARLIER, SEPTEMBER 1988

I t was my favorite day of the week: Friday. Classes were over, homework was finished, and I was minutes away from clocking out at work. The party had been planned at our student center during the first week of college, and by week three, we were ready.

Jocelyn's mom didn't care if we partied at her house; in fact, she said she preferred to keep an eye on us since most of us were eighteen and nineteen. She figured if we were going to drink we should be somewhere safe, and we didn't want our parents to find out. That was the ultimate downfall of attending the local community college—most of us still lived at home.

I knew if Mama found out, there would be hell to pay. It didn't matter if I drank or not; just being there would get me put on lock-down. That's why I usually spent the night with Jocelyn.

Mama somehow knew more about my private life than I did. She said God talked to her. Although it was irritating when God ratted me out, I secretly wished he would talk to me a little bit too.

The time clock punched my card, which read Jack's Department Store in bold letters across the top. I replaced it in the time card holder and said goodbye to my coworkers as I made my way down the employee hall and out the back of the store. Car lights shone in my face as Jocelyn honked her horn. I waved as she pulled around the parking lot. The backseat of her maroon Camaro was filled with giggling friends as I slid into the passenger seat.

"Hey, Lacey!" they all chimed.

"Hey, y'all. I'm so glad I'm done working. Oh my God, if I had to listen to one more whiny child in the store I swear I was going to smack the hell out of someone."

"I have no clue how you do it all. You work, go to school, edit the college paper, and still find time to party on the weekends," Tammy said.

"I wouldn't call watching you fools get drunk partying, but I do love hanging out with you, especially when the guys show," I said.

"One of these nights we're going to get you so drunk! No more of this, 'no thank you' shit," Tammy chided. "What's your reason for not drinking again?"

"My reason? I like my teeth in my mouth and not scattered across the floor," I replied. "My mom would beat my ass." My jaw clenched at Tammy's constant nagging.

"Y'all leave Lacey alone," Jocelyn said. "If she doesn't want to drink, she doesn't need to. Just because y'all are drunks doesn't mean she needs to be lying on the floor next to you." She laughed, her blue eyes dancing as she glanced at me.

Jocelyn—we all called her "Joss"—had a way of smiling even while putting you in your place. She spoke with a soft, sweet voice even when she was pissed, but she didn't have a mean bone in her body. It was the opposite, actually—she made sure no one got too crazy and would even hold your hair back if you were puking. She was the glue that held us together.

However, it was her downfall too, being a mom to us. She rarely stopped to have fun herself. Once you became friends with her you realized she'd been the parent from a young age. She not only took care of her mom and brother, but she dealt with her mom's drunk boyfriends on top of it. She often stepped in and told them to leave when they got physical.

Joss could've had a bad attitude about a lot of things, but she didn't. She embraced the people she loved and held them close. Thank God I was one of them.

We turned onto the road to Joss's house, and the cars filled both sides of the long driveway. She lived a few miles off the main road, so there wasn't much concern about the cops showing up. A house full of loud music and underage drinkers was a cop's wet dream.

Everyone filed out of the car, chattering a mile a minute about which guys were supposed to show and who called dibs on them. I loved them; they were my friends, but sometimes the competition got stupid. Joss and I usually kicked back and laughed at what asses they made of themselves to get laid. Joss kept her legs closed unless she was in a committed relationship, and I still held the V title among most of my friends. Eighteen, in college, and a virgin, but it was my choice. I hadn't met anyone that I loved enough to let it go, and the other reasons were, well, nothing I had ever shared with anyone before. Some secrets you just didn't share.

We all went into Joss's cozy house. I followed Tammy into the kitchen and settled in at the table.

"Here ya go," Tammy said as she plunked a Diet Coke on the kitchen table in front of me. "I give you shit, but I love ya."

"You can be a bitch sometimes, Tammy, but you have my back when I need it," I said, grinning and enjoying giving her a hard time. My can clinked against her glass full of rum and Coke and drank up to friendship.

Our toast was interrupted by a loud noise in the living room.

"What the hell was that?" Tammy said, turning and running out of the kitchen. The commotion was so loud that I had to follow her. Guys, about six of them, laughing and hollering entered Joss's living room. Several of them were already drunk.

We stood in the dining room doorway and waited to see if more were coming.

"Oh my God! They're all hot!" Tammy elbowed me excitedly in the side.

"I'm lookin', give me a minute," I said as I peered around her.

They were so loud that I hadn't heard Joss approach us from behind.

"I hate to break up your ogling fest you two, but Lacey, your mom is on the phone. You can take it in my room so she can't hear the party."

"You're kidding right?"

"Wish I was, but she really is on the phone," Joss said.

"Shit," I muttered and slipped through the kitchen and family room to avoid the crowd. I closed her bedroom door to seal out the noise of the growing crowd and picked up the phone.

"Hello?"

"Lacey, it's Patsy, you need to come home."

"What? Why?"

"It's your mama. Just come home."

"Patsy, is she okay? Is she sick? You gotta give me something," I said. My stomach tightened as I remembered the last time Patsy asked me to come home.

"We can get her through this; we just need to work together."

"Okay, okay, I'm on my way."

"Thank you," Patsy said.

I didn't bother saying goodbye. My eyes squeezed shut while I hung up the phone and released a harsh breath. Nothing good ever came out of those calls. I grabbed my purse and jacket and asked Joss for a ride back to my car.

The party had tripled in a less than an hour. The obnoxious but gorgeous group of guys stood in the middle of the room, surrounded by the majority of the girls at the party. I navigated my way through the crowd, and just before I reached the front door, an unfamiliar hand tugged at my arm. Turning slowly, I melted on the spot. The most piercing blue eyes greeted me.

"Are you leaving?" he asked.

"Yeah, family emergency," I said.

"Well shit, that sucks—I'd hoped I would get to talk to you tonight. What's your name?"

"Lacey. Yours?" I tilted my head and waited for his response.

"Walker. Are you coming back?" he asked as his mouth curved into a smile.

The combination of his blue eyes and smile sent me into a mental tailspin. If a guy could be hot, beautiful, and breathtaking all at once, he was it.

"I doubt it." My brows knitted together. I couldn't believe my dumb luck.

He reached over to the coffee table, grabbed a pen and paper, and wrote something on it.

"Here's my number," he said and handed it to me. "Call me. Please."

I glanced at it to make sure a phone number was really written down, and that it wasn't a joke.

"Gotta go, Walker. Thanks for your number," I said, turning toward the door. My pulse quickened, and I chanced a quick look over my shoulder to find him staring at me. He attempted a sheepish smile and waved. I couldn't help but smile in return.

The warm air clung to my skin as Joss and I walked to her car. Even though fall lingered around the corner, it couldn't get here fast enough. I hated the Arkansas heat. I also hated the mosquitoes that were big enough to carry a small child away.

Joss opened her car door and grinned at me from ear to ear.

"What was that all about?" she asked as we slid into our seats.

"He gave me his number. It's probably his grandpa's, but hey, I got a number." I half-shrugged and smiled.

"Uh huh," Joss said as a lopsided grin spread across her face. She knew darned well I hoped differently.

"You gonna call him? If you don't, I will," she said as her car roared to life.

"You're full of crap, Joss. You wouldn't do that to me."

"I don't know, that was the hottest guy I've ever seen."

"I can't disagree with you, but for now, I need to deal with Mama."

"Did she say why she wanted you home?"

"No, it was Patsy who called, so that means something's up," I said, rubbing my forehead.

"You do realize you're eighteen, right? You don't need to run home whenever she says to."

"Wish it were that simple."

Joss knew when to let it go, and we rode in silence until she pulled up to my car.

The mall was dark and empty and my car was the only one in the parking lot. It creeped me out a little that no one else was around. I knew mall security was inside, but that didn't help me out any.

"Thanks, Joss, I really appreciate it." I reached across the seat and gave her a hug. "Enjoy the rest of the party."

"Don't worry, Lacey, I'll throw more parties," she said. Her nose crinkled as she smiled. I loved her smile. That smile made life a little better because you knew you had a good friend.

"I'll wait to make sure your car starts."

"Thanks, Joss," I said as I closed her car door.

3

I didn't drive the speed limit. I drove right under it until I realized my heart was pounding so hard it was making my head hurt. Life was a roller coaster with Mama, never knowing what to expect from one minute to the next. Patsy wouldn't call me home for any reason at all, though. It was something big.

I reached our street and stopped on top of the hill for a minute. The car idled while I stared down at the two-story log home, but it was hard to see the house in the darkness. Even though we had neighbors across the street and here on the hill, our house was well hidden at the end of the cul-de-sac. The grass was overgrown, and the trees were so thick in some places that you couldn't see the house at all. That's how Mama liked it. She went to great lengths to protect her privacy.

I pulled into the driveway and hopped out of my Mustang, Georgia. Mama and Patsy had bought her for me not long after graduation. Most of the time throughout high school I'd driven Mama's car, since she rarely went anywhere. I came home one afternoon to a car in our driveway and asked if we had company. They toyed with me for a while and finally told me it was mine. My face lit up brighter than a Christmas tree when they handed me the keys. That had been a great day, not only because of the car, but because Mama had stayed in a good mood. Those days were few and far between, though.

Pursing my lips, I took a deep breath and tried to control the rapid pounding in my chest. Rex and Ruger met me at the base of the stairs and demanded my attention. I reached down and pet them both as they licked my hands and face. They always got so excited when I arrived home that they'd beat me half to death with their tails. They were good dogs, and nothing got by them. They barked at anything and everything, and that was one of the biggest reasons I'd never tried to sneak out of the house. I wouldn't have a chance. Not only would they wake Mama, but the rest of the neighborhood as well.

As I climbed the stairs to the side door, I heard Mama and Patsy arguing. I quietly opened it and stepped into the kitchen, unsure of what to expect. A large coffee mug flew through the air and smashed into the kitchen cabinet to my left. It broke into a million pieces.

"Dammit, Patsy, you're just jealous! You're jealous that I hear God better than you do. I call long distance, two thousand miles away, just to find someone else with the same gift so I can save your sorry ass from going to hell!"

I assessed the situation as quickly as possible: shattered cup, Mama's hands bunched into tight fists, and her face reddened with anger. Mama's size alone was intimidating, but when she was mad, her presence was overwhelming.

"That's not true, Lynn. I brought it up because $932 is a hefty phone bill we can't afford to pay. That's the only reason I asked you to cut back on the calls," Patsy said.

"Mama, I can help pay it," I said and stepped forward.

Both Patsy and Mama finally acknowledged I was standing in the room.

"Lacey, that's sweet of you, but it's not your responsibility," Patsy said. Her large, brown eyes flashed with gratefulness.

"Patsy's right, Lacey. You can't even take care of yourself and stay out of trouble long enough to be of use to anyone else."

I tried to shake off her words, but they still stung.

"Patsy just doesn't want me to talk to anyone else," Mama whined.

My breath hitched, recognizing the shift in her voice. We both did; we'd witnessed it a million times.

"Mama, I love you and I don't mind helping at all. You don't ask me to pay any rent, so let me help."

"You and Patsy do whatever the hell you want to do." Her chin jutted upward as she turned around and walked to her chair. She picked up the remote control and turned on the TV like nothing had happened.

I shot Patsy a look. Relief washed over her face and she tucked a stray curl behind her ear. It was over, for the moment anyway. I'd talk to her about the bill later. I set my purse and books on the kitchen table and picked up the pieces of the coffee mug that were scattered all over the floor. I put them in the trash and arranged the dirty paper towels on top so no one could see the remnants. It was yet another moment where I swept something up and hid it so others wouldn't see anything broken.

Patsy sat on the couch and acted as though she was watching TV. I glanced over at Mama. Her eyes were closed and she was gently rocking in her chair, which meant she was most likely praying. Hopefully, things would remain calm for the evening. At least tomorrow was Saturday so if Mama was in a bad mood I had an excuse to leave.

The descent downstairs into the basement was a welcome relief. I reminded myself that I needed to clean the family room; books and papers had piled up over time. Some of it was mine—I used the area to spread my books and papers out for research and homework—but a lot of it was Mama's stuff. My bedroom was through the family room and tucked away in the back corner. If you hadn't been back there before, you would never find it. That's why I picked it.

My feet kicked through the pile of dirty clothes on my floor, placing my purse and books on my dresser, and flopping onto my bed. I was exhausted from classes, work, and Mama not having a good night. A hot knife ripped through me every time she was upset with us. Part of me wanted to run, but even the thought of not having Mama in my life immediately brought tears to my eyes. She knew me so well; she knew what I could do and what I couldn't.

The realization of how many times she was right when she heard from God terrified me. I stared at my buttercream-colored bedroom walls and remembered the times I'd been caught toilet papering someone's house, lying about where I stayed the night, and committing a multitude of other sins. There was no way she could have known about those incidents, so God must really tell her stuff. And the last thing I wanted was to burn in hell.

Mama's voice startled me from my mental descent to fiery darkness. I couldn't make out what she was saying, but she sounded unhappy. The phone clattered against the cradle and her heavy footsteps fell across the living room floor above me. The tone and volume of her voice were enough for me to stay downstairs and out of her way.

Her chair creaked and I released a slow sigh, listening for a few more minutes. But I didn't hear any arguing or loud voices. I glanced at the clock and groaned. How could I be so tired at 9:45 P.M.? If I were still at the party, I wouldn't even consider crashing out this early.

The party brought my thoughts back to Walker and a small smile passed my lips. I'd never seen eyes so blue, and his dark hair made them even more prominent. He had grabbed my attention when the group arrived at the party. They were all hot, but he was by far the best in the group.

I grabbed my purse off the floor and rummaged for the small piece of paper with his phone number on it. Maybe I would call him tomorrow . . . or not. My pulse raced with the mere thought of picking up the phone and calling a stranger, but he'd asked. A familiar fear peeked its head, and a part of me wondered if the phone number was really his.

I folded the paper and put it back into my purse. Hopefully, I wouldn't talk myself out of it, and I would call him tomorrow.

4

Sunlight streamed through my curtains, and I rubbed my eyes, glancing at my alarm clock. It was 9 A.M. Stifling a yawn, I sat up on the edge of my bed and slid into my fuzzy slippers, pausing for a moment to listen, but only silence responded. Hope flickered through me.

As much as I loved Fridays, I hated Saturdays, and made sure I was scheduled to work every weekend. If I wasn't, I volunteered to take someone's shift. My coworkers thought I was a great team player who needed the money, which was true, but I also needed a legitimate excuse not to stay at home.

As I made it halfway up the stairs to the living room, my skin began to itch with the tension in the air. I hesitated and considered going back downstairs, but my stomach growled and propelled me forward.

Mama sat in her favorite chair, and Patsy was on the couch.

"Morning, Lacey."

"Hi, Mama," I said, walking over and placing a kiss on her cheek.

"Does anyone want breakfast?" I approached the kitchen.

"No, but get yourself something to eat and then I want to talk to you," she said.

Patsy stared at her feet. Unable to read her face put me at a disadvantage. My skin tingled with the all-too-familiar feeling that something was up, but I couldn't tell which one of us was in trouble.

"What's your schedule today?" Mama asked.

"I leave in a few hours and work from noon until six."

"Well, this won't take long. You received a phone call last night after nine o'clock and you're aware of the rules."

"Who was it?" I asked between spoonfuls of Grape Nuts.

"Some boy named Walker."

My spoon stopped midway to my mouth.

"Walker?" I squeezed my eyes shut as I realized which one of us was in trouble.

"Do you know a Walker? Don't you lie to me either. Who's Walker?"

"I met him last night, but I never gave him my phone number."

"Well, how in the hell did he get it then, Lacey? You're lying—it's written all over your face."

"No, Mama, I swear I just met him last night. Maybe Joss gave it to him."

"Tell me who he is and who gave him the number if it wasn't you. Your friends know not to hand out your information, and they don't call after nine."

"Mama, I'm sorry. I'll find out and make sure it doesn't happen again."

"Yes, you will. I pay for an unlisted phone number, and that means I don't want it given to other people."

I got up from the table, rinsed my bowl, and loaded it into the dishwasher.

"I need to get ready for work."

"No, I'm not finished yet. Come sit down."

I winced and grabbed the blanket off the back of the chair. This was going to hurt, and I might as well get as comfortable as possible.

"Are you lying to me about going to work today?"

"What? No." I tried to remain calm, but my heart knocked against my chest, and my head began to throb in rhythm with it.

"Where did you meet Walker?"

"At Joss's last night. Her brother invited friends over and he introduced himself."

Her eyes narrowed as she searched my face. I had nothing to hide, but I'd been defending my interest in boys since the age of thirteen. I'd been a late bloomer, and when I had my first kiss I told Mama about it. She screamed at me for an hour, calling me a slut and a whore. By the time she finished, I had promised myself never to share those first moments with her again. I took the piece of me that wanted a good relationship with her, locked it away, and buried the key.

Mama turned to Patsy. "What do you think, Patsy? Do you think she's lying?"

My gaze focused on Patsy and I mentally reminded her that she owed me for last night, and in no way was I required to come home and help diffuse the situation. A flat tire could have easily happened, leaving Patsy to fend for herself.

Patsy glanced at me briefly as fear flickered across her face.

"No, I think she's telling the truth, Lynn," she said. Her body tensed up as the words left her mouth.

We both waited in silence for Mama's reaction.

"Lacey, you're not trustworthy enough to date boys. You've been boy crazy since you were in kindergarten and have made horrible choices since you were thirteen. I thought, after all this time of praying for you, it might help, but there's something deeper here. I've been praying more, and God has shown me you are possessed by a demon. It's a demon of lust, and it draws you to these boys who just want to sleep with you. Then, you give out our phone number to anyone who pays any attention to you. You don't show any regard for me, Patsy, or even yourself. I've told you before, and I guess I'll say it again to get it through your thick head. You don't give out my telephone number unless you ask my permission first. I've told you that over and over again. Yet, here you are giving it to some boy you met for five seconds."

"Mama, I didn't give it to him," I snapped.

I sank back in the chair realizing that my frustration had gotten the better of me.

"Shut up, you filthy demon! You won't take my daughter!" Mama spat.

Silence spread through the air like a bad disease and Mama glared at me. I didn't dare utter another word—I'd said too much already.

Fear flowed through me, and I tried to ignore the small voice inside my head telling me she was right again. A heaviness settled inside my chest as I realized she was telling the truth. I had made some wrong choices with guys. For whatever reason, I liked the bad boys. No matter how hard I tried to hide it, she always found out. It was exhausting, and I was tired of screwing up and I was sick of hurting Mama. My eyes filled with tears.

"Mama," my voice came out as a whisper. "I'm sorry. I don't want a demon. I'll keep praying and change."

"That's what you always say, Lacey, but nothing changes. Don't you understand how much I love you? Don't you recognize that I'm protecting you from making mistakes? Lacey, you're my baby. I realize you're eighteen, but you'll always be my baby. I'm saving your soul. I'll keep fighting and praying for you until we win this battle."

Her expression softened as she began rocking. The squeak of the recliner was the only sound in the room. I glanced at Patsy. She remained tense and quiet.

My gaze dropped to the blanket, and I flicked a piece of lint off of it. Tomorrow I'd need to tell Walker not to call again. There was no way I could date anyone right now; I was too screwed up. No one wanted to be in a relationship with someone who had a demon. There was a bigger choice that needed to be made and I had to stop things now before anything else happened.

"Go get ready for work, Lacey," Mama said.

She didn't need to say anything else, and I wasn't stupid enough to sit there any longer. I wiped a tear from my cheek as I went downstairs and got ready for work.

5

"Hey, Lacey," Becky said as I walked into the children's section of the department store.

"Hey, Becky. Was it busy this morning?"

"Not too bad. It's so nice outside that I think people are at the lake instead of shopping today."

"That could be good or bad I guess. There's nothing worse than standing around for six hours," I said as I punched my ID number into the register.

"Well, since tomorrow's Sunday and a new sale is starting, I changed the signs for the petite section. You only need to take care of the ad for your department."

"Thanks, Becky."

"You okay, hun? You seem a little down."

"Yeah, I'm good."

"Okay then, see ya later."

Becky waved and walked down the aisle past the fine jewelry and men's suits departments. She'd taken me under her wing when I first started working at the store. Although she was in her forties, we worked well together and had become friends. I'd thought about talking to her at times, but if she ever found out how messed up I was, she wouldn't want anything else to do with me. I didn't want to lose her.

No one understood how Mama heard God. They didn't realize how special her gift was. Even though she hurt me sometimes, I couldn't let my friends talk bad about her. She was still my Mama.

The day moved along quicker than I had anticipated. Although the children's department was small, it typically stayed steady with customers. We sold great clothes, and some of the kids were beyond cute. I wasn't sure I wanted kids personally, but I figured working around them would take care of any baby cravings for years to come.

I glanced at the clock: 5:45 P.M. Only fifteen minutes left.

"Hi, I was wondering where the toddler shirts are?"

I froze immediately, recognizing his voice. My eyes flicked up and met the same pair of intense blue eyes I'd seen at Joss's last night.

"Walker? What are you doing here?" I tried to hide my surprise, but I never expected him to show up at my job.

"Well, I was a little concerned about calling you last night. Your mom wasn't too happy when she answered the phone. Since she wouldn't let me speak to you I decided to call Tammy and ask her where you worked, so here I am," he said. His eyes gleamed as he rested his hands on the counter and leaned toward me.

"Tammy? Did she give you my phone number too?" I crossed my arms in front of me.

"Yeah, after you left the party she came over and started talking to me. I'm sure she's nice, but I wasn't interested in anything other than getting your phone number. She was cool about it and helped me out."

My brows knitted together as I realized who had caused me so much grief with Mama.

"Walker, Tammy wasn't being cool about it, she was mad. She knew Mama would be hot pissed if you called after nine."

"Lacey, I'm so sorry, I did call late. I just wanted to talk to you and make sure you were okay. You mentioned leaving due to a family emergency." He stepped back from the counter and ran his hand through his dark hair.

"It's alright, Walker. It's not your fault. Tammy was playing her games. I'll deal with her later."

"Am I allowed to call anymore?" His jaw tightened as he waited for my response.

"I'm not sure. Besides, what if I don't want you to call me?"

"Then say the word, but all I ask is that you go out with me one time before you decide."

I bit my lip and leaned back against the counter. My brows knitted while I reminded myself about the promise I'd made earlier, but he was amazingly hot and my entire body tingled at the thought of being alone with him. Even Mama's warnings couldn't compete with him standing in front of me. The longer he stared at me, the more the arguing in my head quieted. But just when I was about to agree, all the years of "stranger danger" surfaced. I didn't know anything about him. My face paled as hundreds of scenarios played through my head.

A smile spread across his face. "It's okay, Lacey, I won't kidnap you. We can grab a bite to eat and stay in public, alright?"

I laughed—my face had betrayed my thoughts. I really needed to work on that.

"Let me ask Mama," I said.

He lifted one eyebrow. "Is it really a good idea to ask her? I don't think she likes me."

"I'll take care of it. I'll meet you out front in ten minutes."

"Perfect!"

He walked away, looked over his shoulder at me, and smiled from ear to ear.

The second he turned away, reality crashed down on me. What was I about to do? My fingers balled up as I stared at the phone. One dinner wasn't going to send me into a demonic frenzy, right? Couldn't I could control myself for a few hours? I grabbed the phone and punched in the numbers before I changed my mind.

Mama answered and I told her I was going to grab a bite to eat with Joss after work. I couldn't tell what kind of mood she was in, but that wasn't my biggest problem at the moment. Even though I'd already decided against it, I was going to spend time with Walker, the exact thing I had told myself I wasn't going to do. Arguing with myself was a moot point now; I'd already said yes. And even though I realized it was wrong, I wanted to go out with him.

6

S onic was packed. Walker had chosen Sonic so we could eat in his car and talk without anyone bothering us but still be surrounded by people. Sonic and Central Avenue were the places to be on Friday and Saturday nights.

The occasional horn honked as high school and college students drove up and down the street and scoped the scene for friends and parties. Sometimes I was in the long line of cars, but Mama didn't approve of cruising the strip. She said it was a hotbed for demons, drinking, and sex. I had no idea if she was right or not but I wanted to hang out with my friends, so the rare times I went, I kept it on the down-low like everything else. So far God had kept his mouth shut about it, but I couldn't figure out why he told her some things and not others. And would he tattle about me having dinner with Walker tonight? My lips pursed, pushing the concern out of my head.

Walker pulled his car into the only parking spot available, slid the gearshift into first gear, turned the engine off, and released the clutch. He made it seem so easy. His little brown Nissan radiated character. I wondered if he would teach me to drive it. I'd never driven a stick shift and it would be a good excuse to spend more time with him if I wanted too, but the jury was still out.

We ordered and the waitress brought our food. I hadn't realized how hungry I was until the aroma of french fries filled his car.

"So, where did you graduate?" Walker asked between french fries.

"Lake Hamilton, home of the wolves," I said and grinned. "You?"

"Fountain Lake."

"Wow, you live way out in the sticks, huh?"

"It's not too bad. I'm closer to town than you are." He laughed.

"Yeah, I guess so."

"Besides, I work at the country club so it's close," he said as he took another french fry.

"Oh? What do you do at the club?"

A slow grin crept across his face. "I'm a lifeguard."

"Oh," I said, not hiding my surprise. My mind drifted to him sitting in the lifeguard's chair with no shirt on, ready to dive in at any given moment.

"Well, it's good to know that if we ever swim together I'll be in good hands," I said and grinned.

I took my seat belt off and turned to face him. His blue eyes captivated me. It would be so easy to lose myself in them forever and never care. A soft patch of hair shadowed his upper lip. My gaze lingered as I wondered what his lips would feel like against mine.

"What are you thinking?" he asked and trailed his finger lightly across my cheek.

I blushed and silently cursed my pale skin as I reached for his hand. His fingers intertwined with mine. They were strong, rough, and soft all at the same time.

"I'm not good for you, Walker." I glanced down, embarrassed that those words had slipped out of my mouth. No way had I intended to say anything like that, but my mouth had a mind of its own. My plan had included ending the night with a thank-you and letting Walker go, but instead, it was turning into a tug-of-war between my heart and my brain.

"Lacey, I highly doubt that," he replied and squeezed my hand.

"How would you know? We just met." I dared to glance at him. If he knew what I meant he would kick me out of his car right then, leave, and never look back.

Walker leaned his head against his seat as he ran his free hand through his hair. His eyes settled on my face.

"If we date, you're going to hear things about me and my ex-girl-friend. You and I share some mutual friends and enemies."

"You have enemies? What the hell? I mean how old are you anyway?" I asked, dropping his hand. Maybe I wasn't the worst of us after all.

"Nineteen. And no, that's not what I meant," he said, laughing.

"What's so funny?" I asked and folded my arms across my chest.

"Not enemies in that way, but there are grudges and rumors. You know what high school was like."

I nodded, remembering all too well what it was like being caught in the crossfire and rumors. Not to mention I'd managed to piss off a few mean girls myself.

"Well, what do you mean exactly?" My hands dropped back into my lap.

"My ex, her name is Brittany. We dated for three years. She . . . how do I say this?" He paused and shook his head. "She was a handful. I didn't realize it for a long time, though. I even asked her to marry me."

"What? Seriously?" My eyes grew wide with the realization of how serious they had been.

"Yeah, I was crazy about her. It wasn't until we got into a fight and she threw the engagement ring into the lake that I finally saw who she really was. When we worked out the fight the next day, she demanded I buy her not only another one, but a bigger one."

"Shit, Walker. That's just rude!"

"I agree. So, I doubt you saying you're not good for me is true. I have a feeling you're exactly what I need."

He reached over and took my hand again. My face flushed with the warmth of his skin.

"I would never do anything like that even if I were pissed at some-one. You don't treat people that way."

"Yeah, she didn't understand that. I broke things off with her about four months ago."

"Do you still love her?" I asked.

Walker paused for a minute and stared out the car window. My breath hitched as he processed the question.

"Lacey, I was with her for three years. She was my first and I was hers. I'll always care about her, care what happens to her, but I'm not in love with her. If I had been honest with myself I would've realized that I hadn't been in love with her for over a year. I don't want that kind of relationship. We fought all the time. I don't want to be with her. Go out with me again, Lacey—give us a chance to find out who's not good for whom."

The expression on his face said he was telling me the truth, or maybe I just wanted so badly to believe there really was an amazing guy sitting across from me. And, even more than that, that I could do this; that I could keep things under control and work really hard to get better. There was only one way to find out.

"I'd like that too, but I need to get your full name. I've already been on one date with you, and I don't even know your name. There's no way I can make a case with Mama if I don't present all the information."

His warm laugh filled the car. "It's Walker Tate Farren. What's yours?"

"Lacey Anne Beaumont."

"Well, Lacey Anne Beaumont, do you have plans tomorrow?"

"No, it's my day off."

"You do now," he said and squeezed my hand.

7

The morning sun peered through my bedroom window as I kicked and untangled myself from my blankets. I'd agreed to a second date with Walker before he drove me back to my car. That's what I wanted, but I also didn't want Mama to find out.

The constantly looming question in the back of my mind was, what if Walker found out how messed up I was? My decision was selfish. However, I was eighteen and what was the harm in going out with him again to find out if he might be a good guy?

I'm not sure I struggled with that as much as with telling Mama. Maybe if I prepared a case to present to her after a few dates, she'd realize I was capable of making good decisions.

I tossed the blankets off and glanced at the clock: it glowed 8:30 A.M. Late enough to call Joss and fill her in.

"This better be important for you to call me this early in the morning," Joss muttered.

"I woke you—I'm sorry."

"Don't be because I bet you're gonna tell me something juicy," she said, not bothering to hide her yawn.

"Well, I can always call back if it's too early."

"Oh hell no, spit it out. I'm awake now, so fess up."

Joss didn't care what time I called her, but if I did, I made sure I had a good reason.

"I have a second date with Walker later today," I blurted.

"Oh my God, Lacey, that's great! But you said *second* date."

"It wasn't any big deal, just dinner after work."

"Wait, you need to fill me in on the first date. You can't leave me hangin' like that, Lacey. Did you call him?"

"I didn't call him, he showed up at work."

"What? How did he find out where you worked?"

"Tammy and I were in the kitchen when the group of guys came in and then Patsy called. My guess is that she saw Walker and me talking and when I left she thought she'd speak to him herself. Walker said she started flirting with him. He was polite, but he shut her down and asked for my phone number. She assured him it was okay to call my house after nine last night."

"Oh, shit."

"Oh, shit is right. She knew not to give my number to anyone, and Mama doesn't allow calls after nine unless someone's dying. Anyway, Mama gave me hell about it and demanded to know why I would give a strange guy our unlisted phone number. That took forever to explain. And, right after I'd won the tug-of-war inside me and decided I should *not* date him, he showed up at work. I turned around and there he was. I about hit the flippin' floor."

"Wait, back up a minute. How did he find out where you worked?"

"Tammy! Joss, he was so sweet trying to make sure I was okay last night, and then he realized, after speaking to Mama on the phone, that it wasn't the best idea he'd ever had. He apologized for calling too late, but it was Tammy who told him it was okay and where I worked. She frustrates the crap out of me."

"Yeah, me too," Joss sighed. "She does some stupid stuff, but when it comes down to it, she will back you up in a heartbeat. Between us, she thinks she's the third wheel in the group."

"Okay, okay. I'll let it go and not slap the shit out of her, but she has no idea what trouble she caused. No one does."

Joss was silent for a moment. "Lacey, I realize your mom is difficult. She's too strict and controlling. You know I still like her, but when are you going to move out? You don't need to stay."

"You don't understand."

"I do understand. You've told me before that she has a special relationship with God. I get it, but are you sure she doesn't say those things to manipulate you?"

"Forget it. Forget I called." I flopped back on my bed and rubbed my head.

"Lacey! Don't you dare hang up on me. You called to talk to *me*, remember? We can leave Mama alone for now. Let's talk about Walker."

I paused for a moment and brushed my irritation away.

"Joss, what am I going to do?" I groaned.

"What do you mean what are you going to do? You're going to get up and eat breakfast. Then you're going to take a hot bubble bath and shave your pits, legs, and the Garden of Eden. After that, you're going to go on a date with the hottest guy I've ever met. Lacey, I'm serious: put on your big-girl panties and go out with this guy!"

We broke into massive giggles. I held the phone away from my ear and struggled to pull air into my lungs.

"Joss, stop! I can't breathe!" I gasped as tears ran down my face.

"Take a breath, you'll be okay." A moment of silence filled the phone line as we regained our composure.

"I'm scared," I muttered.

"Why? I get being nervous, but what's up?"

I sighed and stared at my bedroom ceiling.

"What if going out with him is a mistake? What if I fall for him and he's a huge asshole?"

"Then he's a huge asshole. You learn from it and move on."

"Why is everything so simple for you, Joss?"

"It's not. You know I take care of David and mom. It's a matter of breaking things down and keeping it simple. Try and keep that in mind. You're going on a date with a gorgeous guy. When was the last time you went out with anyone? Go on a date, kiss him, laugh, live for a few minutes and leave your mom, school, and work behind for a little while."

"Okay, okay, you're right. It's just a date, right?"

"Yes, have some fun!"

"Joss?"

"Yes?"

"Did you see his eyes?"

"They were hard to miss. I told you, if you don't want him, I'll take him. Between that dark hair, those blue eyes, and that incredible ass I wouldn't think twice about it."

"You're such a liar—you'd never do that to me."

"Nope, I wouldn't, but it's a hell of a lot of fun giving you shit."

"Okay, I'm going to make some breakfast. Thanks for listening."

"Anytime, and I expect full details tomorrow."

Her laugh hung in the air as we ended the call.

8

Three hours later, I pulled my car into the Kmart parking lot. Kmart was an old store, and even though I'd never stepped foot in it, the parking lot was usually full. Today, however, there were only a few cars. My shoulders tensed; someone could easily spot me and tell Mama.

My nerves sent a flush across my cheeks, and I rolled down my window, hoping the fresh air would help. My heart pounded as I glanced at my watch—I'd arrived fifteen minutes early. The wait sucked, but I didn't want Mama asking any more questions than she normally did. She'd seemed content when I told her I would be with Joss at the mall. Fear crept down my spine, and I prayed I could pull it off and not get caught. The likelihood of anyone recognizing me once we got to Lake DeGray was slim, but I was still worried.

The seconds ticked by as I glanced at my watch again. Only two minutes had passed. No longer able to sit still, I stepped out of my car and paced back and forth. What if he didn't show? What if this was a joke? What if we spend the day together and he doesn't like me? The warm air clung to my skin, and I sighed as Joss's voice filled my head: "Then you'll get over it and move on."

I pulled my hair back and put it in a ponytail. It was still muggy, but I hoped it would be nice at the lake today and not too crowded.

The sun beamed down on me as I paced around my car, leaned on the bumper, and then brushed off my butt. It was impossible to keep dirt off a car this time of year, and the last thing I wanted was a big dust print on my backside for our second date.

A sigh of relief rushed out of me when Walker pulled into the parking lot.

"Hey! Get in," Walker said, opening the passenger door for me from the driver's seat.

I couldn't control my smile as I checked for my car keys in my purse, locked my car door, and climbed into his car.

"Hi," I said, trying to tame the crazy smile that spread across my face.

"Hi yourself," he replied.

His gaze fell across my face and paused.

"Is there something on my face?" I said, rubbing at my cheeks and mouth.

"No," he said, laughing. "You're beautiful, Lacey."

"Oh." I mentally swore as my cheeks reddened.

"I didn't mean to embarrass you," he said as a smile tugged at the corners of his mouth.

"No, it's fine. Um, thank you," I muttered.

"I can be somewhat forward. I don't mean to be, I just don't have a good filter on my mouth sometimes."

"Isn't that a guy thing?" I glanced at him, laughing.

"Probably. Are you ready?"

"Yes, let's get the hell out of here."

Forty-five minutes later, we pulled into a more private area of the lake and unloaded his car.

Walker shook out the plaid blanket and we sat down facing the water. The sun sparkled off the ripples, and the breeze brought in the smell of the water. It was perfect.

"I brought strawberries," he said as he opened the picnic basket.

"Oooh, I love strawberries." I grabbed one, plucked off the green stem, and popped the whole thing into my mouth. My cheeks bulged as I tried to move the fruit from one side to another, realizing what I'd done. I giggled, bringing my hands to my face and peering at him through my fingers.

Walker tried not to laugh but didn't succeed.

"Did you just do what I thought you did?" he asked.

"Maybe?" I mumbled around the food in my mouth.

"Oh my God, that's awesome. Can't say I've seen a girl do that before!"

I chewed my strawberry before I spoke again. My face flushed and matched the color of the fruit as I swallowed.

"What, be rude?" I reached for another one.

"No, I've met plenty of rude girls. I've just never seen a girl eat like that." His laugh filled the quiet picnic area.

"Well, I tried to warn you last night, but you didn't want to listen. Sorry, I'm nervous," I said, wiping my clammy hands on my jeans.

"I don't care, it was funny. I want you to feel comfortable with me."

I stared at him for a moment, still holding the strawberry in my hand. He reached for it and gently put it in my mouth. I took a bite. His eyes never left my face.

"I'm glad you're here."

"Me too, Walker." As hard as I tried not to, I meant it.

"There's something about you. I mean other than the obvious."

"What do you mean, 'the obvious'?" I asked as I made air quotes.

"You're beautiful, gentle, and funny. You don't find that combination often. Hopefully you'll let me hang around long enough to figure it out."

"Maybe." A small smile tugged at the corners of my mouth.

"Do you want to take a walk on the beach?" he asked and extended his hand.

"Yeah, I'd love to." I accepted his hand and he pulled me up. We stood so close that his breath brushed against my cheek. He held my gaze as his fingers brushed across my hand. A tingle ran up my arm and swirled through my body. If I responded like this to holding his hand, I wasn't sure I could handle it if he kissed me. But the more time I spent with him, the more I wanted to find out.

A ski boat whizzed by in the distance and broke my train of thought. I used the distraction to step back and take a breath. I'd promised myself I could handle this date and not do anything stupid. This was either going to be a perfect opportunity to show Mama I could make good choices, or not.

We reached the beach and I slipped off my sandals and rolled up my jeans. Sand squished through my toes, the water splashing against the rocks.

"Do you water ski?" Walker asked.

"I've tried, but I don't stay up long. I'm pretty wobbly and only manage to smack my ass on the water, giving myself a massive bikini wedgie on the way down. You?"

"No, I can't say I've ever had a bikini wedgie," he said, smiling. "I used to go with my dad, but that was years ago, before my parents divorced." He frowned slightly and turned his attention toward the lake.

"How long have they been divorced?"

"Since my little brother was six, so seven years now."

"Mine too—I mean, they're divorced. I've always wanted a younger brother."

"Really? You can take him. He's a brat."

"I'll give you Krissy, my older sister," I said. "We can trade." My voice filled with excitement at the idea of getting rid of her.

"How old is she?"

"Twenty-three. She's away at college."

"So, you'll trade me a bratty younger brother for your older sister who doesn't live at home? That sounds like a deal I can't pass up," he said.

Laughter bubbled up inside me. He was right, but I'd always wanted a brother. Surely, they were less of a pain in the ass than an older sister, but I never found out.

"I think our parents might object to our idea. What's your brother's name?"

"Garrett."

"Oooh, I like it. You guys live with your mom?"

"Yeah, for now."

There was a beat of silence as I waited for him to elaborate, but he stuffed his hands in his pockets and stared at his feet. Dammit, I'd asked the wrong question. Concern tugged at me while I tried to figure out how to break the awkward silence when he finally saved me.

"Lacey, I want you to meet my family and I'll tell you all about them, but for today can we not talk about them?"

"Walker, of course, I'm so sorry. I didn't mean to be rude or nosy. It's so not my business."

"Stop, you didn't do anything wrong. Come on, I want to show you something. You need to put your shoes back on so you don't cut your feet, though."

I wasn't sure why he didn't want to talk about his family, but I understood it all too well. Secrets were familiar to me. And, for today, I wouldn't ask him to share his.

I bent down to slip my shoes on, taking a moment to soak him in from head to toe. He ran his hand through his hair, leaving the short, dark strands rumpled. The urge to fix them crossed my mind, but I decided he wore it well. His shirt was halfway tucked into his shorts and halfway untucked. He appeared comfortable in his own skin. I wanted to be comfortable with his skin as well, and I found myself thinking about running my hand over his chest and stomach. My focus returned to my shoes and I chided myself for not keeping my word.

"Do you need help?" he asked as his eyes twinkled.

Had he realized I was checking him out or if he was trying to be nice?

"Huh? No, no, they're just a little stubborn sometimes." My cheeks reddened as I focused on actually slipping the strap over my heel instead of imagining him without a shirt.

As I stood up, he reached for my hand and led me forward. Silence filled the air and I followed, enjoying watching him climb the hill in front of me. I wasn't sure what sports he played, but he definitely played something. The tight muscles in his legs flexed as he moved with ease up the rocky path. A few minutes later he stopped and turned, helping me the rest of the way up the hill. He guided me over to a small clearing in the trees.

A gasp escaped me. "My God, it's beautiful," I whispered.

"I've never brought anyone here before."

"Really? Not even Brittany?" I asked, not taking my eyes from the lake.

"No, she wouldn't understand."

The sun cast a warm orange and pink across the tops of the trees as it began its slow descent. There were gentle ripples across the surface of the lake as the fish jumped and nipped at the bugs. I held my breath and absorbed the moment.

"You get it, though. Your expression says it all," he whispered.

"It's amazing watching the sunset from up here."

"It reminds me that no matter how crazy life gets, there's something greater," he said. "I'm not sure what it is, but it's there and it helps."

We stood in silence as the sun continued its descent behind the trees. I realized then there was more to Walker than beautiful eyes and a hot body.

"Walker." My voice came out a hoarse whisper and betrayed my emotions.

He turned to face me. "Lacey, there are a lot of things going on in my life and I'll share them with you later; I promise. But for tonight, I just wanted to look at you while the sun sets. I wanted to see the light on your hair, look into the most amazing green eyes I've ever seen, and let everything else go except us. I'm in trouble already. You're going to kidnap my heart and make me fall in love with you. I knew it the minute I laid eyes on you at the party."

"What? Walker, you don't know me." The words tumbled out of my mouth, but they contradicted the emotions that churned inside me.

"I realize it sounds crazy, but I want to be with you, Lacey. Go out with me—let's talk until three in the morning and fall asleep on the phone together. I'd like you to meet my family and eat dinner with us, learn everything about you. Please say yes, that you want the same thing."

"What exactly are you asking me, Walker?" My eyebrows furrowed as I tried to wrap my head around what he was saying.

"I don't want to share you with anyone else. I want to spend every possible moment with you."

"Walker, there's so much we don't know about each other. And, I told you last night I wasn't good for you," I said.

"No, I'm not okay with that," he said and shook his head. "Spend time with me and give me a chance."

The sunset painted the sky in rich pink and orange hues, but as beautiful as it was, guilt gnawed at me. I knew I shouldn't let this happen, but the pounding and ache in my chest told me I wanted differently. He wasn't the only one that had experienced it—when our eyes met at the party, we'd said so much more than hello.

"Don't break my heart, Walker. You're too good to be real, and as much as I want you, you scare me. I would never forgive myself if I said no, and I might not forgive myself for saying yes."

He released my fingers and brought the back of my hand so close to his lips that his breath caressed my skin.

"I'll take care of you like no one ever has before, Lacey Beaumont," he said, brushing his lips lightly across my hand. He brought my other hand up to his mouth and grazed it with a soft kiss.

I bit my lip and struggled to still my shaking knees.

"Lacey," he whispered as another soft kiss landed on my left palm and then my right.

Heat flooded my body and an ache swirled through me.

He slipped his arm around my waist and pulled me within an inch of his body. His fingers brushed against my cheek as he feathered kisses across my forehead, nose, and cheeks. He paused, our lips almost touching as his hand slipped under my shirt and teased the small of my back. I gasped as I grabbed his arms to balance myself.

"Lacey," he whispered, still not kissing me as his fingertips played gently across my back and up my spine. My legs wobbled as I leaned into him, bringing our bodies against each other. He stepped backward into a tree to balance us. His breath quickened as his reaction grew and I released a soft sigh as I allowed my body to fully lean into him. His fingers continued a slow and steady caress on my back as he planted light kisses along my neck. I couldn't handle much more. I wanted to kiss him; I needed his lips on mine.

He pushed a wisp of hair from my cheek and gently ran his fingers down the side of my face. He tilted my chin up toward him until I met his eyes. An intense ache washed over me as his hand slid down my side and wrapped around my waist. Pulling me in tighter, his soft mouth brushed across my lips. He tugged at my bottom lip and brought his mouth down on mine. My lips parted and welcomed him as I tentatively touched the tip of his tongue with mine. A groan rumbled in his chest as I brought my arms up around his neck. His salty and sweet taste filled me.

Walker lifted me up and I instinctively wrapped my legs around him as he turned and leaned me against the tree. I could feel his desire as he leaned his hips into me. My grip tightened on his arms as his lips moved from my mouth to my neck and then trailed down to my collarbone as he slipped my shirt buttons open. The hint of my bra peeked out of my shirt as his fingertips danced over the lace trim. I grabbed the back of his hair as his hot breath burned my skin. He gently pulled my bra back and lightly grazed my nipple with his tongue.

"Shit! Walker, stop. Walker!" I said and pushed him away.

He stepped back so fast he almost dropped me on the ground.

"Lacey, oh my God, are you okay?" he asked.

"Walker," I said as I adjusted my bra and struggled to button my shirt. "Shit, shit."

"Did I hurt you?"

I buried my face in my hands, embarrassed that I'd allowed my hormones to completely control my actions. Guilt flooded through me as Mama's earlier words whispered through my thoughts.

"No, I'm sorry. I'm so so sorry I did that. Listen, I'm—" my voice faltered. I stared at the ground trying to find the right words. He stepped toward me and placed his hands on my arms.

I chanced a quick glance at him, but I couldn't stand to watch the disappointment register on his face when I told him.

"Tell me—what did I do? I'll make it right," he said as his concern deepened.

"Walker, I'm a virgin," I said, staring at the ground. "I didn't think things would progress this far and a part of me was afraid that if I told you, after your relationship with Brittany . . . that you wouldn't want to go out with me again."

Walker threw his head back and laughed.

"It's not funny! What the hell is wrong with you?" I said, attempting to pull my arms away.

"I thought I hurt you. I'm sorry. Come here," he said as he wrapped his arms around me and pulled me to him. He kissed the top of my head as he rubbed my back. "Lacey, I'll take anything you're comfortable giving me and no more. You set the rules and I'll follow them. We can take a break, find something else to do, and I'll stand under a shitload of cold showers. God, you are so beautiful."

My head tilted up, searching his face. Was he serious?

"Really? You're okay with stopping?" I asked. My eyes examined his face for any signs that he was lying but didn't find any. The earlier tension slipped away from my shoulders.

"Yes, I really am. I was telling you the truth when I said I just wanted to spend time with you. It doesn't matter what we do—watch movies, go hiking, hang out at home with my family—it's fine. As long as I'm with you." He brushed a few strands of hair from my face.

"And kiss me? You still want to kiss me right?"

"I want to kiss you forever," he whispered as he brought his mouth to mine.

9

I couldn't believe that Walker and I had already been dating for three weeks. A smile eased across my face as I pulled my car into the college parking lot and searched for a space. Monday mornings weren't as busy because no student in their right mind wanted an 8 A.M. class. But I didn't mind; it was just another excuse to not be home.

With my English composition and psychology books in tow I made my way to my first class. Mrs. Jones entered the classroom as I settled into my seat.

"Good morning, everyone. I hope you all caught up on your reading assignment over the weekend," she said, smiling as though she knew better.

As she continued to talk I glanced out the window, my mind drifting to Walker sitting at the pool, half-dressed. The country club closed the outdoor pool in the beginning of October, which meant that Walker was babysitting at the indoor pool today. A soft sigh escaped me and I leaned back in my seat. I suddenly had an overwhelming desire to swim this afternoon.

The morning flew by and my stomach growled as I walked from psychology class across campus to the student center.

The student center was packed as I pushed through the door and searched the tables for Emma. A group of kids gathered around the Ping-Pong table and cheered as a fast-paced game took place. I meandered through the line at the vending machines and continued my search. Most students came to unwind between classes and grab a bite to eat, but it was also party-planning central. If you were searching for a party, the student center was the place to ask around. If half the campus hadn't been underage drinkers, I'm sure flyers would have been posted.

Emma and I hadn't seen each other since school started, so we had agreed to start meeting on Mondays and Wednesdays for lunch to catch up. Between my course load, job, and her nursing classes, we understood that times like these could separate a friendship, and we didn't want that to happen.

Emma and I met during our sophomore year of high school. She'd been the new girl from an even smaller town, and she'd landed in my English class.

The first time I spent the night at her house, I tossed my glasses on her bed and, not realizing they were there, she sat on them. I got so excited trying to tell her my glasses were getting smashed that I sent myself flailing off the edge of her bed and flat onto the floor. The only thing Emma could see were my feet sticking straight up in the air. When she leaned over to see if I was okay, she said my face was almost purple from laughing so hard. There was no turning back after that. She could make me laugh no matter what happened in my life, and I loved her for that.

Emma's aunt and uncle attended the same church as my cousins, so she was already familiar with all the nasty lesbian rumors about Mama and Patsy. Although her parents kept an eye on her, they always let her spend the night, and they invited me over often. For a few years I'd fit almost seamlessly into their perfect family—or so I told myself—but you can only hide ugly for so long before everyone sees it.

"Lacey!" Emma yelled over the noise of the crowd.

I waved as I made my way to the table and smiled as I noted her hair color of the week. Emma had a lot of fun with her hair, but this time it had taken a wrong turn, leaving her with hot pink, spiky locks. Although it was an accident, it fit her: spunky and fun.

"Is it busier than normal?" I yelled, sitting down and unwrapping my sandwich.

"Good Lord, I'm thinking so."

"How are you?" I smiled, glad to have time with her.

"Labs are kicking my butt, Lacey. What in the world was I thinking wanting to become a nurse?"

"That you get to change bedpans and wipe old-people ass?" I laughed.

"Right?" she said as she threw a grape at me.

"You're in a smiley mood today," she said as she peered at me over her glasses. "What gives, Lacey Anne?"

I giggled. I couldn't slip anything past her even if I'd tried.

"Guess?"

"You passed algebra?"

"Crap, thanks for ruining my mood. I hate that class!"

"You'll pass it, keep studying. Hmmmm. You're moving out?"

"Emma, no," I said, laughing.

"Then quit torturing me and spill. You're glowing." She paused as she leaned across the table and peered around as though anyone could actually hear our conversation, "Crap! Lacey! You're not pregnant are you?"

"No, Emma—you have to have sex to get pregnant, from what I remember in our sex-ed class."

She feigned relief as she ran the back of her hand across her forehead. "That's good. I could imagine your mom now."

"Emma, knock it off. You're taking all the fun out of it!"

"Okay, Lacey, what gives?"

I leaned on the table and propped my chin on my hand.

"I'm dating someone." An uncontrollable grin spread across my face. The Joker had nothing on me.

"Whaaat? Who? When? Where? Fill me in!" she squealed as she set her sandwich down, picked up her drink, and situated herself to hear the full story.

"Well, there's not a lot to tell, but his name is Walker. I met him at Joss's party last month and we've gone out for three weeks, and . . . he's gorgeous, Emma!"

She leaned farther across the table and her eyes widened as I told her how we met at the party, Tammy's rude attempt to distract him, the repercussions of Walker calling after 9 P.M., and our first few dates.

"First of all, Lacey Anne Beaumont, you're in big trouble for holding out on me," she said, waving her finger at me.

"I'm sorry, I just didn't want to say anything until I knew it was real. And, I haven't seen you to tell you," I said.

Emma leaned back in her chair and bolted upright again.

"Holy crap, Lacey, your mom doesn't have any idea?"

"No! Dammit, Emma, what am I going to do?" I asked and slumped in my chair.

"Well, so far he sounds acceptable, but in order to fully support this relationship I need to meet this Walker Farren. Second, I do *not* want to be anywhere close by when you tell your mom you're dating him. She does *not* respond well to you dating. Granted, your last choice was complete gutter material, but maybe this one's different." She took a sip of her iced tea.

"Emma, I'm in trouble. I shouldn't be with him, but I like him, and I mean *really* like him. He's different—there's something special about him."

"Well, good grief, don't knock it. Who cares why as long as he's good to you? And who says you're in trouble? Because your mom says you make bad choices? Well, the last one wasn't a hit by any means, but that doesn't mean you're not capable of having a good boyfriend in your life. Besides, everyone knows she hates men."

"Emma! I don't want to talk about this again," I said. A frown crept across my face at how quickly the conversation had turned in an uncomfortable direction.

"Lacey, you know I love you, and I even like your mom, but you need to recognize things for what they are. Your mom isn't right all the time. In fact, she's wrong about a lot."

"Emma, I can't talk about her right now. I wanted to tell you about Walker," I said, sliding my chair back to leave.

"No, wait, Lacey, I'm sorry. My timing sucks. Don't go." Emma tilted her head to the side, brought her prayer hands together, and turned the puppy-dog eyes on. She made me laugh every time.

"Okay, but no more talk about Mama. Not right now, okay?"

"Promise," she said as she saluted and grinned. "When do I get to meet him?"

"I'm not sure, maybe next week? He's taking me to meet his mom and little brother this Friday. I'm really nervous, but he assured me it'll be okay."

"Wow, meeting his mom already, huh? He must really like you. Impressive!"

"I hope so." I picked at the corner of my notebook. "Emma, I'm scared. I've never liked anyone this much before. It's weird. It's almost like I've known him forever—like we've met before and somehow found each other again."

"Alright, you've lost your mind now!" Emma said and smacked her forehead. "You're talking about reincarnation or something silly."

My soda spewed across the table as I burst into giggles. I grabbed a few napkins to soak up my mess before it reached our books. I shook my head and smiled.

"Mama would really be praying for my soul," I said, laughing. "What would I do without you, Emma?"

"Well, lucky you, you won't ever find out," she said and winked.

10

I didn't manage anything productive in my journalism class that afternoon after talking with Emma about Walker. My mind constantly drifted toward him, and I couldn't wait until Friday when I would meet his family. I wouldn't see him tonight since I had to work, but I promised I'd call him as soon as possible after my shift.

The minutes ticked by slower than molasses at work, but I finally pulled my Mustang into the carport at home. I would talk to Mama for a few minutes, but I intended to make it quick.

"Hi, Mama," I said as I opened the door. "How was your day?"

"It's been hell," she said.

Her words stopped me cold and I considered stepping right back out the door. If I were smart I'd leave before it got bad, but one look at Mama and I couldn't. We were family, and family stuck together. Not to mention that I wanted to tell her about Walker. Maybe this was my opportunity: show her some support, and then ease into the conversation.

"Why? What's wrong?" I put my purse on the stairs and sat in the rocking chair farthest away from her.

"Where have you been?"

"At work—I told you I had classes and work tonight. Gosh, Mama, if I forgot to tell you I'm really sorry. Why didn't you call me?" My foot jiggled as the tension mounted between us.

"Shut up, Lacey." Her eyes narrowed as she stared at me. "You ruined my day. I've told you over and over that God gave me special gifts. I feel it when you're telling me the truth or lying."

"Mama, what are you talking about? I went to my classes today, worked on the newspaper, and then went to work. I'm confused. What you're talking about?" Fear knotted in my stomach as I tried to keep my voice even and non-defensive.

"Are you sneaking around with some boy?"

My heart stopped. What did she mean? Had she seen me with Walker somewhere? How did she know? Did God tattle on me again?

"Mama, I don't understand what you're talking about."

"I was praying all day, worried about your safety and praying for your demons to leave. I kept having this awful feeling about you. Then God told me you had snuck off with a boy. So who is it?"

"Mama, I was alright—you shouldn't have worried about me. You can ask my teachers, I was at school and work, nowhere else." I stood up slowly and walked to the kitchen for some water; my heart was pounding so hard that my mind turned fuzzy.

The cold water hit the back of my throat and I attempted to calm down, and then placed the glass on the counter. I hadn't heard the recliner creak over the running water. The moment that I began to turn away from the sink, Mama grabbed my hair, pulling me backward. I tripped and stumbled over the kitchen chair, but managed to grab the table and break my fall.

"You're lying and you know it you little bitch! You've been my worst enemy since you were born. All you've ever done is bring pain into my life with your lies and slutty ways. You're nothing, and you'll never amount to anything as long as you keep living your life this way." Her face darkened with each word.

My mind screamed at me to move back and put some space between us, but my feet refused to obey. Those words shouldn't hurt anymore, but they did. Every one of them cut me and it was only a matter of time before I would bleed out.

"Mama, calm down, I didn't do anything," I whispered.

"Who is he!" she screamed, leaning forward with her arms straight at her sides. Her fists were clenched so tightly that her knuckles were turning white.

"Mama, please, you don't understand!" I pleaded, starting to crumple into myself. My feet felt like they were nailed to the floor.

11

My eyes peeled open slowly and I quickly closed them to regain control of the spinning room. Overwhelming nausea hit me and I groaned. Why was I on the floor, and why in the hell did I ache like I'd been hit by a semi-truck?

I opened my eyes again and blinked away the grit. My breath caught in my throat and I slowly sat up. I searched around the kitchen and living room, but they were empty. Oh my God, Mama had shoved me and I'd hit my head on the floor. Terror shot through me as I remembered the argument, but where was she? I half-expected her to be in the recliner, but it was empty.

Standing slowly, I searched the kitchen and living room again, but I didn't see her.

"Mama?" my voice was raw. "Mama?"

My feet drug across the floor as I left the kitchen and went to her and Patsy's bedroom. I found her lying on the bed, probably praying.

"Mama?" I asked cautiously, refusing to get too close. She didn't reply.

"I'm sorry. I didn't mean to upset you."

Still no response. My gaze traveled to her nightstand. A few pills were scattered on the table and the bottle laid empty on its side. I grabbed the bottle and recognized her sleeping pills. My stomach clenched.

"Mama!" I screamed, shaking her. "Mama, I'm sorry! No!"

"Stop, Lacey," she responded, her voice heavy with sleep. "Stop touching me."

"Mama! What did you do? How many did you take?"

"You don't care about me, Lacey. I'm tired of being hurt by you and everyone else. I don't want to be your mother any longer."

"Mama, don't say that." Tears flowed down my cheeks as I struggled to see through them. "How many did you take?"

"Stop being dramatic, Lacey. I only took two. I knocked the bottle over by accident."

"What?" I grabbed the bottle and read the recommended dosage. Take two at bedtime.

"You're okay? You just said you didn't want to be here anymore." My hand brushed the tears away.

"I don't, but you're not important enough to kill myself over."

My mouth dropped open. How could she say something like that? Didn't she love me? I clenched my hands as her words sunk into me like hot needles.

At that moment, I didn't care if she lived or died. I left her room, grabbed my purse, and ran downstairs and into my bedroom. The door closed behind me and I slid to the floor as the tears rushed out. My body shook as my tears turned into gut-wrenching sobs. Her words rang through my mind again: *I don't, but you're not important enough to kill myself over.*

I hated her. I fucking hated her. My breathing came in short gasps. I needed to leave. Joss or Emma would let me stay with them, but the moment I thought it, guilt flooded through me. A large stone sunk into the pit of my stomach, along with any hope.

No matter what, I couldn't. Mama had prayed all day on Sunday for the demons to leave me, but they hadn't, and I'd hurt her. I couldn't do that to anyone else. My heart constricted at the thought of staying or leaving. Exhausted, I curled up on the floor and drifted off to sleep.

1 2

My entire body hurt, and my head throbbed with each step I took. I'd never regretted working in the children's department as much as I had today. And, to make it worse, we were busy, and I didn't get off work until 9 P.M. The arguing and shrill squeals of children playing filled my world for hours. I could only imagine that no hangover was as torturous as this.

My personal hell kept me from thinking about much else. A continual slow loop of last night's events played over and over in my mind. I assumed I smiled at the customers, but I couldn't recall any real conversations.

In between the constant replay I considered leaving again, but I kept coming back to the same conclusion: I couldn't hurt anyone else.

I searched Catholic churches in the phone book on my dinner break instead of eating. Maybe a priest could perform an exorcism, but I had no idea how to even begin that conversation. *Hi, I'm Lacey, and I'm possessed. Can you help me?* It scared me to think they wouldn't understand; only Mama would and without her, what would happen to me?

If I could I'd just clock out, go home, and crawl into bed. Unfortunately, that meant I would see Mama, and I had no idea what to expect. I couldn't deal with her right now. Instead I called home and talked to Patsy. I listened as Mama gave me permission to stay the night at Joss's house. Honestly, I didn't think she wanted me to come home either.

"Thanks, Patsy," I said, hanging up the phone.

My next call was to Joss. She could tell something was wrong by the sound of my voice, but she didn't ask any questions.

We closed at 9 P.M., and by 9:15 I'd counted the till, turned it in, clocked out, and stepped outside. A few coworkers were smoking and laughing in the parking lot. I waved goodbye and headed to my car. Most nights I tried to park close to the lamp posts so I could see around me, but tonight I hadn't paid much attention.

"Lacey."

Startled, I stumbled backward and dropped my keys and purse.

"Lacey, crap, I didn't mean to scare you," Walker said, stepping into the light.

"Shit, do you make a habit of lurking around people's cars?" I winced at the sharpness in my voice.

"Not generally—I thought you would see me standing here." His hands were shoved in his pockets and he wasn't smiling.

"I'm sorry, I didn't mean to sound mad. You just scared me."

"You never called last night."

"What? Oh God, Walker, I'm sorry. It, it was . . ." my voice trailed off. I couldn't tell him what happened. I couldn't tell him that Mama suspected I was seeing him and shoved me so hard that I'd hit my head and blacked out.

"Hey, are you okay?" he asked. He took the opportunity to step closer. "You've been crying."

"No, not today at least."

"Your eyes are puffy."

"Well, thanks, that's just awesome. CoverGirl can only do so much I guess. What are you doing here?" I asked and crossed my arms over my chest.

"Lacey, look at me. You never called last night and I got worried. I didn't want to call again and take the chance of your mother answering the phone. So, I waited for you tonight and figured I'd talk to you after work. Maybe I'd done something wrong and you were upset with me."

"No, Walker, you didn't do anything wrong." I bent down and picked up the items that had fallen out of my purse.

"Let me help," Walker said. We picked everything up in silence. He had somehow managed to move closer to me by the time we'd finished gathering my belongings and had stood up.

"Hopefully we got everything," he said as he rubbed my arm. "Talk to me."

Even in the dark, his blue eyes radiated. I found myself wanting to kiss him for caring enough to show up at work and check on me.

My pulse raced as I stepped into him, wrapping my arms around his neck.

"Thank you," I said.

He pulled me against him and rested his cheek against mine. His warm breath tickled my ear as he held me.

"I have no idea what's going on Lacey, but don't tell me you can't see me anymore. We're just getting started."

He knew what I'd planned to say. After last night, I realized I'd put myself and him in danger concerning Mama. It was selfish of me to stay with him, to even want to date him. I couldn't tell him, though, so I let him hold me as silent tears slid down my cheeks.

"Have you eaten dinner?"

I shook my head no.

"Okay, let's get you some food and talk."

"You can drive my car," I said and handed him the keys.

He unlocked and opened the passenger door for me. Mama thought I was going to be with Joss, and I needed to find a phone and call her. She expected me to report back when I was out with my friends.

"I need to find a phone and make a few calls first."

He didn't ask any questions and drove through the mall parking lot to the nearest pay phone. Luckily there wasn't any traffic when I called Mama. Patsy answered the phone again. I told her I was at

Joss's and we were heading out to grab a bite to eat. Then I called Joss and told her I was with Walker and that I'd arrive in a little while.

"Take your time—I'll leave the house unlocked for you," Joss said.

I got back in the car and Walker drove us to a restaurant where we could talk. A headache formed while I struggled with what I was going to tell him. The hostess guided us to a booth in the back corner. Grateful it wasn't crowded, I slid into my seat across from Walker.

We ordered our drinks and food. I'd skipped dinner and hadn't realized I was hungry until we walked in and I could smell the food cooking.

My eyes lingered on the window as the traffic went by. The silence hurt but the words were going to hurt more, so I delayed the conversation as long as I could. I wanted to delay it forever, but that wouldn't be fair to him. So I would settle on spending the last few minutes with him that I could. I wanted to engrave him into my memory: his eyes, his dark hair, his kindness, his soft kisses. If I managed that, I would have a piece of him forever.

Walker held my hand; his thumb rubbed the back of it as he searched my face. My cheeks heated and I mentally swore for not hiding my emotions better. Emotions tore me in a million directions. I wanted to be with him. Oh my God, I was falling for him.

It would be another story if he ever found out, though. If he knew who I really was, or the things I did. And, for the first time in my life, I was a little bit scared that if I told him Mama had thrown me on the floor, he'd confront her. I couldn't risk that either.

"How was work?" Walker asked.

"Busier than I hoped. There were a ton of incredibly loud children, and when you're trapped in a small area that echoes, it's rather tortuous. Most of the time I don't mind it, but today I did."

The waitress brought our drinks and I slipped my hand away, found some aspirin in my bag, and downed a few. I folded my hands in my lap. Walker leaned back in his seat and sighed.

"Just say it, Lacey. I can't stand it. Your silence and small talk is tearing me up."

His raw honesty caught me off guard and I stared at him, taking a deep breath.

"Walker, it's not . . ."

"You, it's me," he said, finishing my sentence.

"It's true—there's so much you don't know. My life is complicated, I'm complicated, and I don't want to suck you into a black hole along with me. I care too much about you."

He leaned forward. "Say it again, Lacey."

"I care about you, Walker, I do. I'm crazy about you."

Relief spread across his face and in the next moment I snatched it away from him.

"But it's not enough. Just because I want to be with you, spend every waking moment with you, stay in your arms, and kiss you until my lips are numb doesn't mean it's the right thing to do. It's not the best for either of us and I'd be selfish to do it."

"How in the hell would that be selfish?" he asked as his dark eyebrows rose. "Tell me. If we want the same thing, how is that selfish?"

He leaned forward on the table as his intense stare burned a hole through me. This was worse than I thought it would be. I'd pushed him, and I couldn't lead him on any longer. I wanted to be honest and end the torture for both of us.

Our food came and the next several minutes were filled with complete silence as we ate. I racked my exhausted brain for any possible way I could make this work, but last night's events kept playing over and over in my head.

Yet, at the same time, if I allowed myself to really think about it, I could fall in love with him. In less than a month, he'd shown more respect and fought for me more than anyone else in my life. No one, especially not a guy, had ever cared enough to show up at my job, scare the shit out of me, and talk me out of breaking up with him. I'd never had to fight him off physically like with other guys. Those jack-asses hadn't even bothered to buy me something to eat. Walker asked nothing of me except my honesty.

I dipped a fry into my ketchup and then tossed it onto my plate.

"I can't do this, Walker." I threw my napkin on the table, grabbed my purse, and flung some money on the table. Before I realized it, I'd turned and walked out of the restaurant without so much as a glance behind me, and for the millionth time in the last twenty-four hours, tears ran down my cheeks.

My feet stumbled out the front door, into the parking lot, and I gasped for air. I struggled to see through the tears as I searched for my car. A horn blared at me as a pickup swerved to avoid hitting me.

I found my car and fumbled through my purse for the keys. His footsteps echoed in the against the pavement as he approached me. I bit my lip to stop the tears. My breath came in short, raspy gasps as I dug around frantically in my purse.

"Lacey, you left your keys on the table," Walker said as he jangled my keychain.

I closed my purse.

Unable to turn around yet, I frantically wiped at my tears, rolling my finger under my eyes to eliminate any possibility of raccoon eyes. I leaned forward, my hands on my car, and tried to regain my composure.

"It's been a terrible day, Walker. I thought I could handle things, but apparently I can't."

"You can't drive—I won't let you. So, regardless of whether you want to be with me or not right now, you're stuck with me. I'll take you home."

"No!" I spun around. "I mean, I'm going to Joss's house tonight."

Walker shoved my car keys back into his pocket.

"Okay, I'll take you to Joss's and someone can pick me up there. But I wanted to make sure you're alright first," he said.

"No you don't, Walker. You want answers," I said, kicking at the ground.

"That would be nice under the circumstances. Just take a breath and listen for a minute. Try and think about things from my side, Lacey. We've dated for almost a month and you've always called when you said you would, but not last night. I waited and waited. Of course I'm upset. And worried."

He paused and ran his hand through his hair.

"I wanted to call you so bad, but I remembered what you said about your mom when I called that first night. The last thing I wanted to do was piss her off. The next best thing I could think of was showing up at your work. I couldn't think of anything else. Were you okay? Had I lost you already? Why hadn't you called? Today lasted for years and I was scared of what you'd say to me tonight. But, you didn't say anything. In fact, you told me every reason you thought we *should* be together and in the same sentence shattered any hope I held for us moving forward. So think about that for a minute, Lacey. Think about how I'm feeling right now. How I want to wrap my arms around you and keep you safe from whatever you're running from. Tell me, or I'm left to draw my own conclusions and it starts with something bad at home, which means I'm going to hurt some motherfucker if they laid a hand on you."

I froze, unable to breathe as his words sunk into my head and traveled to my heart. I'd already hurt him without meaning to.

"You can't run from yourself," I whispered.

"What?" he said and moved closer.

"You can't run from yourself," I said louder. "When you're the problem, if you run, it just follows you. No matter what I do, no matter how hard I try to change, I'm not getting better."

Confusion clouded Walker's face as he struggled with my words.

"Are you sick?" he asked as his voice hitched.

"I . . ."

He didn't step any closer and wrap his arms around me. He didn't promise things would be okay this time.

"Yes, Walker, I'm sick." I bit my lip and forced the tears back. I was so tired of crying.

"What? No, I don't understand. You don't seem sick."

"Do you believe in God?"

"Yeah, I mean we're not best friends, but I think he's out there. What does this have to do with you being sick, Lacey?"

"Angels? Do you believe in angels?"

"I guess so," he said as he ran his hands through his hair.

"Do you believe in fallen angels?"

"What? Lacey, for shit's sake, are you dying? How sick are you?"

"No, Walker, I'm not dying. It's not that simple."

He bent over for a second as though my words had removed the fist from his gut and he could breathe again. I hated seeing his reaction, but it would hurt more in a minute. I took a deep, ragged breath, realizing that in a moment I would be left empty.

"Do you believe in fallen angels, Walker?" I asked again.

"Guess so. I've heard the stories in Sunday school about Lucifer and the fallen angels. The same thing most of us learned, I guess—they turned on God and he kicked them out of heaven. They were evil and did all sorts of messed-up crap. I don't understand what this has to do with you being sick, though, Lacey."

"Walker, I'm . . . I'm possessed. By demons."

"What the fuck?" he said more than asked as he took a step backward.

13

"If I'm around you I'm going to hurt you. I don't want to hurt you —anything but that. This is bad enough. I'm so sorry, I should have never agreed to go out with you." My arms crossed in front of me and waited for him to get pissed.

"Lacey, I want to make sure I understand. You're telling me you're possessed, like *The Exorcist* kind of possessed?"

"I haven't watched the movie, so I'm not sure."

"You spoke with a priest? Is that who told you?" he asked as his brows knit together in confusion.

"No, it gets complicated."

"Tell me," he demanded.

I paused and tried to gather the words to tell him something other than what had actually happened last night, but I failed.

"The reason I didn't call you last night was because Mama suspected I'd been dating someone. She didn't know who, but she has this relationship with God and he . . . he just tells her stuff. There's no way she should have known I was with you. I've worked hard at hiding it. She would have said no because I would hurt you, and as long as I'm possessed I can't date anyone. It's not you, it's everyone, Walker."

"Keep talking, Lacey." An edge clipped his voice, but I couldn't tell if he was mad at me or the situation.

"She said when I turned thirteen I became possessed. She said these demons make me act like a slut, attract guys who aren't good for me, make bad decisions, and hurt everyone around me." I stared at my feet, unable to watch as the truth dawned on him. We couldn't be together and now he understood why.

"What happened last night? Tell me everything."

"I got home and I couldn't wait to call you." My gaze searched his face as I talked. I wanted him to understand how much I already cared about him, but his eyes held a stony gaze, almost cold.

I'd finally revealed the ugly I'd tried to hide for years. Resisting the urge to run, I forced the words out of my mouth. He deserved the full story and I had nothing else to lose. I'd already lost him.

"The moment I walked in the front door . . . Mama hadn't had a good day. She told me God had told her I'd been sneaking behind her back and seeing someone. She demanded I tell her who, but I didn't. I tried to calm her down and then I made the mistake of walking into the kitchen for a glass of water. She got mad. She . . . she grabbed my hair."

My brain struggled to form the words as I hiccupped through my tears. Walker stared at me. I would rather a hot knife stab me over and over than have him look at me like this.

"I . . . she . . . shit. She grabbed my hair and threw me backward, calling me a slut and a whore. She started praying and telling the demons to leave me. Fortunately, I caught myself on the kitchen table, but then she moved so fast. Mama's big, and when she prays she gets a little excited. She shoved me and I hit the floor. I don't know how long I was unconscious, but when I woke up, she was in her bedroom, so I just went to my room after that." There was no way I could tell him the rest; that was as much truth as I could handle at once.

"Let me make sure I understand this," Walker said. "You're telling me that your mother has been saying you're possessed by demons, and that on more than one occasion when she's prayed for you, she's physically hurt you?"

I answered him with my silence.

"What does your dad say?"

"I haven't seen my father in years. It's just Mama and Patsy now."

"Who the hell is Patsy?" His voice still sounded cold and clipped.

"Mama's roommate."

Walker took a few steps back and covered his face with his hands. He would probably leave at any moment. At least I was so numb that I wasn't crying anymore and I could see to drive to Joss's house by myself.

"Okay, I'm still working this out. Give me a minute," he said.

He paced back and forth in front of me for a few moments. One second he searched the sky and then he glanced back at me. Confusion danced across his face, and then anger. This was it. The next words out of his mouth would shatter my heart into a million pieces and send me crawling back to Mama begging her to help me get better.

"Where does Patsy sleep?"

"What?" I asked in disbelief.

"Where does Patsy sleep? Does she sleep in her own room? You said she's your mother's roommate right?"

"Yeah, they share the bills, sort of . . . but no, they sleep in the same bedroom." I shook my head as the words came out of my mouth. This wasn't something new and I realized what he was implying; my friends had said it for years.

"She sleeps in the same bed with your mother?" he asked.

"It's not what it sounds like, Walker. Mama has a gift—she has this relationship with God and he tells her things. She sits there all day and talks to Him like you and I are talking right now."

Walker stepped back and ran his hands through his hair. "You're serious aren't you?"

"What? Why would you ask me something like this? What the hell is wrong with you?" My voice stepped up an octave. "Screw you, Walker!"

I turned to open my car door. It refused to open and I remembered that Walker had my keys in his pocket.

"Not yet, Lacey." His voice had softened. "I didn't mean to upset you, but this is some crazy shit and I'm trying to process it. It's not every day your girlfriend tells you she's possessed by demons."

"What?" I said, turning around to face him. "Walker, you're not listening to me! I can't be your girlfriend. I'm possessed."

Walker closed the gap between us and placed a kiss on my forehead. My eyes flicked up to meet his.

"Lacey, I can't tell you everything that's going through my mind right now, but I do know this."

Looking away, squeezed my hands into fists, and attempted to control my shaking. I was pretty sure that nothing he was about to say could breathe life back into my broken heart.

"Look at me, Lacey," he said as he lifted up my chin and forced me to meet his eyes. "You're not in any way possessed by demons—not one, and not a hundred. Your mother is fucking crazy, and you're right, she won't like me or any other guy you bring home."

I shook my head frantically, denying what he was saying. He didn't understand. I tried to turn away from him, but he refused to let me go.

"Stop, don't turn away from me. I'm sorry, but you're not possessed. You don't behave in a way that would harm other people, you're not mean, and you don't lie, steal, rape people, or hurt kids or animals do you?"

I didn't even have to think before answering those questions. No, I'd never done those things, not in a million years.

"Okay, we'll get through this. I can't imagine how tired you are right now. Did you go to the hospital? Do you have a concussion?" he asked as his face filled with concern.

"What? Oh . . . I'm not sure, I never thought about it," I said, rubbing my head.

"It's been long enough that you're okay, but let's get you to Joss's for now."

"I don't understand, Walker. You shouldn't want anything to do with me."

He touched my cheek and wiped away the remnants of my tears.

"You're braver and stronger than you'll ever realize, Lacey. Please just trust me when I say there's nothing wrong with you. You aren't possessed. Don't push me away anymore. Let me help you."

The next several moments were filled with complete silence as he waited for my response. I wanted to trust him. And what if he was right? What if there wasn't anything wrong with me? Did I dare reach out for the one piece of hope that anyone had ever extended to me? Did I dare trust him and what he said? I wanted to, and I wanted him.

A chill shuddered through me as I realized I'd just shared my darkest secret with him. I'd kept it so buried that I'd wondered if I even held the key to unlock it any longer. No one knew including Emma and Joss. No One. Ever. I was terrified of losing the few people in my life that I allowed in.

"You don't need to say anything else, Lacey. You've been through enough tonight, but remember what I said."

He leaned down, brushed his lips against mine, and pulled back. I wrapped my arms around his neck and drew him back to me. He gently kissed me and ran his fingers through my hair. My mouth opened and invited him in, my tongue tentatively touching his. Our kiss deepened, and his arms enveloped me in a warm cocoon as I melted into him.

"You crazy kids break it up!" someone yelled from across the parking lot.

"Crap," I said as I broke the kiss, embarrassed. Walker laughed as he dug my keys out of his pocket and unlocked the passenger door to let me in.

14

"**L**et's get you to Joss's house."

As he drove he occasionally planted kisses on the back of my hand and smiled. Maybe he thought I might run off again or do something crazy. I wanted to trust him, but there was a part of me that expected him to call me tomorrow and break things off. Who could blame him? I'd just opened a whole can of crazy.

He pulled into Joss's driveway, turned off the car, and held onto my keys. "There's been a small change of plans—don't move," he said and kissed me before he got out of the car.

Puzzled, I watched him knock on Joss's door. Joss opened it, peered around him to make sure I was in the car, and then let him in. I'm sure it was only for a few minutes, but I wondered what in the world they could be talking about for so long. I was left alone with no radio, only my thoughts.

My hand covered my mouth as I stifled a yawn and leaned my head back, closing my eyes.

"Hey sleepyhead, wake your ass up," Joss suddenly said through the car window.

I smiled and opened the door. "Sorry, I didn't realize how tired I was," I said and reached to unbuckle my seatbelt.

"Nope, keep it buckled. Walker is going to take care of you tonight. You're going to stay at his house okay?"

"What? Joss, no!"

"Hey, it's alright, I'll take care of your mom. It's almost midnight so she won't call tonight anyway. You focus on getting some sleep and feeling better. I'll talk to you tomorrow, alright?" Her tone shifted from playful to gentle and motherly. Walker had told her something. I glanced at him as he got back into the car.

"I seriously doubt his mom is going to let me stay the night," I said, sighing.

"He already called her from my house, and she's expecting you both. Now hush, and go. I'll talk to you tomorrow. Everything will be okay, promise." She reached in and gave me a hug.

"You promise things will be okay, Joss?" I struggled to push down the panic in my chest.

"Yes. I've never lied to you, right?"

"No, never."

She smiled as she closed my car door.

Walker started the car and we pulled out of the driveway.

"I think I'm mad at you, but I'm not sure," I said.

"Why would you be mad at me?"

"Because you just went into my best friend's house and convinced her that I should spend the night at your place. And your mom actually said it was okay? Shit!"

"What?" Walker asked, a hint of worry threaded through his voice.

"I look like hell and I'm going to meet your family! How could you do this to me? And all I have to wear is this ugly work uniform!"

Walker tried to hide his grin.

"Tell you what," he said. "I'll let you take a hot shower and brush your teeth, and you can sleep in one of my T-shirts and my sweats. You'll just need to tie them really tight so they don't fall down." He laughed. "I wouldn't be upset if they fell down, but you might. I have a younger brother who walks around with a hard-on, so we'll keep you covered. You can grab some of Mom's makeup in the morning if you need too. Honestly, I can't wait to wake up with you in the morning, even if your hair does stick up in every direction."

I appreciated the darkness as my face flushed at the thought.

15

Thirty minutes later, we pulled into a gravel driveway. A small, two-story red-brick home stood at the end of the road and only a single light shone from inside. Large oak and maple trees lined the road, their leaves just starting to change color. I hoped I'd be able to come back in a few weeks to see them when they were at their most brilliant.

Walker pulled into the carport next to a black Camaro.

"Is that your mom's?" I asked, getting out of the car. "It's beautiful."

"Yeah, she loves that car. She won't let me drive it, though."

"Really? Why? You're a good driver," I said.

"It's fine. Let's get inside," Walker said as he held open the screen door.

Walker quietly unlocked the door and led me into the dark kitchen and to the left into his bedroom.

"This is your room?" I asked, surprised.

"Yup, this is it," he said and placed my keys on his dresser.

"You can put your stuff anywhere. I'll tell Mom we're here." He kissed my forehead and left me alone in his room.

I noted the golf trophies on his dresser and almost laughed, but I was too nervous. Golf is not the sport I imagined him playing, but the proof sat in front of me. Although I was curious, I was afraid to touch anything, and wrapped my arms around myself. My eyes caught the picture of a younger Walker with a baseball team, and I walked over to it. His eyes and dark hair were unmistakable.

"That was about four years ago," he whispered as he wrapped his arms around me and nuzzled my neck with a kiss.

"You haven't changed much, just the ability to grow facial hair instead of peach fuzz," I laughed.

"Mmmhmm."

"Where am I going to sleep?" I asked, turning toward him.

"In my bed," he said as he tried to keep a straight face.

"Where are *you* going to sleep, Walker?" I cocked my head and placed my hands on my hips.

"Well, my plan was to let you shower and then tuck you into bed and crawl in beside you," he said, testing the water.

"You did *not* bring me over here to get me into bed!"

"Shhh, Lacey, no, not like you're thinking," he said, laughing softly.

"Then you better explain before I grab my keys and drive back to Joss's," I said. My eyes narrowed as I waited for his explanation.

"No, I told you at the lake you set the rules. I won't try a thing, I promise. I just want to hold you tonight. That's all," he said as a soft smile spread across his face.

My gaze dropped to my feet, and I paused as his words sank in.

"You promise? You'll just hold me and nothing more?"

"I promise," he said as he held up his hands like he was surrendering.

"We can try it, but if you cross a line, Walker Farren, you can sleep in your brother's room." I glared at him for extra emphasis.

"You're seriously cute when you're exerting yourself," he said and kissed me again. He turned to his dresser and pulled out a T-shirt and sweatpants for me.

"I hope these will work. You're pretty little, but I think they will." He took my hand, led me into the bathroom, and grabbed a towel and toothbrush for me.

He closed the door behind him. I suddenly realized how weird it was that I was standing in my boyfriend's bathroom getting ready to take a shower and spend the night . . . with his mother at home. I slipped off my shoes and clothes and turned on the shower, half expecting the door to open at any moment with a pissed-off mom or Walker inviting himself back in. Either way, I wanted to get into the water and hide behind the curtain.

I stepped into the spray and let the water flow over me as I took a deep breath, rubbing the remaining makeup off my face and washed my hair. The bathroom filled with the scent of vanilla as I soaped my body. I wished it would wash away the pain, too. Not just the physical ache from last night, but the sharp pang in my heart every time I thought about Mama and our fight.

Placing my hands on the wall in front of me, I leaned into the hot water, my body heavy with exhaustion.

I turned off the water, grabbed the towel, dressed, and brushed my teeth. The bathroom door creaked slightly as I opened it and then made my way through the darkness and back to Walker's room.

I'd never allowed any of my boyfriends to see me without makeup, not to mention not wearing my own clothes. I stepped into his room and stood at the foot of his bed. He lay in the middle of his bed with his eyes closed. He was still wearing his polo shirt and jeans.

"Close the door," he whispered.

I turned the knob and pushed the door quietly closed.

"Come here," he said and patted the bed next to him.

"My hair is still wet," I replied.

"It's okay, the pillow will dry."

I crawled into the bed and slipped under the covers. Walker slipped in next to me and we faced each other, mere inches apart.

"You're so beautiful," he whispered.

"You don't need to say that, Walker. If you haven't realized it, I'm already in your bed," I said.

"I'm serious, Lacey."

My breath hitched as our eyes locked. A faint hint of Polo cologne lingered on his skin, and I resisted the urge to bury my face against his chest and listen to his heartbeat. I wasn't sure how I planned to sleep with him so close, but at the same time, part of me felt relieved. I was safe, for the first time I could remember.

He lifted my chin and kissed me. "You need to get some sleep," he said as he pulled away.

"I'm not sure how you expect me to with you in the same bed," I said.

"Turn around."

As I rolled over, Walker scooted up behind me until the back of my head was touching his chest. I began snuggling the rest of my body into him, but he put his hand on my butt.

"If you move any closer, I'm going to come undone—and I mean that in the literal sense," he whispered.

I wanted to be with him, but I wasn't ready to give him all of me yet, so I stopped and accepted it for what it was. Besides, I was still trying to figure out if he was going to leave me after everything I'd told him tonight.

The warmth of his body and his steady breathing lulled me to sleep within minutes. I didn't dream.

16

The sound of voices and aroma of coffee and bacon woke me the next morning. I glanced at the empty place on the bed next to me and then looked at the clock. Crap, it said 7 A.M.—classes started at 9 A.M.

I threw the blankets back, rifled through my purse for my hairbrush and a hair tie, and walked quietly to Walker's dresser mirror and almost shrieked in horror. My hair stuck up in multiple directions and my eyes were swollen. My eyes searched around for water and found a glass on his nightstand. I grabbed it, stuck my brush in it, and ran the brush through my hair, smoothing the crazy strands into place. Hopefully he wouldn't drink the water later.

"How is she?" came a woman's voice from the kitchen. I stopped and realized that I was about to walk out of my boyfriend's bedroom and into the kitchen to meet his mother for the first time.

"Crap, crap, crap!" I muttered as I continued to work as fast as I could to get my hair manageable and in a respectable ponytail. Stepping back, I straightened Walker's T-shirt and pulled up his sweats so they wouldn't drop to my ankles the moment I walked into the kitchen.

My pulse raced while I shook my arms out, took a deep breath, and opened the bedroom door. My bare feet didn't make any noise as I stepped into the kitchen. Walker stood with his back to me, cooking breakfast. Slowly, I peered around the corner at his brother while he sat at the kitchen table and picked his nose. I stepped back and muffled my giggles against my arm. How gross, but he was thirteen. My attention flickered between Garrett and Walker again, and I noticed that they looked nothing alike. His sandy-brown hair and dark eyes were in stark contrast to Walker's.

My eyes closed for a moment while I gathered my composure and then entered the small kitchen. At the same time, the woman who had spoken earlier walked through the door on the opposite side of the room. I stopped short. A beautiful but abnormally thin woman stood at the other side of the room and returned my gaze. She allowed me a moment to gather my surprise and then she smiled.

"Good morning, Lacey," she said as she slowly made her way to the kitchen table. The squeak of wheels echoed through the room as she pulled her oxygen tank behind her.

"Hi, Mrs. Farren," I replied quietly.

"Mom, wait, I'm coming, let me help you," Walker said. Within two steps, he was by her side and guiding her to the chair.

I stood in awe and then realized that the eggs and bacon were going to burn, so I stepped in and finished cooking.

"Good morning," Walker said as he kissed me on the cheek and wrapped his arms around me.

"Hi," I said, smiling at him. "Mrs. Farren, thank you for allowing me to stay last night," I said, peeking around Walker. "Hi, Garrett," I smiled.

Garrett sat at the table with his mouth open. I guess no one had bothered to tell him that his brother had company.

Grateful for the cooking distraction, I turned my attention back to the food.

"Let me get the biscuits out of the oven," Walker said as he patted my butt and scooted me out of the way.

"Walker!" I hissed, "Your mother is sitting right over there."

"I know," he said, teasing me and laughing. "Go sit down and talk to her. She wants to speak to you."

My eyes grew large.

"No, she's not upset at all that you're here, just the opposite. It's safe, I promise," he said and stroked my cheek with his thumb.

I approached the kitchen table and pulled out the chair next to Mrs. Farren, smiling as I slipped into the seat.

"I don't mean any disrespect at all, Mrs. Farren, but this is really strange. I've never stayed at a boyfriend's house before," I said and bit my lip.

"It's okay, Lacey. Walker called me last night and I said it was fine." Her eyes filled with compassion.

I turned to Walker and tried to figure out exactly what he'd told his mom.

"Uh, well, thank you again," I said as I refocused my attention on her.

"You can call me Susan."

"Are you sure?" I asked.

"Absolutely," she said and sipped her coffee.

"Okay, Susan," Garrett piped up.

"Not you, young man." Susan laughed and spiraled into a hard coughing fit.

Walker was next to her in an instant. "Garrett, get Mom some juice."

Garrett hopped up, grabbed some juice, and brought it back to Susan. After a couple of minutes, her cough settled and Walker put the food on the table. He took the seat across the table from me.

Guilt filled me as I realized why Walker hadn't wanted to talk about his family that day. I had selfishly shared my secrets with him, and not once did he say anything about his mom being sick or having to take care of his family.

Walker nudged me under the table. I glanced up—he'd realized what I was thinking.

"Lacey, Walker says you're in college. What's your major?"

"Communications," I said between bites of egg. "I was going to major in journalism, but then we conducted an interview with a family whose son had fallen on an iron fence. He was still alive, but the fence post had speared right through his chin. I had to interview the parents while the medical team tried to get him down without killing him. All I wanted to do was hug the parents and tell them he was going to be okay."

"Cool!" Garrett said.

Walker reached over and smacked the back of his head. "Not cool, bro. Show some manners."

I hid my smile, but peeked back at Garrett and winked at him.

"How do you plan on using your degree?" Susan asked.

"Honestly, I'm still figuring it out. I love writing. I'm the editor of the college paper and I write my own column."

"I didn't know that," Walker said. "She works full-time at Jack's Department Store in the mall, too," he said to his mom.

"Busy girl with a lot of goals I bet?"

"Yes, ma'am."

"Susan is fine, Lacey, really," she said.

"Okay," I said, smiling.

"What are your plans today, Walker?" Susan asked.

"I have to work and later today I was going to take Lacey to meet Aunt Linda."

"Oh, that's an excellent idea. Linda is my sister. You'll like her."

"Yeah, for an aunt she's actually kinda cool," Garrett chimed in.

"Garrett, are you ready for school? Did you get your paper done? Isn't it due this week?"

Garrett collapsed back in his chair and groaned.

"What kind of paper, champ?" I asked.

"English and it sucks!" he whined.

"Well, if your mom and Walker don't mind, maybe you can wait a little while and I'll help you tonight after I meet your aunt?" I waited for Susan and Walker to approve.

"Yeah!" Garrett said. "Please, Mom? I'll even do the dishes."

"You're on," Walker said and piled all the plates in front of Garrett before Susan could respond.

"That's fine with me as long as Lacey doesn't mind. Lacey, why don't you come with me and we'll find some clothes for you to wear today. I'm sure Walker likes you walking around in his T-shirt, but we need to get you into clothes that fit better." She smiled.

Walker helped her up and the three of us walked back to her bedroom.

"Shut the door behind you, please, Walker," Susan said. Walker nodded and winked at me as he stepped out of the room, the door closing softly behind him.

Oh shit, she brought me back here to tell me what a horrible person I am. I took a deep breath before I turned toward her. I opened my mouth to apologize again, but she cut me off.

"He didn't tell you I was sick, did he?" she asked.

Susan's question caught me off guard.

"Uh, no, no he didn't. I had no idea at all. I shouldn't be here . . ."

"Lacey, stop honey, there's no reason to apologize. I did want to talk to you without the boys around, though. And I was serious about getting you some clothes—I think you'll find some jeans that are too big for me now. They're hanging in my closet. I think they're a size three, so they should fit you okay."

I turned to find them as tears welled up in my eyes, unable to imagine a size three being too big.

"These?"

"Yes, they're just some comfortable Levi's but I think they'll fit you. You can borrow any shirt you like as well."

I grabbed a light-blue V-necked shirt and held it up for her approval.

"That's fine," she said, nodding.

"Susan?"

"I was diagnosed with stage-four lung cancer. The doctors are only giving me about six months to live, maybe less."

"Shit," I said as I sat down on the bed next to her. "Oh, gosh, Susan, I'm sorry. I didn't mean to swear."

Her laugh turned into another coughing fit. I sat helplessly and waited for it to end.

She straightened back up and drew in a slow, raspy breath. "It's okay, both my boys swear sometimes."

"Is this what you wanted to tell me? Your diagnosis?"

"Yes, I could tell by the expression on your face that Walker hadn't said anything. I don't want you to feel uncomfortable. Ask me anything you want."

"Does it hurt? Are you in pain?"

"Yes, all the time. That's why Walker helps so much."

I wasn't sure what to say.

"He didn't tell me details, in case you're wondering," Susan said.

"About?"

"Why you're here. He said you and your mom had gotten into an argument and asked if you could stay here for the night."

"Oh," I said and stared at my feet.

"Lacey, I realize there's more to it, and I know my son. Whatever it was, it was bad enough for him to step in. He's in love with you and honestly, he hasn't been this happy in years."

Confusion clouded my face. "Even with Brittany?"

"I thanked God the day he came in and said he'd broken up with her for good. Some people bring out the worst in each other. Brittany isn't a bad person—she's young and selfish, but she's not a bad person. But when she and Walker were together it became a toxic relationship for them both. I recently recognized something in him that I haven't seen in years: hope and happiness. It's you. No matter where this relationship goes, I wanted to thank you for giving me the gift of seeing my son with someone who's good for him." She reached out and squeezed my hand.

"Susan—" I tilted my head back and tried to contain my tears.

"It's okay, you don't need to say anything at all. I just wanted to tell you. Whatever is going on in your life, let him love you. Let him in. You couldn't be in better hands."

The tears won and slid down my face. "Can I hug you?" I asked quietly.

"You don't need to ask again," she said and wrapped her frail arms around me.

After a moment, she pulled away. "You're welcome here anytime, okay?"

"Are you sure? I don't want to intrude, ever, especially with—"

"Bringing happiness and laughter into my home is always welcome, especially now."

I smiled, grateful for our talk.

"Go get dressed. Help yourself to anything of mine you need. We girls should stick together," she said as her eyes lit up.

"Thank you, Susan. I'll see you later today."

I frowned as I looked at my watch and realized I didn't have time to talk to Walker about his mom or last night. It would have to wait until after classes.

17

The late-afternoon light peeked through the trees at Walker's house. Although it was October, it seemed as though fall started later and later in Arkansas. I kicked at the leaves on the sidewalk and knocked on the front door. My heart fluttered at the thought of seeing him again after what had ended up being a long day of classes.

"Hey, Lacey," Garrett said as he waved me in.

"Hey, buddy, how was your day at school?"

"Stupid," he replied. "Walker's in his room, just go in."

"Thanks," I said as I made my way to his room.

"Hey," I said.

"Hey, yourself," Walker said as he tied his shoe. "Are you ready to go meet Aunt Linda?"

He stood up and pulled me in for a kiss. It was weird being with him in his bedroom while his mom was in the living room. Mama would have never allowed it.

"Almost," I said and wrapped my arms around his waist. "Your mom . . . why didn't you tell me, Walker? I unloaded all my crazy shit on you last night and not once did you mention your mom and what you're going through. You have enough to deal with—why am I here with you?"

"You're here because I want you here. I was going to tell you about Mom, but it wasn't first- or even third-date material. I wanted to go out with you for a while and make sure before I brought you home. I didn't want to send you running."

"I'm not the one that should be running," I said. "We never talked about our conversation in the parking lot last night. You never said much—I mean, not about what's wrong with me."

"We will, but for now, I want to introduce you to Aunt Linda. We can talk after you meet her."

I nodded, but I didn't understand why he wanted to wait.

"Trust me," he said as he kissed the top of my head and took my hand. I followed him as he walked from his bedroom to another door off the kitchen.

"Where are you taking me?" I asked.

"You'll see."

I followed him up a set of stairs to another door, which he knocked on.

"I didn't realize your Aunt Linda lived above you, Walker."

He smiled as I squeezed his hand and we waited. Moments later the door opened and we entered another house.

"Hi, Aunt Linda," Walker said and hugged her.

She chuckled and patted his back.

"Hi, Lacey," she said as she extended her hand to me.

"Nice to meet you, ma'am."

"Call me Linda, please." Her face lit up with a warm smile as she motioned for us to come in.

It was obvious that Linda and Susan were sisters. Walker got his blue eyes from his aunt. She was shorter than Susan, but shared the same cheekbones and hair color.

"Aunt Linda bought this place when Mom got sick so she could help take care of her when I couldn't be around," Walker explained.

I attempted a smile as I struggled with what to say. What were you supposed to say when you found out your boyfriend's mom might only have six months to live?

"Make yourselves comfortable," Linda said.

We followed her to the couch; Linda sat in the chair on the other side of the coffee table and folded her hands in her lap. Walker took my hand as an uneasy gnawing tugged at me. I had plenty of experience with sensing uncomfortable situations, and I didn't like this one. Plus, I was confused as to why Linda was staring at me, too.

"It's okay," he whispered and rubbed his thumb across the back of my hand.

"I can tell by the surprise on your face that you're confused about why Walker brought you here other than to say hello," she said. "I'm a mental health therapist, Lacey."

"What?" I jumped off the couch. "Walker? How could you? You brought me here to lock me up?" I tried to step around his feet to leave, but he was too fast. He grabbed me and pulled me into his lap.

"Lace, wait, it's not you. Aunt Linda isn't here to diagnose you or anything close to it—please give her a minute to explain . . . for me."

"I'm sorry, Lacey," Linda said, "I didn't mean to scare you. You're in no way being diagnosed with anything. It's the opposite, actually. Walker told me a little bit about your mother."

"Walker!" The humiliation crushed my chest. "How could you? I told you that in confidence. I trusted you." I tilted my head back and closed my eyes. If I squeezed them hard enough maybe this would all disappear.

"The reason he said something is because he knows that there isn't anything wrong with you, Lacey. I wanted to talk to you and help you understand that you're not demon-possessed or anything close it. There's also information I have that could help you at home."

I turned to face her. "I'm not possessed? Are you sure? You've only met me for a few minutes."

"Let me ask you a few questions so we can clear this up."

"Okay," I said as a little bit of the tension eased from my shoulders.

"Do you black out or lose periods of time?"

My eyebrows furrowed as I thought about her question. I'd never blacked out before that I was aware of. Surely someone would have told me by now.

"No. I remember what I do during the day, a month ago, and farther back."

"Okay, good. Have you ever harmed yourself? For instance, cutting?"

"No, oh God, no."

"What about animals? Do you hurt them?"

The questions grew more absurd by the moment.

"What? No!"

"Okay, and are you violent? Do you ever experience bursts of anger and harm others even though you were fine a few minutes before?"

I shook my head and tried to process what Linda was asking me.

"Lacey, those are a few of the typical signs that someone—if you believe in possession—would exhibit. Often it's another cause, such as an undiagnosed mental illness. Someone doesn't walk around for years with something like this without it being detected."

"You don't understand. I appreciate your help, but . . . Mama is different, she has this relationship with God that most people don't understand."

Walker rubbed my arm.

"Do you trust Walker?" Linda asked.

I turned to look at him. I did, or at least I wanted to.

"Yes."

"He's spent several weeks with you, correct?" She didn't give me time to answer. "Walker has assured me that he hasn't seen anything wrong with you other than you've been hurt. Take a minute to think about the questions I asked and your answers. You were horrified at the mere thought of harming yourself, someone else, or animals. These are not signs of someone with a demonic possession problem. Lacey, you're not in any way walking around with a demon or demons inside you."

"Are you sure?" I asked, my voice barely above a whisper. "Are you sure there's nothing wrong with me?"

"I'm positive," she said with a gentle smile.

I sat there for a moment and tried to wrap my mind around what Linda was telling me.

"Linda, if what you're saying is true, then what *is* wrong with me?"

"Why do you think anything is wrong with you?"

I didn't answer.

"Let's do this. Let me ask some questions about your mother. I think that might help you understand some more. Is that okay?"

"Yeah," I replied. I slid off Walker's lap and onto the couch next to him.

"Walker mentioned that your mom has a roommate. What's her name?"

"Patsy." I stared at my shoes. My cheeks burned with the question. Here I was, once again, explaining Mama's situation. "Yes, they share the same bedroom and the same bed," I blurted.

"Is their relationship healthy?" she asked.

"What do you mean by that? Where's this going?" I was unable to hide the exasperation in my voice.

"I'm trying to get a clear picture, or the best picture I can, to explain some things. But first I need more answers." She waited patiently for me to indicate we could go on. I was so focused on the conversation that I almost forgot Walker was next to me.

"They fight," I said. "I don't mean they just argue, which they do too, but Mama gets hot pissed. Sometimes she hits Patsy. A few weeks ago, Mama had Patsy pinned down on the floor. Mama had a butcher knife in her hand and she screamed that she was going to kill her. Mama's big and super strong when she's mad. I just walked right back downstairs. I don't think Patsy or Mama even realized I'd witnessed the fight. So, I guess now that I think about it, no. They don't have a great relationship."

"Tell me more about Mama. Is she angry a lot? Is she in a good mood one minute and the next she isn't?"

"I guess. I honestly stay away as much as I can. I work and go to school so it helps me stay out of the house."

"Does your mom work?"

"Does sitting in her recliner praying for everyone count as a job?" I snapped.

"That makes you angry?"

"Of course it makes me mad. She never wants to go anywhere or do anything. She's always in that damned chair praying. The minute one of us walks in the door she's sitting us down and explaining everything we're doing wrong and what demon needs to be prayed out of us," I hiccupped.

I covered my face to hide the tears from Walker. Walker hadn't said a word, but he pulled me closer and kissed the top of my head. I wasn't sure if I wanted to crawl into his lap or run. I'd never shared any of this with anyone. He was going to break things off with me for sure.

"What do your mom and Patsy fight about?" Linda asked.

"A few times, Mama accused Patsy of wanting to leave. I don't know if it's true or not. Mama doesn't like Patsy to be out her sight very often. Even when Patsy's at work, Mama calls her. Patsy has even come home from work to talk to Mama."

"I know this is difficult, Lacey. Have you spoken to anyone about this before?"

"Only a little bit—Mama always stopped it. Somehow she finds out what I've said and she doesn't allow me to schedule appointments with a counselor anymore. She says I'm always trying to turn people against her and that I'm her enemy."

"Did you ever tell anyone about your mom hitting Patsy?"

I shook my head no. "You're the first person I've ever told—you and Walker, anyway." I didn't dare glance his way.

"Do you consider her to run the family?"

"Yeah, everyone does what she says. I'm not sure if it's because we think she's right or because we're scared."

"You're afraid of her?" Linda leaned forward in her chair.

"I don't remember a weekend I was home that she hasn't threatened to kill Patsy or hit her. I don't want her to come after me too." My words choked me as I spoke them.

"Has she come after you?"

I shook my head. "Not like that."

"But?"

I didn't answer her. I wasn't ready to tell anyone else about my argument with Mama.

"So, you don't think I'm sick?" I asked, redirecting the conversation.

"No, I don't. I think your mom is."

"What do you mean?"

Linda leaned back in her chair and crossed her legs.

"Lacey, I can't say anything for sure since I've never met your mom. Off the record, we might be dealing with several possibilities, including bipolar, borderline personality disorder, or narcissism and depression. It's difficult to say, but I can promise you two things: you're not demon-possessed, and no matter what, the violence you're living with is not normal or acceptable. Your mom doesn't have a right to hit you, Patsy, or anyone else. Ever. Do you understand?"

"She doesn't mean to," I said, "I just say the wrong thing. She can be okay and then I say something I shouldn't have and I've started the war."

Silence hung in the air for a moment.

"Lacey," Linda said gently, "she can't get better as long as you're making excuses for her."

"I . . . can she get better? Are these things you mentioned curable?" I asked, ignoring part of what Linda had said.

"It would take a lot of hard work, Lacey, but people get better all the time."

"This is a lot to take in," I muttered, biting my lip.

"I agree. It is a lot. Let me give you some information to read concerning some disorders. Maybe it will help you understand mental illness a little bit better. Your mom needs help, Lacey. However, you're not responsible for her. You can't change her—she has to want that for herself."

I reached out and accepted the brochures from her.

"Thank you, Linda. Thank you for talking to me and I'm sorry I was snappy."

I stood up, walked out the door, and left Walker and Linda sitting in her living room. I hopped down the stairs two at a time and went straight out the front door. My head pounded with each step I took as the tears streamed down my face. What if Linda was right? A part of me wanted her to be right. I didn't want to be possessed, but I didn't want Mama to be sick either. And, if all of that was true, how was I going to help Mama?

"Lacey?"

"Susan, what are you doing out here?" I asked, walking down the path to the patio. I attempted to wipe away my tears as I approached her.

"Well, I do like to come outside sometimes and sit under my oak tree. Have a seat and join me." She smiled and pointed at the available chair.

I pulled the chair out from the small table and sat down.

"I'm sure whatever Linda said is a lot to take in. I can only guess, not having all the details." She arranged her oxygen tank at her side as she shifted in her chair. "It was my idea."

"What do you mean?" I asked. I wrapped my arms around myself and leaned back into the outdoor chair.

"When Walker called me last night, he was so upset, Lacey. He wouldn't tell me exactly what happened, but he wanted to talk to your mother."

"What? Oh my God, Susan, no! He can't do that!" I shot forward in my chair as my eyes grew wide at the thought of Walker showing up at my house.

"I realized that. That's why I told him to bring you here and suggested you talk to Linda. It was all me."

"Why would you want to help me? I don't even know you," I said as I leaned back again.

"Well, you do now." She laughed, which followed by a coughing fit.

"Susan, I'm sorry."

"Lacey, you need to stop apologizing. None of this is your fault, honey. You didn't ask for problems with your mom, nor did you ask

Walker, myself, or Linda to help you. There are some things I can still do before I leave this earth. If one of them includes helping you, then I gladly accept."

I leaned forward and rested my head in my hands as I cried. No one had ever said anything like that to me before. Susan remained silent as I cried.

"I'm a mess," I said as I tried to wipe away my smeared makeup. My eyes had already been puffy from the crying and lack of sleep even before I came over.

"Did Linda tell you?"

"No, and she won't. Walker won't either. It'll need to come from you."

"Okay," I said and bit my bottom lip. "Linda thinks my mom might have a mental illness."

"I'm sure that's a lot to think about," Susan said.

I nodded. "I don't know what to think right now. Mama always told me it was my fault she acted like she does."

"That's a lot of power she's giving you."

"What?" I asked, surprised. "I don't have any power, or I'd be able to make Mama stop hitting Patsy or throwing me on the floor . . ." My voice trailed off as I realized what I'd said. "She's not a bad person, Susan. I love her very much."

"I know you do, or you wouldn't have protected her secrets this long. The hard part is understanding that you can't save her, nor is it your job to do so. She's grown, she knows right from wrong, and she also realizes that help is a phone call away. Your mother sounds like an intelligent woman."

"She is," I nodded.

"So are you, Lacey. Take some time to think about everything Linda talked to you about. You can talk to her, Walker, or me anytime."

"Thank you," I said.

"You're always welcome," she said and flashed me a warm smile.

18

"Hey," Walker said as he crawled into his bed next to me.

"Hey," I whispered as his strong arms wrapped around me. "I guess I fell asleep. It's all this stupid crying."

"It's okay, I wanted to check on you," Walker said and brushed my cheek with a kiss.

I rolled over to face him.

"I feel like hell. My eyes burn from crying,"

"You're beautiful, and your eyes are even greener if that's possible."

"What time is it?" I asked as I rubbed my face.

"It's six o' clock," he replied.

I sighed and peered out his bedroom window at the large oak tree.

"Walker, what if your aunt is right? What if nothing's wrong with me?"

"There's not a doubt in my mind that she's right, Lace. I knew there must've been something going on with your mom even before we talked last night, but what you told me took it to a different level. She can't hit anyone. That's never okay."

"If she's sick, how did I not know? How did I not see it?" I asked, covering my face with my hands.

Walker gently pulled them away.

"You can't blame yourself. We all believed what our parents told us when we were growing up—we didn't know any different. You couldn't have known it wasn't normal because it was *your* normal."

"I still don't understand everything. Like, how did she find out you and I are together? I mean, we've been out to the lake, the mall, dinner, and other places so I guess anyone could have seen us."

"Yeah, there were always other people around, except when I took you to watch the sunset at the lake. No one was around then, I checked."

"Oh, I guess I wasn't paying any attention." I giggled as I thought about that day.

"You haven't laughed in a while," Walker said.

His gaze traveled up my face and held my eyes. If I let myself, I could get lost in his eyes for days. They were warm and safe.

"I love you," he whispered.

I stared at him, speechless. No guy had ever told me he loved me, and I'd never said it to anyone in a romantic way. I'd never been in love before, until now. Not only had he accepted me even after I'd revealed the worst parts of myself, but he had taken me home and kept me safe.

My heart belonged to him; I couldn't fight it anymore. He was the best thing that had ever walked into my life, and I was going to hang on to him with everything I had.

"I love you too, Walker."

He smoothed my hair away from my face and kissed my nose. My hand slid around the back of his neck and I pulled him to me. I wanted every part of him against me, wanted his warmth to fill me. Not just my body, but my mind, my heart, and the core of my being. I loved him. I loved this man for his strength and his ability to love me despite my craziness.

He placed a trail of kisses along my cheek and neck as he rolled me over onto my back. I wrapped my legs around his waist and pulled him as close as possible.

"I love you, Lacey. I've loved you from the moment I saw you at the party," he said as he continued planting kisses down my collarbone and to the V of my T-shirt.

My fingers slipped under his shirt and I gently ran my hands over his back and shoulders. I wanted to touch him forever. His skin burned under my touch and I welcomed the heat building between us.

I moaned as he continued kissing me, and his hand moved slowly up my stomach and stopped at the edge of my bra. He kissed my earlobe and finally my lips. His mouth was warm and gentle. I opened my mouth and invited him in, accepting him and everything he meant to me. I tilted my hips toward him and he groaned in response. His kiss deepened, our urgency for each other growing.

I slid his shirt up and broke the kiss only long enough to slip it over his head. His muscles tensed as I ran my nails down his back.

"You feel so good," he said as he nuzzled my neck.

I slipped my shirt over my head and tossed it on the floor. Thank God I'd chosen my cute black bra.

"Lacey—" he said and abruptly sat back on his heels. "Lace, I didn't just say I loved you because I wanted to sleep with you. You don't have to do this. I don't want you to ever question why I told you I love you, ever. It's not about that, no matter how beautiful you are lying in my bed half-dressed." He sighed and ran his hand through his dark hair.

"Walker, I'm not ready yet, but we can do other things until I am. I love you. I want to feel you on top of me, explore your body, and make you feel good—make you happy in every way possible."

"You do, Lacey. You're so amazing it blows my mind. Your strength and gentleness, with everything you've gone through, is something I haven't seen before. You still have faith and hope in people. Sometimes I'm in awe of how you can focus on the positive things. I can't believe I'm going to say this, but let's put our shirts back on and take a break." He sighed and rubbed his face.

My hands covered my chest and I unwrapped my legs from around his waist. I'd misunderstood him and thought he was okay with making out . . . everything but sex. Apparently, I was wrong, and before I could stop them, tears pooled in my eyes.

"Hey! Wait, no, Lacey. No . . . shit, I'm so sorry," Walker said as he pulled me to his chest and wrapped his arms around me. "I'm an ass. I didn't mean it the way it came out. I want you, I want to be with you, kiss you, run my hands over your body, and do anything you're okay doing. The reason I stopped is because you've been through a lot in the last few days. If I move too fast, you'll doubt me, and I can't have that. I need you to trust and believe me when I tell you I love you and that I'm going to be there for you. Let's wait for a little while so I know you're going to be okay. Being with someone for the first time is a huge step and I love you enough to slow down."

"You're sure? But you and Brittany had sex and I don't want to lose you."

Walker laughed. "Yeah, we did and look how we turned out. You don't understand what I'm saying—I want to have sex with you. What I don't want is for you to think I told you I loved you just to get you into bed. We need to wait. You just found out some big news about your mom and you're hurt and vulnerable. My job is to protect you, not hurt you more. Sleeping with you right now would hurt you and us in the long run, and—ouch! What the hell?"

I smiled at him with a crooked grin.

"I'm not sorry I pinched you. I needed to make sure you're real," I said, giggling.

"You're supposed to pinch yourself, not me!"

"Well, you just said you didn't want to hurt me so I figured it was the best path to take."

Walker wrestled me back down on the bed and tickled me until we gasped for breath. I'd forgotten what it was like to have fun and not worry about the moment I walked back through the door at home.

"Shit," I said. "I just remembered I have to go home tonight." I put my shirt back on as the moment of happiness slipped out of the room.

"Now?"

"Not yet, I have to be home by eleven," I said, glancing at Walker's clock. "There's still some time left. But, I need to call Joss, though. I'm sure she's waiting to hear from me."

"The phone is on the nightstand. I'll give you some privacy. When you're done, come find me," he said as he tugged his shirt on and closed the door behind him.

I dialed Joss's number and she answered on the second ring.

"Hey, you."

"Hey, I just wanted to say thanks for helping last night and see how you're doing," I said.

"I'm okay, but tell me how you're doing. Walker was really upset when he came in last night."

"Honestly, I'm clueless, Joss. I told him some stuff and the next thing I knew I'm spending the night with him. His mom's really awesome, though."

"You can tell me when you're ready, but Walker did say your mom hit you . . ." Joss's voice trailed off. "What I don't understand is why you didn't tell me about it."

"I didn't have time to tell anyone between when it happened and when I went to work. The only reason Walker found out is because he showed up after work and was waiting for me by my car. He wanted to make sure I was okay since I hadn't called him the night everything went down at home."

"It's not the first time though, is it?"

"Joss, I met Walker's aunt, Linda. She's a psychologist and she thinks Mama might be sick, like mentally ill," I said, ignoring Joss's question.

Silence filled the phone line. Joss was taking her time thinking about what to say.

"What do you think after talking to her?"

"I think she might be right, but I'm confused. Mama always said I was the reason she got so angry, or else it was Patsy. She always had an explanation."

"But it was never that she was wrong?" Joss prompted. She intuitively chose the right questions to ask to help me process or think something through.

"No, it was always someone else," I mumbled.

"You can't make your mom do or not do something, Lacey, especially something like hitting you. You should try and stay with Walker again tonight or come over here. I think you need time to process what Linda told you. I'll cover for you on this end, just call me back and tell me where you'll be tonight, okay?"

"What if Linda is right and Mama is sick?"

"Then talk to Linda to see what your options are, but what you need to understand is that it isn't your responsibility to take care of your mom. She makes her own choices, she's grown, and she knows right from wrong. If she wants help, then you need to let someone else help her. You aren't equipped or trained to handle something like this."

"Yeah, okay. Joss, thank you."

"You know I love ya."

"Right back atcha," I said and hung up the phone.

I sat on the side of Walker's bed for a few minutes before I called home, and then talked to Patsy and got permission to stay at Joss's house again. It was almost too easy, and it concerned me that something was wrong. I couldn't hide forever—it was only a matter of time until I'd find out.

Walker was watching TV with his mom and Garrett. I didn't step into the living room right away, but observed how relaxed he was as he held his mom's hand. The familiar theme song to *The Golden Girls* emitted from the TV. This wasn't about what was on the TV, though; it was about doing whatever Susan wanted to do, and just spending time with her. Garrett probably couldn't care less about watching *The Golden Girls*, and I smiled as he laid his head on the back of the couch. He was bored already.

"Hey, Garrett," I said as I crossed the living room. "I think we have some homework to do?"

"Oh yeah, I'd hoped you'd forgotten," he replied.

"No way, champ. Go get your stuff and I'll meet you at the kitchen table in a minute."

"Can I get you anything, Susan?" I asked.

"No, thank you, and I appreciate your help with Garrett's homework. He doesn't like English too much."

"Yeah, I didn't like it either, but I'll make it fun for him. I used to tutor junior high students all the time."

Walker smiled as I turned to meet Garrett at the table.

19

"**M**om said you can stay as long as you want," Walker said as he wrapped his arms around me and pulled me to him.

"Yeah? That might be dangerous," I said as I stood on my tiptoes to meet his lips. "You might not get rid of me."

"I'm okay with that," he whispered.

"Are you sure?"

"Yes. I love you muches, and muches, and muches," he said as he placed soft kisses down my neck that made me giggle.

"I love you too."

"Let's go for a walk," he said.

"That actually sounds good. I could use some air since you're sucking all of mine out of me." I laughed and squeezed his hand.

We told his mom goodbye and walked behind his house to a trail. The night air held a chill—autumn was finally here. I loved fall.

"How are you doing?" he asked as he led me down the trail through the trees.

"I'm trying not to think about it all, but that's impossible. I can't stay with you much longer and if your aunt is right, what am I going to do? She's my mom—I owe it to her to take care of her."

Walker stopped short and turned to face me.

"Lace, you don't *owe* her anything, and you can't take care of her," he said, his voice filled with frustration.

"Why? You take care of your mom," I said with a sharp tone.

"It's not the same. Mom doesn't hit us, for starters. I have Aunt Linda, who helps me, and my mom is *dying*, so I'm not sure how in the hell you can possibly compare the two," he retorted.

Dropping Walker's hand, I took a few steps back. I'd hit a nerve and wasn't sure how to undo it. I hadn't really thought it through—I was just talking out loud.

He ran his hands through his hair and kicked at the ground. I wanted to tell him I was sorry and didn't mean to hurt him, but I just stood with my feet rooted to the ground.

"I shouldn't have said that," he mumbled, looking at his feet. "It makes me crazy that you still want to help your mom after what she's done to you. Every night I'm going to lie in bed and worry about you when you're not with me or one of your friends. I can't protect you and it fucks me up. It fucks me up that I can't be there with you and that I can't help my mom—" His voice trailed off. "The two women in my life who mean everything to me, I can't help!" he yelled as pain flashed in his eyes.

"Walker, that's not true! Don't say that. You're the first person in my life who's cared enough to find out what's really happening behind the scenes. You asked questions, showed up at my job, listened to me, and still loved me when I told you my secret. No one has given me that before. And your mom, she loves you so much. I'd give anything to have what you and Garrett have. You two are her everything and she just wants you to be happy. You're giving her what she wants and needs—time with you. Please don't think any different," I pleaded.

"I can't save her though," he said as he clenched his jaw.

"Neither can the doctors, and they're trained to save people."

Silence filled the space between us. He finally nodded and reached for my hand as we continued down the trail.

We'd just had our first argument and I didn't like it. I had picked a bad time to fall in love. I felt like I was bouncing around like a Ping-Pong ball with everything happening at home, not to mention the added insecurity with Walker. A pang of frustration filled me. I'd bared my soul and shared my darkest secrets with him. Things I hadn't even told my best friends. If he wanted to, he could hurt me more than Mama ever could.

I drew in a deep breath and attempted to clear my head as we reached the pond. The crickets filled the night air with their chirps and the frogs responded. We could create a Disney movie right here.

A smile pulled at the corner of my mouth.

"What are you smiling about?" Walker asked.

"If you could live in my head for a few days, you'd run. I think of the weirdest things sometimes."

"Like what?"

"I was having a Disney moment with the dwarfs singing in the forest. You probably never watched the *Snow White and the Seven Dwarfs*, but that's where my mind went. Images appear in my head when I talk to people or when I'm writing."

"Do you write a lot? I don't mean for class or the newspaper, but just because?"

"I used to write all the time in my journal, but Mama found it and told me it was demons writing their thoughts down. I'd written about how angry I was with her when I'd been asked out on a date. She didn't bother asking any questions, she just said no and refused to give any reason why I couldn't go. By the time she got done with me, I really thought she was right about the demons. I believed her. Hell, I'm still confused. But it was the last time, and I never wrote in a journal again."

"Did you give her a reason to search your room? I mean, if I had a daughter who was coming home stoned or drunk I'd search her room, but only if I had a reason for concern."

"No, I don't like weed and I don't drink. I just came home one day and my room was torn apart. She said she'd spent the day praying and God had told her to search my room. She tossed my journal at me and smiled like she'd just found a bag of stolen money in my room. In her eyes, she thought she'd won and in a way she did, but I never shared myself on paper for her to find and use against me again. The weird thing about it was I still believed her about being possessed. Then, other days I questioned everything she said. I've been battling myself about her for a long time, but I'm the only one. Her friends think she's amazing and so does everyone in the family."

"Are you telling me you're the outcast?" A smile tugged at the corner of his mouth.

"That's kind of funny considering I don't smoke, drink, do drugs, or screw around. Maybe I should start, since that's what they think anyway." I laughed.

"Don't do any of those things because of them—do it because that's what you want to try."

"Mr. Farren, are you suggesting I pick up smoking, or worse?" I giggled.

Walker shook his head and laughed as he led me to a huge oak tree and sat down against its trunk. I situated myself between his legs and leaned into him.

"I'm sorry about what I said earlier." I kissed his cheek and put my head on his shoulder.

"Me too, I just worry about things when you go back home."

"That makes two of us, but I have to go back tomorrow. I have morning classes and then work from noon to five, though, so at least I'll have somewhere to go."

"I'll meet you after work then. I have a short shift at the pool tomorrow so I'll spend time with Mom and then meet you around five."

"You don't have to, Walker. I know you have other things to do."

"I want to see you, Lace. I need to hold you, even if it's only for a few minutes."

"Okay," I replied as I snuggled into him.

The night was clear with the unspoken hint of promise. I finally had someone in my life who loved me, I might not be demon-possessed, and there was hope for Mama to get help. Maybe God did speak to me sometimes after all.

20

My heart raced as I pulled into my driveway. I'd tried taking deep breaths in through my nose and out through my mouth, but it didn't help. My palms were sweaty and stuck to the steering wheel.

I grabbed my handbag and walked up the porch stairs, attempting to still my trembling hands by shaking them out. One, two, three. I turned the doorknob, plastered a smile on my face, and walked into the house.

"Hi, Mama," I said as I closed the door behind me.

"Hi, honey."

That was a good sign. I approached her and kissed her cheek.

"How are you?"

"Good, much better the last couple of days."

"Really? That's great, Mama!"

"Did you have fun at Joss's?"

"Yeah, Tammy stayed too."

"That sounds fun."

"I need to finish some homework for tomorrow and get ready for work." I paused to make sure she didn't want anything else.

Mama appeared okay, though, almost like nothing had happened a few days ago. I should've known better, but I'd take any good from Mama that I could. It didn't come very often.

I grabbed the stack of clean clothes she'd left for me at the top of the stairs and slowly made my way downstairs and to my room. Unable to see well over the stack of clothes, I made my way toward my dresser by memory. I laid the clothes on top, but they landed in a heap on the floor. Confused, I glanced around.

My dresser was gone and so was my bed. My clothes laid scattered on my floor and every piece of furniture was gone. Only a sleeping bag and pillow were left. I began to shake, thinking about sleeping on the floor. Part of our house was underground and giant spiders appeared in the family room and my bedroom. I was terrified of them and everyone knew it. They weren't little tiny spiders, either —they were large and they jumped. Mama called them wolf spiders. Now, with no furniture, I would be on the floor for them to crawl on.

I ran out of the room and up the stairs.

"Mama! Where's my furniture?" I couldn't control the fear in my voice.

"I sold it. If you want to stay with your friends for two or three days at a time, you don't need furniture anymore. After I prayed about it, God told me your demons are too attached to worldly possessions. I only did what was right for your healing."

"What? Are you serious? Mama, you're teasing, right? You sold my bed and dresser? Why? I don't understand."

"I just told you. Apparently you don't think family is important enough to come home to."

"That's not true at all. Just because I spent a few days with friends doesn't mean I don't want to be here. Mama, I'm on the floor now with the spiders."

"Guess you'll learn to kill them then, won't you?"

At that moment, the front door opened and Krissy walked in.

"Hi, Mama," she gushed as she ran over and crawled onto her lap like she was three.

My mouth dropped open. Krissy hadn't been home for almost six months. She lived on campus at college and didn't make it home often. I had no idea she was coming.

"How's my angel?" Mama asked as she hugged Krissy.

"Good. I've missed you so much, though. I love college, but it can't take your place." Krissy giggled as she hopped out of Mama's lap and got comfortable on the couch. She hadn't even glanced at me.

"Don't you have classes, Krissy?" I asked her. "What are you doing home on a Thursday morning?"

"Well, I hear you've caused a lot of trouble for Mama, and that's why I'm here for a few days, to make sure she's okay. I'm going to talk to her first and then I'll be downstairs to speak to you."

The color drained from my face as I realized what Krissy had said. Mama had called her to come home, which meant that Krissy hadn't gotten the real story.

The story Mama told was usually twisted. It was always someone else hurting Mama, not her shoving me or pinning Patsy to the floor. If she ever did share any of that with Krissy, she'd put a spin on it so she'd be the victim, and Krissy was worse than I was about believing it. She never questioned anything—she fell for every word out of Mama's mouth.

I turned and made my way downstairs as calmly as possible. I went into my bathroom, locked the door, and turned on the water. Then I puked up every bit of the breakfast that Walker and I had cooked together.

The cold water calmed me as I washed my face and flushed the toilet. I leaned my forehead against the mirror, closed my eyes, and thought about the last few days with Walker and his family; my time with Susan, Linda, the meals together, and the sound of everyone's laughter. In the moment, I could almost imagine Walker's arms around me, his soft kisses, and when he whispered *I love you muches, and muches, and muches.*

My stomach calmed as I remembered that Walker and his family weren't the only ones who knew what was going on at home—Joss knew, too. As long as I could get out of the house, I now had safe places to go.

Regardless if I was or wasn't demon-possessed, what Mama did wasn't right. I hadn't done anything wrong. No demon had acted out through me and made her take my furniture. All my friends who still lived at home spent days at someone else's house. We were in college, for God's sake.

I stopped and giggled as I realized my thought process. Mama's behavior wasn't okay or normal. *We* weren't fucking normal. Before I could stop, the giggles turned into choked tears once again, but behind the tears, for the first time in my life, a small glimmer of hope appeared.

21

I had almost forgotten Krissy was home until she appeared in my room about an hour later, leaning against my bedroom wall.

"Guess your chat with Mama went well?" I asked. "I'd offer you a place to sit, but as you can see, I have no furniture." I crossed my arms in front of me and leaned against the opposite wall.

"I heard you pushed Mama."

"Is that what she told you? You're never here, but you believe anything she says. And what did she say about Patsy? Did she mention that she pinned her down on the floor and held a butcher knife to her throat? Threatened to kill her?"

"Yes, Lacey, she did. Patsy realizes Mama gets depressed and she still said those horrible things to her. She asked for it."

My mouth hung open. I thought I'd been prepared for anything Krissy was going to say, but she blindsided me.

"I'm sorry, what?" I snapped.

"You don't know, do you? I'm not surprised. Mama can't trust you with anything. I don't blame her," she spat.

I wanted to slap the smug expression off her face and into next month.

"What, Krissy? What's so important that Patsy asked to have a knife pulled on her?"

"You're so stupid, Lacey. Mama told Patsy she remembered her uncle raping her and Patsy said she deserved it. That's why Mama got so pissed. Patsy deserved it."

I stared at her, stunned. Mama hadn't said anything about her uncle or being raped. As awful as it was, Mama still didn't have the right to treat Patsy that way. But then again, I'm not sure how I'd react if someone close to me said I deserved to be raped. I might beat the hell out of them too.

"Yeah, I thought so," Krissy said.

"I had no idea. That's horrible. How old was Mama?"

"Sixteen. She said he reeked of alcohol and came into her bedroom one night, placed a pillow over her face, and raped her."

We were both processing this information not only as Mama's daughters, but as women, thinking about what that must have been like. The horror of being hurt by someone you loved, by family, and not being able to stop it.

The silence weighed heavy in the air between us.

"I do worry about her, Krissy. It's different since you left. You're not around very much so you don't see the fights." I tugged at the string hanging from the hem of my T-shirt.

"It sounds like it, but you can't push her."

I'd forgotten the real reason Krissy was here. Mama had said I'd pushed her instead of the other way around.

I hesitated while I considered telling Krissy what had actually happened, but it wouldn't change anything. And, I didn't want to deal with it anymore. I couldn't get past the fact that Mama had been raped and the awful things Patsy had said to her.

"If you hurt Mama again, I'm going to call the cops and press charges against you," Krissy said and smirked.

What the hell? Was I ever going to stop being surprised by what came out of her mouth? I wanted her to leave and get out of my empty bedroom, and the only way for that to happen was to give her what she wanted. I was trapped, and if I tried to defend myself, Mama would start casting demons out of me. Krissy wouldn't acknowledge the truth even if it were a poisonous snake that had sunk its fangs into her.

Mama had got me. She'd won, and all I wanted was to go to work and get out of this hell hole.

"I understand." And I did. All too well. I was considered the outcast of the family, the crazy one.

Krissy stared at me for another moment before she left my room and went back upstairs.

I searched the rubble on my bedroom floor, found my tote bag, and stuffed it with some clothes in case I found myself unable to come home again. Then I carefully laid my books for class on top of the clothes so nothing would appear suspicious. At least I could hide it in my car and be more prepared than I was last time.

I headed for the shower and got ready for work. Once again, I was grateful for my job. It was so much more than a paycheck.

22

The store was busy, and I welcomed the distraction. The time passed faster than I'd hoped, and I dreaded going home to not only Mama but Krissy as well. Mama surrounded herself with believers, which left me alone. It wouldn't matter if I tried to talk to Krissy and Patsy about mental illness. They believed whatever Mama told them.

My break arrived and I clocked out, grabbed my purse, and walked down the mall to Wyatt's Café to meet Emma. We'd missed our regular lunch meeting earlier in the week and had rescheduled. I had so much to fill her in on; there was no way I could do it in an hour. A smile spread across my face as I found her waiting for me at the restaurant door.

"Hi!" Emma said and hugged me.

"Hey," I said and hugged her back. "How are you?"

"Good, just the same ol' thing with classes. I've come to realize that you truly have to love taking care of people to be a nurse or doctor. I'm studying some really gross stuff!"

I couldn't help but laugh. Emma had a big heart and was genuine in everything she said and did.

"What about you? Are you still dating Walker?"

I couldn't stop the huge smile even if I'd wanted to.

"That says it all. You lit up like a Christmas tree! Lacey Anne, are you in *love?*"

My laugh filled the busy restaurant.

"Emma, I really need to master my poker face when we're together."

"You go right ahead, I can read you no matter what expression's on your face."

"Am I that easy?" I asked.

"Sometimes, but I'm familiar with you and *all* your moods."

We grabbed our food and found a booth in the corner of the restaurant. I'd hoped for a bit of privacy, but it wasn't going to happen.

"Okay, now that we're settled, fill me in," Emma said between bites.

"Things are great. He's so good to me. I've met his mom and brother too. Actually, I spent the weekend with them."

Emma's fork clattered to the floor as she stared at me with her mouth open.

"I'm sorry, you did what?"

I handed Emma my spoon to eat with.

"It wasn't like that at all, so you can close your mouth."

"Are you sleeping with him? Do you love him? Oh my God, are you using protection? Are you on the pill?"

I shook my head as the questions kept coming.

"No, we aren't sleeping together—yet. If you give me a minute, I'll explain everything," I said.

I couldn't help but laugh. When Emma got excited, her questions came at you like rapid fire. When she was upset, it was like dodging little torpedoes.

"Mama and I got in a fight. She found out I was with Walker."

Emma gasped.

"Yeah, right? I have no idea how she found out either."

"I do. God told her." There was no mistaking the sarcasm in her tone.

"Well, it doesn't matter, but in a nutshell—" I put my fork down and stopped eating. "Emma, she pushed me. I fell and hit my head hard enough that I blacked out."

Emma's spoon clattered to the floor. At this rate, she would be eating with her fingers.

"Are you okay?" she asked in disbelief. "Why didn't you call me?" Her expression transitioned from shock, to worry, to anger in a matter of seconds.

"I didn't have time," I said. "It happened so fast, and I was upset. I was afraid to call anyone, so I just stayed out of Mama's way until the next day when I went to work. Then, after work, Walker was waiting for me. I hadn't called him that night and he finally got me talking. I told him more than I should have." A moment of silence filled the space between us as I took a drink from my Diet Coke.

"What do you mean? You should have told him about her hurting you!"

"Emma, keep your voice down, please."

"I'm sorry, I'm just upset."

"Hang on, there's more. I also told Walker that I was possessed by demons."

Emma stared at me, her expression unreadable.

"Explain, please," she said firmly.

"For years, Mama has told me I'm possessed by demons. I was afraid that if I told anyone they wouldn't want to stay around me. You'd think I was crazy and your parents sure as hell wouldn't allow me around you and your brother. I was scared, and no matter how hard I tried to get better, it never worked. Plus, I thought if I told anyone about what was going on, no one would understand. And they didn't."

"Lacey."

"Don't, Emma," I said, cutting her off. "Let me finish, and then you can say whatever you need to."

She nodded.

"I told Walker everything." I leaned back in my seat and moved my food around on my plate. "That night I planned to stay with Joss, but when I told Walker what happened, he took me home with him instead. His mom said it was okay. Isn't that nuts?" I asked and took a breath.

"Anyway, we didn't sleep together," I continued. "I stayed with his family, but where it gets really interesting is when I met his Aunt Linda. She's a mental health therapist and she talked to me about Mama. She thinks she's sick, Emma. That Mama is mentally ill. She also said that I was in no way demon-possessed."

I put my fork down, no longer hungry. It was Emma's turn.

"I had no idea. Everyone knows your mom has control issues, but Lacey, I had no clue what was going on. I should have put it together—and I should have done something!" Her eyes grew wider as she talked.

"Stop, it's not your fault. I've kept this quiet for a long time. I mean, how do you tell someone you're possessed?"

"But you're not. That's insane, and it pisses me off that you believed it—that she said it so many times that it became the truth to you. Honey, if you want to see possessed, I'll show you what that looks like. You can come over and watch *The Exorcist* with me. You've never acted like that, especially the head-spinning thing," Emma said and attempted a smile.

Emma's classic humor announced itself during tense situations. It was her way of coping when she didn't know what to do.

"I'm not sure I want to watch it, but I appreciate the support."

"You need to move out, Lacey."

"I can't. She's my mother, and it's my responsibility to get her help. Don't you understand? She's sick, but she can get help."

"I'm sorry, what did you say? No. No way. She is *not* your responsibility."

"Emma, I'm serious."

"So am I, and she's abusive. Why in the world would you think it's your responsibility to get her help?"

I flinched at Emma's words, each one stinging me like tiny needles.

"What if it were your mom?" I leaned forward, daring her to answer any differently than I had.

"I'd leave. I would leave and call for help when I was in a safe place."

"I'll keep it in mind," I mumbled, leaning back in my seat again. "But right now I have to wait until Krissy leaves."

"Jiminy Christmas! Krissy is home? Why? For what?"

"Mama told her we got into a fight and I shoved her."

Emma laughed so loud that people turned around and stared at us.

"What's so funny about that? I wanted to slap the shit out of Krissy the moment she showed up and you think it's funny?"

"What I think is funny is the idea that you would ever shove your mom, first of all—not to mention the fact that you wouldn't even be able to move her. No offense, but your mom isn't a small woman. I guess if you got a running start, maybe?"

I smiled at the thought of me backing up and running headfirst at Mama. I'd watched too many cartoons, and Emma wasn't helping.

"So, you told Walker and his family and they took care of you?" Emma asked.

"Yeah, they're really great. Walker has been amazing, even with everything that's going on with him. I was shocked when I met Susan."

"What do you mean?"

"She has stage-four lung cancer. She doesn't have much longer to live. Walker and Linda have been taking care of her."

Emma gasped. "I'm so sorry."

My heart sank as I thought about the situation. Not only was I in love with Walker, but I was already closer to Susan and Garrett than I was my own family. They were quickly becoming my new one.

"Me too."

"So, what now?"

"Well, I'm trying to believe I'm not possessed, and sometimes it's easy for me to think I'm not, but there's a part of me that tugs at my sleeve and says that no one understands except Mama. It terrifies me to think she's right."

Emma leaned across the table.

"She's not right, Lacey. She's just using it to control you and everyone else in the house. She's found exactly how to feed on one of people's biggest fears—dying and going to hell. That's not okay."

"I hope you're right."

"I am. You need to trust me. And I'm not the only one telling you the truth. You have several of us, including Walker's aunt. I'd think her word was good for something, right?"

"Yeah. Listen, I'm sorry I took up the entire dinner telling you all the crap that's happened. Thanks for listening to me."

"I'm always a phone call away, but I still think you should reconsider trying to help your mom. I'm not trying to be mean—I'm just trying to protect you."

"I know," I mumbled.

Emma and I walked back to Jack's Department Store and made plans for next week. She made me promise I'd call every day and tell her where I was staying and what was going on.

23

Most of the time I was happy to get off work, but not tonight. The only thing that would make it tolerable was meeting Walker for a few minutes before going home.

I pushed through the back doors at work and stepped into the early evening air. It was perfect. The stars danced in the sky as I walked across the parking lot. I found Walker leaning against my Mustang and hurried toward him.

"Hi," I said as I unlocked my car door and tossed my purse onto the passenger seat.

"You look amazing," he said as he kissed me. "Mmmm, peppermint," he whispered against my lips.

"You like peppermint? It's my lip gloss. I'll have to use more of it."

"I like peppermint on you," he said as he drew me in for a deeper kiss.

I lost all sense of time and my surroundings as we kissed. I could have stayed in that moment forever, with his body against mine. I never wanted to let him go.

"I love you muches and muches and muches," he whispered against my cheek.

A giggle escaped me as his whisper tickled my ear.

"I love you too, Walker. You're the best thing that's ever happened to me."

The cars slowly dissipated from the parking lot, and only a few were left. I didn't have much more time with him, but I hopped up on the hood of my car and wrapped my legs around his waist.

"How was your day?" I asked.

"I ran some errands for Mom and picked Garrett up from school. He was really excited—he got a B on the paper you helped him with."

"That's fantastic! I'll congratulate him when I see him next."

"Thank you for helping him. It meant a lot to Mom, too."

"How is she?"

"About the same." He paused for a moment and played with my fingers.

"Lace, I never know what to expect. When I wake up in the morning, my first thought is, did she make it? One of these days I'm going to walk into her bedroom and she isn't going to wake up. It's going to be over. It makes me sick."

I pulled Walker in for a hug and gently rubbed his neck. There weren't any words I could say that would make anything better; I could only promise to be there with him when it happened. I'd lost friends before, but not a parent or sibling. I wasn't equipped to help him through it, or even myself for that matter, but I loved him and would be there for him and Garrett. Aunt Linda was there as well.

"Walker, what happens to you and Garrett when—?" I couldn't finish the question.

I hadn't thought about where they would live. Would he stay here? Would he find his dad and move? Did he have another relative that lived out of state? Was I going to lose him too? I bit my lip in an attempt to hide my panic.

"We're staying at the house. Garrett will move upstairs with Aunt Linda and I'll live downstairs."

I tried not to show my immediate relief. It was selfish that I'd even had the thought when Walker was losing his mom, but I couldn't help it.

"Would you be sad if I left?"

"It would shatter me times three."

"What? Times three?"

"Walker, I love you. I'm closer to your family than my own." My voice hiccupped as I fought back the tears. "I can't lose all of you. Losing Susan is bad enough."

Walker leaned in and kissed me softly. He wanted to make me feel better, but he couldn't when he felt worse than I did.

He pulled my hips forward and into him. His response to our kiss gave me something much better to think about. My fingers slipped underneath the waist of his jeans and I tugged. Heat spread through me as my mind raced with thoughts of his chest and stomach muscles beneath my hands. I wanted to be in his bedroom. I wanted him.

"Lacey Anne!"

Walker and I snapped to attention. I peered into the darkness, but I'd already recognized the voice of the person who said my name. There was no mistaking her.

"Son of a bitch," I mumbled as I slid off my car and grabbed Walker's hand.

"So this is how you're spending your time?" Krissy asked as her eyes traveled up and down Walker. "Won't Mama love to find out about this." She was almost rubbing her hands together with the excitement of her discovery.

"I'm Walker," he said as he extended his hand to Krissy.

"So you are," she said, ignoring his extended hand.

"Krissy, you can't tell Mama," I stammered.

"Oh, but I can, little sister. And I will."

She almost couldn't talk she was smiling so hard.

Walker stepped in front of me as he realized who she was and what was unfolding.

"I don't think that's a good idea, Krissy. I realize you've been away at college, but there's been a lot going on. Lacey and I aren't doing anything wrong. There's no reason to say anything to anyone."

"That's where you're very wrong. I'm not sure what Lacey has been telling you, but I'd be happy to set you straight," she said as she pushed her pointer finger into his chest.

I didn't even have enough time to step forward before Walker grabbed her hand.

"If I want you or anyone else to touch me, I'll make it unmistakably clear."

I couldn't see Walker's face, but I couldn't miss the sharp tone in his voice. He was pissed.

"And let me make something else clear. Whether you like it or not, I love Lacey."

Krissy's laugh echoed through the parking lot.

"You're just as stupid as she is. Let me give you a tip for your own well-being, Walker. Stay away from her. Lacey is dangerous. She rips through people's lives like a tornado, destroying everything around her and only leaving pain in her wake. She will lie to you about her family, lie to you about her school—hell, she'll lie to anyone about anything. You can't believe a word she says."

"Krissy, stop! Walker, it's not true."

"And here's the icing on the cake. She's a mental case, crazy, she does bizarre shit and then blames anyone she can. She even shoved her own mother last week during a fight!"

"That's not true," Walker said, taking a step toward Krissy. "You're not getting the truth, Krissy. Did you even ask Lacey what happened and who pushed who?"

"I didn't have to, Mama told me everything," Krissy said as her chin jutted upward.

"I suppose she said demons made Lacey push her? Made Lacey act that way?" Walker asked as he closed the gap between them.

If I hadn't been so shocked that Walker had stood up for me, I would have laughed my ass off at the stunned expression on Krissy's face. No one had the balls to get in her face. My heart grew faster than the Grinch's at that moment—Walker didn't believe my family's vicious lies.

"I know the truth, Krissy. Maybe it's time you did too."

Krissy took a few steps back and then walked away. It was then that I spotted her car on the other side of the parking lot. If I was lucky, she'd trip over a rock and eat pavement. It served her right for what she'd said.

Krissy pulled out of the parking lot and Walker wrapped his arms around me. I snuggled against him as his heart pounded against my cheek. He was mad. I had just witnessed firsthand Walker Farren getting pissed.

"Are you okay?" he asked.

I nodded. I didn't want to let him go, ever.

We stood in silence for a few minutes until I pulled back.

"Walker, she's going to tell Mama. There's nothing I can do to stop her. I'm in deep shit."

"I'll come with you and meet your Mom, then. Maybe it will help calm her down."

"You can't. She hates it if I bring someone over without asking. It will make things worse, if that's possible."

"What do you want me to do? You can't stay there with them."

"Walker, I have to go home, and tell Mama I'm dating you before she does. In fact, I'm glad Krissy showed up. I've wanted to tell Mama anyway. I love you. I don't want to hide our relationship anymore. It's time—I just wish I'd told her sooner. This is my fault. If I'd already told Mama, Krissy wouldn't have anything to hold over my head. She still doesn't. I won't give her the satisfaction. I'm sorry."

"Stop, you can't apologize for your sister. She's responsible for her own actions, not you. Call me later?"

"I'll do my best. It might be tomorrow, though. I have class at nine and a break at noon."

"I'll be there," he said and kissed me on the forehead. "I'll be there."

Our hands slipped apart as I searched his blue eyes.

"I love you—" I began.

"—muches and muches and muches," he finished.

I got into my car and locked the doors, peering in the rearview mirror as I pulled away. Within a few short minutes, Walker had protected me and then stood helpless as I drove away. I wanted to reassure him that everything was going to be okay, but I couldn't. I couldn't even tell myself that.

Guilt reared up its familiar head as I once again realized I shouldn't have brought Walker into this messed-up situation. I suspected that Krissy was at home telling Mama what she'd seen and I was going to walk into a shitstorm.

My mind raced with exit strategies: where the doors were, where I should stand or sit while Mama was casting demons out of me and screaming. I had my bag packed and hidden in my trunk, so I had enough clothes to make it a few days.

I mentally kicked myself all the way home for not being honest with Mama, but it was no use now. I'd screwed up and it was time to confess.

I pulled my Mustang into the driveway and took several deep breaths. My hands shook as I gathered my purse and stepped out of my car. Maybe I should have stayed with Walker. Instead I'd pretended that I wanted to be brave. I was eighteen, almost nineteen. Legally, I didn't have to come back at all.

I leaned against my car and closed my eyes, thinking about Walker, Susan, and even Garrett picking his nose the first time I saw him. My decision was made and, I was going to talk to Mama because I loved them. I loved all of them and I wanted to spend as much time with Susan as I could before she left us.

It was Susan's support that moved my feet up the steps, across our porch, and through the front door into our living room.

24

The image in front of me was shocking. I blinked a few times, thinking the light was too bright after standing outside in the dark, but the picture before me didn't change.

Mama sat in her chair, Patsy on the couch, and Krissy in the recliner. They didn't even look at me as I came in. In fact, they were watching TV and laughing.

Disbelief filled me as I stared at them for a moment until Krissy waved at me to close the door.

I walked to the kitchen table and put my purse and books down. My plan was to have everything close in case I needed to make a run for it, but this wasn't what I was prepared for at all.

"What are y'all watching?" I asked, barely able to hear my own voice over the pounding in my ears.

"*Miami Vice,*" Mama said, not really paying much attention to me.

I glanced at the TV again, picked up the books I'd left on the table, and made it a few steps before Krissy spoke.

"Oh, I almost forgot to tell you I met Lacey after work today, Mama," she said.

I stopped in my tracks and turned around to stare at her.

"Well, why are you home so much later, Lacey?" Mama asked.

I tried to collect my words, but there was no right way to say it.
"I . . ."

"She was with a boy," Krissy blurted.

I glanced around the room. No one said a word, but all eyes were on me. Mama turned the TV off. That was my cue to run if I was going to, but I didn't want to run. I didn't want to hide Walker anymore. My shaking knees argued with my decision.

"Mama, I'm sorry I didn't tell you first," I said as I shot Krissy a look. It should have sent her to hell, but unfortunately it didn't work. She still sat in the living room with a smug expression on her face.

"Who is he?" Mama asked. Her voice remained steady. The calm before the storm; I recognized it all too well. She was just gathering additional information before planning her attack.

"His name is Walker."

"Oh, so you did lie to me. You said you didn't give him our phone number when he called that night. You also denied seeing anyone when I asked you last week."

"I didn't lie, Mama. Tammy gave him my number and told him it was okay to call. She was being a brat. She knew it wasn't okay for him to call after nine."

Mama stared at me for a moment longer and remained unusually quiet. I leaned against the wall, my books still in my hands.

"So, you've been going out with him for a month now?"

"Yes, almost a month."

"Krissy, how did you meet him?"

"He was all over her in the parking lot at work. They didn't even care that other people were around. They are definitely sleeping together, you can tell by the way they act."

"That is not true!" I yelled. "We are not sleeping together, Krissy, you're just guessing. You met him for five seconds and you already think you have us all figured out!"

"Enough!" Mama sat up straight in her chair. "Sit down, Lacey!"

This was it. I sat in the rocking chair farthest away from Mama already regretting my decision. I shouldn't have come home at all. Krissy was enjoying the entertainment of Mama getting pissed that I was dating someone. Krissy dated all the time, but Mama never found out because she was away at college, so it never became an issue.

"Lacey, I'm glad Krissy spotted you. She just confirmed what God has already shown me. I knew you were with someone that Sunday, but you lied to me then, too. I spend entire days praying for you and this is how you repay me? This is how you treat a family who loves you? You ungrateful little bitch," she snarled.

My breath caught in my chest as she talked. I would never get used to her calling me names.

"Krissy is right and you're sleeping with him, aren't you? Those demons are leading you around on a leash and you just give in to any boy who pays attention to you. There's a part of you that enjoys it, or you would be free of them by now—I pray too hard for you not to be. This is your fault. You want them to stay!"

"Mama that's not true, and just because I'm dating someone doesn't mean I have demons."

Mama's face turned red as she struggled for words. I'd never said anything like that to her before.

"Who told you that?" she spat. "Your little boyfriend? And you believe him? He's just trying to get you into bed, you stupid little girl."

"No he isn't, Mama!"

"You're so naïve you'll believe anything he says."

"Mama that's not true. Please, just meet him and you can find out for yourself. He's a good guy. I think you would even like his mom."

"His mother?"

Dammit, I'd gone too far. When was I going to learn to keep my mouth shut? I wanted to slap the part of me that wanted Mama's approval of my choices, my friends, and my relationships. When was I going to finally accept the truth that she'd never approve of anything I did?

"You've met his mother?" she asked quietly.

I nodded.

"So now you've met his perfect little family who loves you? Is that it? But they have no idea, do they? They have no idea what you do, how you hurt people, how sick you really are."

I couldn't answer the question. If Mama knew the truth, it would be the end of it. She would fly across the room and be on me in a flat second.

"Answer me, dammit!" she said. "You brought this on yourself. You schemed and plotted behind my back and didn't think God would tell me? He put your sister there at the right moment and she loves you enough to say something to me in order to save your sorry ass!"

"That's not true," I whispered.

"What? I didn't hear you." Mama stood up and took a few steps toward me.

"I said . . ." My voice faltered.

Mama's face froze and her body stiffened. Her eyes glazed over and she stared through me. The floor shook violently as she dropped to the ground.

"Mama!" I yelled as I jumped out of my chair and grabbed her hand.

Mama remained rigid as her whole body twitched. Her head tilted back and only the whites of her eyes were visible.

I don't remember who called 911 as I talked to Mama. I didn't know what was happening; Mama had never done anything like this before. Krissy held Mama's head in her lap and tried to keep her from thrashing around, but she was strong.

As abruptly as it began, it stopped. Mama lay still no matter what we did. Krissy, Patsy, and I were all talking to her at the same time. Patsy patted her face and I squeezed her hand, but there was no response.

It seemed like hours before I heard the sirens in the background, but I knew that couldn't be right. A fire station was less than a mile away. They'd be the first to arrive, with an ambulance right behind them.

Strong arms pulled me up to a standing position and moved me away from Mama as the emergency team gathered around her. I stood rooted to the floor in horror as they checked her vitals and rattled off information to each other. They placed an oxygen mask over her face and her eyes fluttered open. She had a fearful expression; she was probably trying to understand why strange men were all around her, and what had happened.

Patsy stepped in and took her hand. She spoke quietly to Mama as the team continued to work on her. Then they wheeled Mama out of the house on the gurney, and I followed.

As Patsy was climbing into the ambulance, she told me to meet her and Krissy at the hospital. Krissy hopped into her car. All the vehicles pulled out of the driveway, and the red-and-blue lights broke through the darkness. This time the sound of the ambulance was for my family, not someone else's.

I stood alone at the front door trying to grasp what had just happened. Then I ran back into the house and called Walker's house. The phone rang six times, and I was about to hang up when Garrett answered.

"Garrett, it's Lacey."

"Hey, Lacey, what's up?"

"Buddy, I need to talk to Walker. They just took my mom to the hospital."

"Shit, really? Walker's not here. He ran to the store for Mom, but he should be back in about thirty minutes."

Thirty minutes would be an eternity, and I couldn't wait to talk to him. I had to go.

"Garrett, can you please ask him to meet me at the hospital as soon as he gets home?"

"Yeah, I will—the second he walks in I'll tell him, Lacey."

"You're awesome, thank you. I have to go."

"Hey, keep us posted. Mom will worry until you call again and tell us you're okay."

"I'm alright, Garrett, but I promise I'll call."

We hung up and I grabbed my purse and keys. It was a twenty-minute drive from Mama's house to St. Augustine's Hospital, but it would be almost an hour-long drive for Walker.

I drove the speed limit, not wanting to get pulled over. There was nothing I could do for Mama anyway, but I was scared. I'd never seen anything like it, and I thought she'd died right there in front of everyone. If Mama died in the hospital, Krissy would never let it go. For the rest of our lives, she would accuse me of killing her.

Dread filled my stomach, and I pulled over just in time to empty the contents of my stomach on the side of the road. I steadied myself against the car as I wiped my mouth. My stomach gurgled again and I bent over as my gut rebelled against anything remaining inside it. By the fourth time, I was dry heaving and grateful nothing else came up.

I took a deep breath, attempting to calm my shaking, weak body. There was no one else to drive to the hospital so I had to suck it up. Sweat beaded across my forehead as I sat in my car and dug through my purse for some gum. Thank goodness I'd stocked up when Walker and I had started dating.

The peppermint flavor filled my mouth and I leaned my head back, chewing for a minute. I willed my shaking limbs to calm down and focused on the cool night air as it dried the beads of sweat on my forehead. It was exactly what I needed, and within a few minutes I pulled back onto the road and headed for the hospital.

25

The parking garage was packed so I found a space in the emergency room parking lot. I locked my doors and jogged into the hospital. A nurse directed me to the room Mama was in, and I rushed down the hall to the ICU and searched each door for her name. The hospital was huge, and it took me almost ten minutes to find her room.

My pace slowed while I approached Patsy and Krissy sitting in the hallway.

Patsy glanced up as I grew closer. I'm sure I looked like hell after puking my guts up on the side of the road, but Patsy looked like hell too. Her mascara had streaked down her cheeks and her dark hair was messed up.

I nodded hello and sat next to her.

"The doctors are with her," Patsy said. "She regained consciousness before we got here."

"Is she going to be okay?" My voice faltered.

"I don't know yet, Lacey."

I glanced at Krissy; she was picking at her fingernails. When Krissy was younger, she used to pick at her nails before the first day of school. When she was anxious about something she fell back into the nervous habit, but she hadn't done it in years. That told me things were bad.

The clock above Krissy's head ticked with each second that passed. After an eternity, a doctor stepped out of Mama's room. He glanced at the chart he was holding and looked at us. His eyes held a compassion that I hadn't seen in other staff members as they rushed around taking care of all the sick people.

He ran his hand through his thinning gray hair and cleared his throat.

"Are you Lynn Beaumont's family?" he asked.

Patsy, Krissy, and I all said yes at the same time.

"I'm Dr. Snider. Lynn will probably be here in the ICU for a few days. We need to run some additional tests. It appears that she had a seizure, but we haven't identified the cause yet."

My mouth dropped with the news. Mama had never had a seizure that I was aware of. I didn't understand how this could happen.

"Does she have a history of seizures?" Dr. Snider asked.

"No, she doesn't," Patsy responded, shaking her head.

Their voices faded into the background as I tried to process the information. I just didn't get it. My mind automatically replayed what had happened over and over. I remembered her getting out of her chair and how red her face was, but it was the same as any other argument.

It was the strange expression on her face that had told me something was different—more than that, *wrong*. I was the only one who'd witnessed it, since Krissy and Patsy hadn't been sitting in front of her.

"Lacey."

"What?" I asked as Patsy broke me out of my thoughts.

"Krissy and I are going in to visit your mom. I don't think you should come in yet. I'm not sure it would be good for her to see you."

"What?" I hiccupped. "Why?"

"Do we really need to discuss this now, Lacey?" Patsy said, frowning.

I stared at her. No words came out of my mouth, and she took that as me agreeing with her suggestion. She and Krissy went into Mama's room and closed the door behind them. And I was left sitting in the hallway by myself.

I sighed and leaned my head against the wall. Its smooth, cold surface sent a chill through me and reminded me that this was real and not a nightmare. Not only was something wrong with Mama, but Patsy had made it clear that I shouldn't be anywhere near her, which meant that Patsy thought I was the cause of what had happened.

Maybe I was. Maybe the news had been too much for Mama.

As that thought took root in my mind and heart, a tear trickled down my cheek. If Walker's aunt was right and I wasn't possessed, then how did this happen? She had to be wrong. Once again, I'd hurt Mama, and this time I'd put her in the hospital. She could've died because of me.

Mama's door creaked open and Krissy slipped into the hallway.

"What are you crying about?" she asked.

I ignored her question and stood up.

"Is she okay?"

"I hope so, but the doctors are running tests," she said. "She'll be here in the ICU for a few days from what it sounds like."

Silence filled the space between us as I struggled for something to say. I hated the tension. Maybe I didn't always like Krissy, but she was still my sister.

"You do realize this is your fault, right?" she said.

"Stop, Krissy."

"No, you need to get this, Lacey. *You* caused this. *You* hurt Mama, just like you always do. What gets me is that she pours all her time into saving you, but you choose to keep hurting people. Do you *want* to hold onto the demons inside you that are ripping this family apart? Are you ever going to get it, or do you have to kill Mama before you'll believe her?"

"I didn't mean to hurt her, Krissy. I wouldn't hurt anyone on purpose. You have to believe me."

"You should've thought about that before you decided to date Walker behind her back."

"That's enough, Krissy," a voice boomed through the hallway.

I turned to see Walker as he approached us. Part of me sighed with relief, but another part was scared to be around him again. I didn't want to hurt him too.

"This is none of your business, Walker," Krissy hissed. "Besides, you have no idea what your little girlfriend did to her own mother."

Walker strolled right past me and stopped inches away from Krissy's face.

"If you want to believe that you go ahead, but I'll give you something else to chew on," he said. "Your mom is very sick—in fact, you might want to have her mentally evaluated while she's here. It's not Lacey's fault and Lacey isn't possessed by demons. It would do you all good to find out the truth. Until then, you need to back off Lacey, and I mean now."

Walker turned away, grabbed my hand, and led me down the hallway.

"Where are we going?" I asked.

"Home, baby. You've had a really rough night, but your mom's in good hands now. Everything's going to be okay."

We didn't talk in the elevator or the parking lot. He found the car, opened the passenger-side door for me, and then slid into the driver's seat. The black Camaro's motor rumbled to life, pulling my thoughts away from Mama.

"You drove your mom's car?"

"Mine wouldn't start, so Mom let me borrow hers."

I nodded and turned to stare out the window as we left the parking lot and drove to his house.

26

I understood now what people meant about being in shock. My thoughts were still at the hospital, and Krissy and Patsy's words rang in my head. If I'd ever questioned where they stood concerning me, I'd gotten a definite answer tonight. Their allegiance was with Mama, no matter what.

I wasn't sure if I was possessed or not, but I couldn't deal with it anymore. If Mama was mentally ill, I couldn't help her. I certainly couldn't help her as long as other people in her life agreed that I was the problem. As soon as the doctors knew what was wrong with her, I would figure out my next move.

Walker parked the car in front of his house, snapping me to attention. I didn't remember the drive at all. I opened the passenger-side door and got out, and he placed his hand on the small of my back as he guided me to the front door and into the kitchen.

He pulled a chair out and motioned for me to sit down. I slid into my seat as he busied himself in the kitchen. My eyes glazed over while he grabbed the tea kettle and put it on the stove as he took some coffee mugs from the cabinet. Silence hung in the air, but he continued to glance at me over his shoulder.

The phone rang and I jumped. He smiled, trying to calm me down.

"Hello? Yes, this is Walker."

I leaned forward, trying to hear if the caller was male or female. I trusted Walker, but I wouldn't put it past other girls to call him even though everyone knew we were together.

Walker's face fell as he listened to the person on the other end of the phone. My stomach knotted as I stood up and walked toward him. Fear gripped me while images of Mama lying dead in the hospital filled my mind. I shouldn't have left. I should've stayed, no matter what Patsy and Krissy said to me.

"Thank you for calling, sir," Walker said, hanging up the phone.

I grabbed his hand as he stared at me. Something terrible had happened, but I was too afraid to ask.

The whistle of the tea kettle broke the silence and he released my hand to turn off the stove. He stood motionless with his back to me, staring at the floor. The silence suffocated me. I needed to know.

"Walker, tell me—what is it?" I said softly. "Is it bad? Tell me. Please."

Walker turned to face me. When he did, the worry in his eyes pierced my heart.

"I just got called for boot camp. I leave for the military on November 17. Before you and I had met I'd talked with a recruiter, but I never heard anything back. I assumed . . . Lace, I didn't know." He ran his hands through his hair.

I stared at him blankly, not comprehending the words that had just come out of his mouth. My mind scrambled as I tried to piece together what he'd said, and then a cement wall slammed into my chest.

Leaving. Walker was going to leave me.

"What?" I whispered. Then I covered my face with my hands as I wilted to the floor and cried.

27

I wasn't sure how much time had passed. The last thing I remembered was Walker telling me he was leaving in three weeks, but I didn't remember how I got into his bed.

"Hey," Walker said. "I'm so sorry, Lacey. I'm so sorry."

His fingers rubbed my arm as I lay still and refused to open my eyes. I was tired of reality smacking me in the face. If I stayed still, maybe I would wake up to another life.

Walker scooted closer to me, spooning me, and rested his chin on top of my head. His hand rubbed my back as I snuggled into him. I could smell traces of his Polo cologne as we spent the next few minutes lying there quietly.

He was going to try to explain everything, not that it mattered. He was leaving and there was nothing I could do about it. I couldn't even stand up to Mama, much less the military.

He tilted my head up and kissed me gently. "I love you."

"I love you too," I replied. "I don't understand, though."

"I met with an Air Force recruiter before we met, Lace. It's been a while and I just assumed that I'd been passed over for the area I was interested in, but apparently not—they just didn't have openings until now."

"Why would you do that while Susan is sick and Garrett needs you?"

"It was the only way I could think of to provide for Garrett and take care of him. I know he'll live with Aunt Linda after Mom's gone, but he's still my responsibility. I figured after boot camp I could request to be stationed in Little Rock so I could visit him a few times a month. He'll be going through so much with both Mom and I gone that I'll do everything I can to get stationed close to him. It's the initial six weeks I'll be in Texas that will be the hardest."

"Six weeks?" I said, my voice breaking.

Walker nodded.

"The timing couldn't be worse," he said. "The expression on your face when I told you broke my heart in two. I'd already talked everything through with Mom before I did it, and Garrett was aware of the plan too. But the last thing I expected was to fall in love—really fall in love—with someone as beautiful as you. You're everything to me, Lacey. These six weeks are going to be the hardest thing I've ever done, but as soon as it's over I'll be back for you. I'll be back for all of you."

"You promise?"

"Yes, I promise."

I leaned my head against his chest and listened to the sound of his breathing as he held me. There wasn't anything else to say right now, so I settled for feeling his chest rise and fall with each breath. Soon, I wouldn't be able to listen to his heartbeat, feel his kisses on my forehead, or his fingers stroking my cheek. I didn't plan on taking another moment with him for granted. He'd made it clear through his words and actions that he loved me, and I loved him too.

I didn't realize I'd drifted off to sleep again.

28

The sound of Walker and Garrett's voices in the kitchen woke me. Glancing at Walker's clock, I gasped. Somehow, I'd slept through the night until noon the next day. I got out of bed and made my way to the kitchen.

Walker and Garrett were standing at the stove and Walker was teaching him how to make hamburgers. I couldn't stop myself from smiling. Walker loved Garrett. He planned on taking care of him as soon as he was able to.

I wondered what it would be like to live with them. Walker and I would help Garrett finish school and graduate . . . it was an enormous responsibility. By the time Walker came home and we were ready to take that on, though, I'd be nineteen and Walker would be twenty. We'd still be young, but we could do it. I would do it for Susan and Walker.

I didn't just love Walker; I'd fallen in love with his entire family. Just because he was leaving for a few months didn't mean I couldn't stay close.

"Hey, Lacey," Garrett said as he turned to the sink to wash the raw meat off his hands.

"Hey, buddy. What are you making?" I asked as I peered around them.

"Walker's teaching me to cook hamburgers." As big as his smile was, it didn't quite reach his eyes.

"Good, I'm starving," I said as I reached over and tousled his hair.

"You might be a girl, but I won't hesitate to give you a noogie," Garrett said, laughing.

"Like hell you will," Walker said as he popped Garrett in the ass with the hand towel.

"Dude! You suck!" Garrett said.

"Yeah, but you'll get over it. Get back over here and turn your burgers," Walker ordered.

Garrett went back to the stove and attempted to turn his burgers, but sent grease spattering across the stove instead. Walker showed him how to slip the spatula under the meat and turn it gently.

I mentally snapped a picture of them at the stove together. I wanted to forever ingrain it in my memory. A pang of jealousy and hurt filled me as I wished things at my home were different, that we were close like Walker and his family. But we weren't, and I was grateful to have a second chance with people who loved me.

"Whatcha thinkin', Lace?" Walker asked as he crossed the kitchen and leaned down to kiss me.

"How awesome you are."

Garrett made a gagging noise.

"Pay attention to your cooking, Garrett," Walker said over his shoulder.

I couldn't hear Garrett's response.

"You hungry?"

"Yeah," I said as I ran my hands over his chest. I was going to miss these moments most of all, being next to him with his arms wrapped around me, safe from everything and everyone. I wished I could stay there forever.

"What do you want for dessert?" he whispered as he gently grabbed my ass.

I peeked around to make sure Garrett still stood with his back to us as I rubbed my hand across his lower stomach and slid my fingers beneath his jeans. I fiddled with the button as I searched his face. His expression changed from wanting to take care of me and shield me to pure need.

I wasn't sure who was right, Mama or Aunt Linda, about being possessed or not, but I was tired of fighting. I was the only virgin left in my group of friends and if that was part of Mama's basis for my condition, then maybe she was wrong. Maybe I was normal, maybe I was in love with someone who thought I was worth fighting for. Regardless, I wanted Walker.

He rubbed my neck in small circles and threaded his fingers through my hair. He tilted my head up, exposing my neck as he leaned down and placed light kisses down to my collarbone. If Garrett hadn't been making so much noise cooking, he would have heard me gasp as Walker stroked my nipple through my shirt. Walker moved me backward from the kitchen into his bedroom as he continued to kiss me. I heard the door shut behind us.

As soon as the door closed, Walker slid one hand up my stomach and across my rib cage. He hesitated for a moment as he came into contact with my bra, and then slid his hands around my back and released the clasp. I wiggled my arms free and let it slip to the floor.

He pulled me up as I wrapped my legs around him. He took a few steps and leaned forward with us together until my back pressed against his mattress. I scooted up toward the head of the bed and Walker settled on top of me. He rolled us slightly onto our sides as he gained more access and cupped my ass. I rocked against him, wishing our clothes weren't in the way. I wanted him like I'd never wanted anyone before. I wanted to touch and kiss him, and I wanted him inside me.

I slid my hands along his back, allowing the tips of my nails to dig into his skin. I tugged on his shirt until he released me long enough to slip it over his head and toss it on the floor. My hands ran over his bare skin as he kissed me. Our tongues danced as we rocked together. I reached for the hem of my shirt and slowly pulled it over my head. The cold air brushed across my breasts as Walker pulled back for a moment to look at me. I searched his face for some kind of clue to move forward. This was the first time I'd been half-undressed with him. My heart knocked against my chest as I waited for his signal. I needed him to do or say something before I put my shirt back on and ran.

"You're going to undo me," he muttered as he lowered himself down on me.

We were skin to skin, and the heat from our bodies made me want to finish what we'd started.

He dipped his head down between my breasts and kissed me. My breathing quickened as he took me into his mouth. His tongue flicked across my nipple as he cupped my other breast. I tilted my hips to him, trying to bring him closer.

His breath was hot against my skin as he rose up and released the button on my jeans and unzipped them. We rolled over onto our sides as he continued to flick his tongue across my nipples, one then the other. I was barely conscious of his other hand slowly making its way across my stomach and down to my panties.

"Don't stop," I whispered in his ear as I dug my fingers into his back.

His kiss became more urgent as he slipped his hand into my jeans and over the thin lace of my panties, and I moved against his hand as he slowly began making small circles with his fingers against my core. I pushed down my jeans so they weren't in the way.

"You're so wet," he whispered as he moved my panties to the side and made contact with my bare skin. Nothing was in the way of his hand and me.

A moan escaped me as he dipped his finger inside me and his thumb circled against my clit. My breaths became ragged as he slipped another finger inside me. I moved my hips with his fingers, taking him in, and wanting more.

I reached down and unbuttoned his jeans. He groaned as I released him and ran my hand along his shaft.

He shifted and allowed me more access as he kissed my neck and worked his magic on me.

I wrapped my hand around him and stroked him in rhythm with his fingers as they slid in and out of me.

"Oh my God. I need you," I whispered. "I need you now."

Our breathing came in jagged, desperate gasps as we touched each other. I tightened my hold on him as I stroked him faster.

"No, baby, not yet—you first. Come for me. Come on baby, let it go," he whispered in my ear.

Chills shot down my spine as I arched up against his hand. His warm mouth covered my breast and I exploded against his hand. I gripped the blanket tightly as he continued his rhythm. Even though I was super sensitive from my release, I didn't want him to stop. I wanted him inside of me, all of him.

I continued stroking him as I nuzzled his ear.

"Walker, come with me this time."

"Oh God, you're driving me crazy," he said as he ground his hips against my hand.

"Are you ready?" I asked, pumping him harder. "Come with me, baby."

He buried his face in the pillow as his hot fluid spilled over my hand. I stroked him faster as he moaned into the bed. His release peaked mine and once again I arched against his hand and released with him.

We relaxed together as he kissed my cheek. He eased his fingers out of me and I wrapped my legs around him. He throbbed against the inside of my leg, and I reached down to stroke him.

"Lace, I don't think this is a good idea."

"Why?" I asked, kissing him along his neck.

"I want you to make this decision when we aren't mostly naked."

"I have—I love you."

"You've been through so much lately, I need you to be sure," he said and stroked my cheek with his fingers.

I adjusted my pillow and met his eyes.

"I'm sure. I have no doubt in my mind."

"It's not going to be the same as what we just did. It's going to hurt and I don't know if I can stand hurting you right now with everything else going on. I don't want you to ever second-guess how much I love you. We don't have to just because I'm leaving. We can wait."

"I don't want to wait anymore. I want you and no one else. I don't want you leaving for boot camp and questioning me, either. I want you to think back to this moment, our first time together, and let it help you get through every difficult time ahead."

Walker let me go and rolled over onto his back as he opened his nightstand and grabbed a condom. It was the first time I'd seen him completely naked. My breath caught as my eyes traveled over his chest, down his stomach, and down to him. He was larger than I thought, and hard again.

I bit my lip thinking about him being inside me, but then I remembered a few minutes ago when we came together. I wanted that with him again. Walker would take care of me. I realized it would hurt, but I trusted him to be as gentle as he could.

He rolled the condom over the length of him.

"Are you sure?" he asked. His voice was rough with emotion and need.

"I'm sure."

"Okay, I'm going to try and make this as gentle as I can."

I nodded. He slowly lowered himself on top of me, the full length of his body against mine. I slid my hands down his back and dug my fingers into his ass.

"I'm going to take care of you first," he said as he lifted up my leg to position us better. Then he grinned.

He took both of my breasts in his hands and squeezed gently. His tongue darted across my nipples, teasing them again. I ran my fingers through his hair and arched into his wet mouth.

Walker trailed soft kisses down my stomach and continued to play with my nipples as he spread my legs apart. His hands kneaded the inside of my thighs.

He ran his tongue slowly along the inside of my thigh. I throbbed with need. He brushed his thumb over my clit and I gasped. His hot breath brushed across my bare skin as he paused for a moment and glanced up at me. I gripped the blanket in anticipation of his mouth.

Finally, he dipped his head between my legs and ran his tongue over my clit as his finger entered me. I tried to raise my body up to meet him, but he pinned my hips against his mattress. His tongue caressed me as his finger slipped in and out of my wet core.

He sucked and licked my clit until I twisted underneath him. I needed him inside me.

"I need you inside me," I said breathlessly.

He sucked harder as his rhythm picked up.

"Baby, I can't . . . I'm gonna . . . Oh God . . ."

I grabbed his hair as he caressed me with his tongue. I wouldn't last much longer. If we were going to do this, it needed to be now.

Walker pulled away, nestling himself between my legs, and met my gaze.

"Are you sure?" He repositioned himself on the bed so he was on all fours above me.

I answered him with a kiss.

He paused for a minute, cupping my breast and kissing me deeply, and then slid his hand down and massaged my clit again. I was still wet.

"I just wanted to make sure you're ready," he whispered.

I nodded. I could feel him at my entrance, and there was a moment of intense pressure as he pushed inside me a little bit.

I gasped as I dug my fingers into his skin. He was right: it hurt. He eased in more as I accommodated him. Once fully inside me, I wrapped my legs around him and lay still. He didn't move either.

"You're so beautiful, Lacey. I love everything about you. I love your heart, your mind, and now your body. I'm the luckiest guy alive."

My pulse raced as I leaned up to kiss him. He responded and pulled on my lower lip with his teeth as he began to rock his hips. His kiss deepened as his gently picked up his pace. He was taking extra care to make it worth me saying yes. I loved him for that. I loved him for loving me. It wasn't as much about the sex as it was my needing to be as close as possible to him. I wanted to give him the one thing I could never give to anyone else, and I was doing just that.

This was a moment I could never change and never get back. I closed my eyes and tried to relax as I gave myself completely over to him.

"Are you okay?" he whispered.

"Yeah," I muttered.

"Okay, good. I was afraid I'd really hurt you."

I answered him with a slight tilt of my hips as I dared to take him a little deeper. My nails dug into his back and he responded with a moan as I tentatively rocked back and forth with him.

Walker trailed light kisses down my neck as our fingers intertwined and we maintained a slow and steady rhythm together. The pain eased the longer we were together and my body molded to him.

"My God," he whispered. "Lace—"

"—I love you," I whispered as Walker tensed and released as I tightened my legs around him.

Afterward, we lay quietly against each other, not wanting to ruin the moment by speaking. I'd done it. I'd given Walker my virginity and I didn't regret it one bit.

29

It was strange sitting at the dinner table with Susan, Linda, Garrett, and Walker after what Walker and I had just done in his room. I wondered if anyone could tell, or if I was acting differently. My heart swelled as I glanced at Walker. I loved him in a way I'd never loved anyone before. I finally belonged to someone who wanted me and loved me in return. My life might be crappy at home, but Walker and his family were quickly becoming mine.

After dinner, Walker and I cleaned the kitchen and washed the dishes.

"How are you doing?" he asked.

"Sore, but I guess that's pretty normal." I smiled at him. My cheeks warmed with the thought of everything we'd done in his bed. A flutter of heat traveled through me as I gazed at him. I stood on my tiptoes and brushed my lips against his.

"I love you muches and muches and muches," he whispered.

I didn't notice as he reached behind himself, dipped his hand in the sink, and doused me with soapy water. My eyes widened as I turned the faucet on cold, grabbed the sprayer, and let him have it. He laughed as he wrestled it from my hands and turned it back on me.

My hair and T-shirt were soaked by the time Susan made it to the kitchen to find out what all the commotion was about.

She stood in the doorway, smiling, and shook her head.

"You two clean it up," she said as she made her way back to the living room.

We burst into giggles as Walker picked me up and twirled me around. Every time I thought times with him couldn't get better, they did.

"We better get you out of that wet shirt," Walker said as he raised an eyebrow at me.

I giggled as I backed away and put my hands in front of me, warding off his threats of tickling me. Right as his fingers met my side the phone rang. I froze in place. The last time Walker's phone rang it was bad news. Although the afternoon had been incredible, there was the constant nagging of the real life that was waiting for me to return so it could chew me up and spit me out.

"Hey, Joss," Walker said into the phone. "Just a minute, she's right here."

I sighed with relief and leaned against the kitchen wall to steady myself.

"It's okay, it's just Joss," Walker said, turning to me. "You can take it in my bedroom and I'll clean up the kitchen."

"No, I helped make the mess. Wait a minute and I'll help."

I walked into his bedroom and picked up the phone.

"Hey," Joss said.

"Hey yourself, how are you?"

"Good, but I got a little worried when I called your house six times and no one answered. Are you okay?"

"Well, it's been a hell of a night and day."

I filled her in on how Krissy had caught Walker and me in the parking lot after work, how she'd told Mama about us, Mama's seizure, and Walker getting in Krissy's face. Joss remained silent as I told her one event after another.

"Are you going to go back to the hospital?"

"Yeah, I need to visit Mama and find out when she's coming home. I haven't heard from anyone since the doctor said we could see her."

"Lacey, you can stay with me while she's in the hospital if you want. You can always stay here if you need us."

"Thanks—I love you for being an amazing friend. I don't think I'll be going home until she's back."

"Are you staying at Walker's?"

"Honestly, I'm not sure. We haven't talked about it."

"Okay, well if you can't, just call me and tell me you're coming over. Mom and I rented some movies so we can hang out if you want."

"I'll let you know."

After I hung up the phone, I returned to a clean and dry kitchen. Walker, Linda, and Susan were watching TV and I sat down next to Walker on the couch. He put his arm around me and I leaned into him and got comfortable.

I'd told Joss everything except that I'd slept with Walker. For whatever reason I didn't want to tell anyone yet. Maybe I just wanted to keep it between Walker and myself for now. I needed something to hold on to over the next few days; something special that no one could take from me.

Susan said I could stay as long as I needed to. I promised to make myself useful: help clean, run errands, and help Garrett with homework. She opened her home to me and I wanted to let her know I appreciated it. I'd never really be able to tell her how much it all meant to me, but I was going to try.

I mentally reviewed my finances and decided I could swing taking some time off until Walker left for the military.

"Hey," I said. "Can I use your phone? I need to call work."

"You don't have to ask, Lace," Walker replied.

I slipped out from under his arm and went into the kitchen to call work. My boss offered her condolences as I told them Mama was in the hospital and requested a few weeks off. I promised to keep them updated on when I would return.

A heavy sigh escaped me as I replaced the receiver. Walker had already given notice to his job so he could spend his last weeks with his family. Even though I was worried about Mama, now I had some extra time with him too.

It was 11 P.M. when Walker and I settled into bed. This time, we didn't snuggle. We made love again and it hurt a little less. Afterward, he wrapped me in his arms and I fell asleep listening to his soft breathing.

30

The next morning, I woke and showered before Walker could see my makeup smeared and hair in every direction. Not that he hadn't before, but I was also sore and wanted a hot shower and a few minutes alone.

I turned on the water, let it warm up, and slipped out of my clothes. My reflection in the mirror caught my eye and I stared at myself. I was different; maybe no one could see it, but something new stirred inside me. Not just physically, but emotionally. Whatever it was, Walker loved me and that in itself gave me hope. I believed in myself a little bit more.

There were moments I was still confused and went back and forth about who was right, Mama or Linda. Was I actually possessed, or was Mama sick? Sometimes I believed Linda, but other times fear taunted me with the possibility I'd caused Mama's seizure and that she was right. But somewhere inside me, a glimmer of hope flickered, and I began to think there was a possibility I wasn't possessed. If I was, how could I love someone so much? And how could I love Susan and Garrett? How could I still love Mama no matter what happened?

After Linda talked to me that day, I'd read the material she'd given me concerning mental illness. The more time I took to digest it and think about Mama's behavior, the more it sank in that something was wrong. We weren't normal, but everyone was too terrified to say anything.

I'd also continued my research at school, since the college library allowed me the time and privacy I needed. I'd grabbed some books and read up on demon possession. Maybe I couldn't explain some of my behavior all the time, but I didn't do the things that the books described.

Even with all the information I'd gained, however, when you're told for almost half your life that you're possessed, the fear doesn't dissipate overnight. A few weeks of new information doesn't erase years of a mom who loves you one second and screams at you the next. It lingers like the fog until small rays of sunlight pierce through it.

It was almost ironic: right when everything around me was falling apart, the most amazing guy had strolled into my life.

I dressed, fixed my hair, and applied my makeup. The house was still quiet, so I made coffee and started breakfast for everyone. I heard Susan's oxygen tank move across the floor as she made her way to the kitchen.

I pulled the kitchen chair out for her and helped her get situated. She smiled as I brought her a cup of coffee.

I finished the pancakes and bacon and piled everything on a big plate, set the table, and sat down to wait for Walker and Garrett.

"We shouldn't wait for them," Susan said.

"Really?"

"Yeah, my mouth is watering." She grinned as she grabbed a few pancakes and drizzled syrup over them. I did the same and giggled. We were like two silly girls sneaking around, and for some reason, it struck me as funny.

"How are you?" I asked between bites.

"Everything considered, I'm doing okay. I'm sorry your mom is in the hospital. Do you plan on visiting her today?"

I played with my pancakes as I nodded. I recognized it was the right thing to do, even if I didn't want to.

"Yeah. I need to find out if the doctors have figured out anything."

"I know I've already said it, but you can stay as long as you need, even after Walker leaves for the military."

"What? No, I couldn't impose."

"You're not imposing. It'd be nice if you stayed some, for Garrett and myself. Honestly, I could use your help if you're open to it. Maybe some with Garrett. I realize you have a full course load at school and you work, but it would still be really nice to have you around."

"Really?"

"Really." She smiled.

"I'd love to, Susan. That would mean the world to me."

"We'll make plans to visit Walker a few times, too. Maybe you could help me drive?"

"Drive your Camaro?" I squeaked.

Susan laughed until her coughing replaced the sound of her happiness. It was a rude reminder that she wouldn't be around long.

"Yes, you can drive my car on the trip."

I grinned at her like it was Christmas morning.

"Besides, now that you and Walker are officially serious and having sex, he'll want to spend as much time with you as possible."

My fork clattered to the floor. I reached down to pick it up without looking at her. How in the hell did she find out?

"It's okay, there's no judgment here. You're both young and in love —I figured it would only be a matter of time. I've told you before, but I'll say it again. I've never seen Walker so happy." She reached over and squeezed my hand.

"How did you know?"

"I know my son, and I could tell your relationship had shifted into something beyond what it was even a week ago. Your connection is deeper. That's what happens when you become intimate with someone. It changes how you view each other and the world. And, if it's a good thing, it strengthens the relationship. You and Walker have a good thing and I want to support and help you both hang onto it while he's in transition. Besides, I have my own selfish reasons."

"You're not selfish at all—the exact opposite, and I'll do everything

I can to stay close and help you and Garrett. It'll help me as well. I don't think I could handle not seeing *any* of you for six weeks."

"Not to worry, I think we have it all figured out."

I squeezed her hand in return.

We finished eating and Susan made her way to her bedroom to rest. I put the plate of food in the oven for when the guys got up.

I'd planned on visiting the hospital today, but we also needed to get Walker's car running again. The crisp morning air welcomed me as I stepped outside and took a deep breath. Fall was in full force now, and the trees boasted bright red-and-yellow leaves. I wanted to take Walker to the pond again and instead of fight, make love to him. The thought of the cold air across our naked bodies sent a chill through me. I promised myself that I would make it happen before he left.

I heard the door close and turned around. Walker stood in the doorway, smiling.

"Morning," I said.

"Morning, beautiful. How are you?"

He approached me and wrapped me in his arms. I snuggled into him and closed my eyes. Every moment, every kiss, every hug was worth a lifetime to me. We would start counting the days before he left soon, and I just couldn't think about it yet.

"Did you sleep okay?"

"Yeah," I said as I stared into his eyes. It never seemed to matter how many times I saw him; his eyes drew me in and I could get lost forever in them.

I rose up on my tiptoes and kissed him good morning.

Then, I snapped back as I remembered what Susan had said.

"Holy shit, your mom found out we had sex!" I squealed.

Walker narrowed his eyes in confusion as he waited for me to clarify.

"Walker, she knows we're sleeping together," I whispered.

"Yeah, she said we could," he replied.

"No," I said, impatiently patting his chest. "She knows we're having sex."

Walker paused as my words registered, and then he shocked the hell out of me with a huge smile.

"What? I was a little bit mortified when she brought it up over pancakes!" I retorted and leaned against his car.

Walker laughed and kissed my forehead.

"Lace, I'm sorry you were embarrassed. I didn't say anything if that's what you're thinking, but Mom was well aware of my last relationship and she probably just figured it was a matter of time."

"So, you didn't tell her? You two are really close."

"No, I wouldn't have said anything, but she isn't stupid either. She figured that when you started spending the night, it would happen."

"Well isn't that a bit presumptuous of both of you?" I huffed and rubbed my arms against the chill.

"Don't get upset. But are you going to tell me that when we slept next to each other the first night, you weren't even considering it? Even a little bit?"

It irritated me that he was right. It also irritated me that they'd assumed we would start sleeping together if we kept dating. And for some reason, I didn't want to admit the truth to him, which was probably silly, but I didn't.

"I had no intention of sleeping with you, Walker Tate Farren, but I fell in love with you, so as far as I'm concerned it's your fault. I have other things to think about than if you assumed we would eventually have sex."

Walker couldn't contain his smile.

"What?" I asked, exasperated by this conversation. I wasn't ready to tell anyone, especially Susan, and here I was having a conversation about my sex life twice before 10 A.M.

"You're so cute when you get feisty. It makes me want to kiss you," he said as he took one long stride, grabbed me, and kissed me with so much passion that I wanted him to take me right there on the hood of his car.

"I love you," he whispered.

"Muches and muches and muches," I replied.

We held each other in silence for a moment and listened to what we were telling each other without saying anything. A cocoon of safety wrapped around me—something I'd never dared dream about before I met him.

I stood on my tiptoes and kissed Walker again. My brain had started reminding me that we couldn't stand around all day; we had things to do.

"How's Garrett been doing in school since I've been helping him?" I asked.

"Honestly, I have no idea, but you can ask him. He likes you, a lot, actually. He hardly ever talked to Brittany."

Walker stopped short as soon as the name escaped his lips. I understood it was a part of his past and a part of who he was, but I hated her name coming out of his mouth. I folded my arms and stared at my feet.

"I'm sorry," he said. "I honestly don't think about her anymore. It was over months before I ever met you."

"I know, but it's hard sometimes. You and Brittany dated for three years, and we're just beginning," I said.

"I know," he said and reached for my hand.

"So, I need to get to the hospital today," I said, changing the subject. "Which means we need to get your car fixed, right?"

"Yeah, I found out what's wrong. I just haven't had time to deal with it."

"Is it anything major?"

"Well, I need a new battery, but it'll still start."

Confused, I waited for him to explain.

"With a stick shift you can push the car to get it moving, pop the clutch, and it'll start. If you're on a hill, it's easy. If you're not, you have to push if fast enough so you get enough speed to pop the clutch."

"I need to learn to drive your car," I said, smiling. His brown Nissan wasn't new, but it radiated character and it fit Walker. "Okay, since I have no clue how to drive a stick shift yet, I'll push."

"Lacey, you are not pushing my car!" Walker exclaimed.

"Hey—I might be little, but I have pushed a car before," I said, quite proud of myself.

"Really?"

"Yup, one of my friend's cars broke down and I pushed it off the highway and onto a side road until we could get help. And yes, by myself, so stop looking at me that way."

"You continue to surprise me," he said as he ran his hand through his hair.

"I'm sure you'll be okay," I said, smiling. "Should we get ready to go, then?"

"Let's say bye to Mom and tell her we're leaving. I wanna see if she needs anything, too."

"I need to grab a few things as well," I said and followed him into the house.

Fifteen minutes later, we were on the road to the hospital. Walker glanced at me several times, shook his head, and grinned. I guess he hadn't believed me when I said I could push his car.

I hated the stench of the hospital. Although they were helping people get better, but people died here, too.

Nurses hustled from room to room, machines beeped, people cried, and it was everything I could do to keep walking down the hallway, get into the elevator, and push the fifth-floor button.

Walker was silent as we walked, but he squeezed my hand as we made it to the ICU floor. I figured he was thinking about Susan; she was often in the hospital for weeks at a time. Guilt gnawed at me. The only reason he stepped foot into a hospital again was because of me, but at the same time, he wouldn't let me go by myself. He would leave me alone in a few weeks, but not until then.

We stopped at Mama's closed door and Walker released my hand.

"I'll be right here, okay?"

I nodded and gently knocked on the door before I pushed it open. Mama was hooked up to more machines than I'd ever seen. My eyes scanned the room and I took it all in. She slept as I stared at her. I was glad she was asleep because I couldn't articulate any words anyway. Tears slid down my cheeks as her chest rose and fell.

Had I done this? Was this my fault? I couldn't stand the pressure building in my chest as the walls dared to close in on me. I opened the door and bolted out of the room.

Walker pulled the door closed behind me, but I couldn't look at him yet. I wanted to find the doctor. It was time I got some answers.

I darted down the hall to the nurses' station and left Walker standing alone by Mama's door.

"Hi, I'm Lynn Beaumont's daughter. Is her doctor available?" I asked.

"Let me page him, hon," the nurse said.

Her voice echoed through the PA system and minutes later a middle-aged doctor came around the corner. I recognized Dr. Snider from earlier.

"Lacey," he said as he extended his hand.

"Hi, Doctor Snider. Thank you for talking to me," I said.

"I didn't see you around when I spoke with Patsy and Krissy. I have a few minutes if you have questions?"

"I do. They haven't told me anything about Mama or what happened, so I'm really confused about why she's still in ICU."

"Let's have a seat," he said as he led me to some empty chairs in the waiting room.

"Lacey, we called in a neurologist and a cardiologist to discuss what was going on with your mother. Several things can cause a seizure, so we wanted to check every avenue. We diagnosed your mom with malignant hypertension."

He paused before he continued.

"Malignant hypertension is a rapid rise in blood pressure, typically one eighty over one twenty or higher. It causes severe headaches, numbness, shortness of breath, and blurred vision, among other symptoms. In your mom's case, it caused a seizure. Unfortunately, we suspect she has high blood pressure and it went undiagnosed for a long time."

"Yeah, she always talked about not feeling well, but we couldn't ever get her to go to the doctor. She hasn't been in years."

"That's what Patsy said as well."

"What caused it, though? I mean, I understand her blood pressure went high really fast . . ." my voice faded as the memory of that night replayed. "But what causes high blood pressure to begin with?"

"There are several factors. A few include diet, weight, lack of exercise, and poor sleeping habits."

"Mama's all of those. She rarely leaves the house, sits in a chair all day, doesn't sleep well, and she's really overweight."

Dr. Snider nodded in agreement.

"But, did I—" I took a deep breath and blurted out my question before I lost my nerve. "Did I cause her seizure?"

"Why would you ask that?" His face filled with concern as he waited for my answer.

"She found out I was dating someone. I was dating him for several weeks before she found out, and she got furious." Shame washed over me and I stared at my shoes, afraid to hear his answer.

"How old are you, Lacey?"

"I'm eighteen," I replied as I looked up at him.

A gentle smile crossed his face.

"I have four daughters and as they reached eighteen and nineteen every one of them waited to tell me about a new relationship until they went on a few dates. It's perfectly normal. And as you get older, the relationship has the potential to get serious. I don't think my daughters would've wanted to tell me about every single date they had in college until they were sure it was someone they wanted to bring home. You didn't do anything wrong, and you didn't make your mom have a seizure. This was a problem that has built up over the years."

"You're sure?" I asked.

His kind smile reappeared. "I'm absolutely confident. You have not made your mother ill. Her choices have."

"So, I didn't cause the seizure by making her angry?"

"It was going to happen one way or another. You're not responsible."

I nodded as I took in his words.

"How long will she be here?"

"I'd guess about a week and then we'll send her home with a diet plan and schedule regular visits to the doctor. They'll help her lose weight and manage her blood pressure. I will tell you that if she doesn't take care of herself, this could be fatal next time," he said gently.

I sucked in a sharp breath.

"She could die?" I hiccupped.

"Yes. I'm sorry to be so blunt, but you're an adult and you need to hear the truth."

"Okay," I said and stood up. "Thank you so much for taking the time to speak with me. I really appreciate it."

"Here's my card. You can call me anytime if you have questions or concerns."

"Thank you, Doctor," I said and shook his hand goodbye.

He walked away, and I sat back down and stared at the card. I didn't cause Mama's seizure. I didn't almost kill her when I told her about Walker. It wasn't my fault. Relief flooded me as I sighed and leaned back in my seat. I tucked the card into the inside zipper of my purse. This was another secret I would keep close to my heart until I needed it.

I glanced at my watch and realized I'd left Walker outside Mama's door for fifteen minutes.

Hurrying back to her room, I spotted Walker sitting in the hallway, head against the wall. My heart stuck in my throat. He was still there waiting for me. I'd taken off on him and he hadn't left me.

He stood as I approached. I ran to him and hugged him as hard as I could. He returned my embrace and held me.

"I'm so sorry I took off. I shouldn't have left you," I said, not letting him go.

"It's okay. I know what it's like when someone you love is connected to machines and cords and . . . and the sinking pit in your stomach because you can't save them or make it better."

We pulled apart and I reached up to kiss him.

"The only thing that's going to make it better is that we're together," I said. "I don't think I could go through this without you. And you know I love you, Susan, and Garrett."

"I know, and I love you too," he said and kissed my forehead.

With so many people in the hallway, I didn't realize that Krissy had approached us.

"Well, isn't that sweet." She eyed us in disgust. "I hope you haven't visited and upset Mama."

"No, she was asleep and I didn't want to wake her."

"That was unusually kind of you," she snapped.

"We just came to visit your mom and talk to the doctor," Walker said.

I squeezed Walker's hand hard at the mention of the doctor.

"Oh?"

"Yeah, I talked to him," I said, "and he told me Mama will stay in ICU while they run tests. He explained her diagnosis."

"Did he explain that you caused her seizure?"

"Shut the hell up, Krissy," Walker said as he took a step forward.

I pulled on his arm and brought him back alongside me, reminding myself of the conversation with the doctor and his card in my purse. I already knew the truth, and nothing Krissy said at this moment could hurt me. I was also smart enough to keep my mouth shut.

"I assume you have to go back to school soon?" I asked.

"Yes, and if I don't get back to take finals next week, I'll fail the term. Patsy has promised me she'll take care of Mama. You, on the other hand, need to knock off your nonsense or I'm coming back and there'll be hell to pay."

"Yeah, I'll keep that in mind," I muttered. "When are you leaving?"

"My flight leaves at eight o'clock tomorrow night, so if you would leave until then, I'd appreciate it. I don't need Mama having another seizure when she sees you."

"Not a problem. Have a safe flight back," I said as I took Walker's hand, turned around, and left Krissy standing in the hall.

"Thank you," I said, looking up at Walker.

"For what?"

"For standing up to her on more than one occasion. It means a lot to me."

"I love you and that's what I'm supposed to do."

"Well, do you remember our day at the lake when I offered to trade Krissy for Garrett and you said that worked for you?"

"Crap," Walker laughed. "Yeah, I remember, but I take it back. I am *not* trading. She's a handful. Besides, Garrett likes you already," he said and smiled.

"I'm glad—I like him a lot too."

3 2

"So, I need to grab some clothes and you've never been to my house. I figure while Patsy and Krissy are at the hospital and no one's there, I'll show you around?"

"Sure, sounds good," Walker replied. "Shall I drive?"

"Well, with all the commotion, I left my car parked here at the hospital," I said, rubbing my forehead. "I should probably take it home, but now I don't remember where I parked."

I was so used to passing the hospital as I drove to work that I'd never realized how big it was. Not to mention, I didn't even remember which entrance I had used. All I remembered was puking on the side of the road and how terrified I was when I thought I'd killed Mama.

"It's okay, we can just drive around," Walker said. "We'll find it."

"What if your car won't start?" I giggled. I wasn't sure why I thought the situation was funny because it wasn't. Stress manifested in weird ways.

"Then I'll have someone jump it—not the end of the world," Walker said, smiling.

I'm not sure how he could always remain so calm, but then I remembered he'd taken care of his mom. He was probably so relieved to leave the hospital that his car not starting wasn't a big deal.

Walker's car started on the first try and after an hour of driving through the hospital parking lot and garage levels, we located my car.

"Oh good, I was beginning to think we'd lost her!" I laughed as I hopped out of Walker's car.

"I told you we'd find your car."

I leaned through the window and kissed him.

"Okay, I'll follow you there?" he asked.

"Yup! See you soon," I said.

I kissed him one more time and then got into my car and pulled out of the parking lot.

The thought of Walker coming over made me nervous. Hopefully the house wasn't a disaster, and someone had at least loaded the dishes so the house didn't stink. Most of the time that someone was me, but I hadn't been home. It was more than that, though. I was about to reveal another part of me that I hadn't shared with Walker yet.

He was about to see where everything happened: the yelling, the praying and casting out of demons, the bloody noses, the place I was knocked unconscious. It was one thing to tell him about it; it was another thing entirely for him to walk in and stand where it had all happened. If I ever told him something happened again, he'd have the full mental picture, and it scared me. He'd already threatened to confront Mama, and now that she was sick that couldn't happen.

By the time I decided it wasn't a good idea to have him over, I had pulled into the driveway and parked my car in the empty carport. I motioned for him to park next to me.

"Here we are," I said.

"Wow, it's a big house," he said, looking around the front of the house and deck.

"Big and empty." I took his hand and led him up the steps and into the house.

"Hello!" I yelled as I closed the door.

No one answered.

"Okay, well, I'm pretty sure no one's here, but I'll show you the house and we'll make sure. As you can tell, this is the kitchen."

Walker stood silently for a moment and took everything in. He assessed the kitchen and slowly turned toward the living room, identifying Mama's chair and the stack of books next to it.

"This is where she knocked you unconscious," he said. Walker's voice carried an edge I didn't recognize.

"Yes," I whispered. It felt like I was cutting myself wide open as I allowed him to step into my world.

I took his hand and led him down the hallway, ready to focus on something else.

"This is Mama and Patsy's bedroom and bath." I took him into the room and opened the curtains to the sliding glass door. "This is the back deck." I led him to the guest bedroom and bathroom and then took him downstairs.

"This is Krissy's room. There's not much here since she's away at school most of the time, which works for me."

We turned the corner into the family room and then I guided him around one more corner to my bedroom.

"This is my room," I said, placing my bag on the floor.

"Uh, where's your furniture?" he asked as he noted the few piles of clothes and the sleeping bag on the floor.

Shit. With everything going on, I'd forgotten that Mama had sold my furniture. He was going to be pissed.

"Yeah, well, that's a long story," I said. "I'm just going to grab some clothes and a few things from the bathroom. I'll be right back," I said, darting past him.

My head pounded with every step. This hadn't been a good idea. I don't know what the hell I'd been thinking—apparently nothing.

I rustled through my bathroom drawers and grabbed some makeup, shaving cream, and razor. I hurried back to my bedroom and rifled through my clothes and threw them in the bag too. Walker stood in silence and stared at me as though I were on display.

I stood up and smiled.

"Okay, well that's it. You've gotten your tour and I've got what I need. It's still okay that I stay with you, right?"

Walker frowned at my question. "I sure as hell don't want you to stay here!"

"It's not as bad as it looks. I mean, it is, but . . . it's over. What's done is done and I just want to move on."

"Where's your furniture, Lace?" he asked again, his voice firm.

Apparently, I wasn't going to get out of this one.

I hugged my bag in front of me. "This was a terrible idea. Not sure what I was thinking when I brought you here." I tried to move past him and get out the door, but he grabbed my arm.

"Lacey, where's your furniture?"

I sighed as I rubbed my forehead. "If I tell you can we leave? Please?"

"Yes."

"She sold it when I stayed with you the first time. It was after our fight and I told her I stayed with Joss. When I came home, my furniture was gone. She said if I wanted to stay at my friend's house all the time then I didn't need furniture." My face flushed and tears threatened to spill over and onto my cheeks.

"She broke my fucking heart," I whispered as the tears broke free. "How? How can someone treat their kid like that? I was gone for a few days after a horrible fight and she sells my stuff! Do you know that we have scorpions and huge spiders down here? Of course you don't," I laughed through my tears.

I pulled my arm away and ran to the bathroom, locking locked the door behind me, and leaning on the counter as the tears rushed out. I didn't want to ugly-cry in front of him.

Five minutes later, I emerged from the bathroom to find Walker sitting on the stairs. My eyes were red, but at least I'd touched up my makeup.

"I'm sorry, baby. I'm sorry she did that to you. Let's get out of here, okay?"

My chest ached as I followed him up the stairs and out the front door. I locked it behind me and another piece of my heart with it.

33

The drive to Walker's was beautiful, and I took a deep breath as I watched the late-afternoon sun dance across the autumn leaves. So much had happened in the last several weeks that my head throbbed just thinking about it, but something about the fall colors, the sunshine, and the coolness in the air gave me some much-needed peace. If I could have only two seasons a year, fall would be the one I would want to last the longest. Unfortunately, it was always the shortest season in the South.

Susan and Garrett were at the kitchen table playing cards when we walked in. It was such a stark contrast from my kitchen to theirs. Not because it was smaller, but because of the life that was there. The love, shared smiles, and sometimes the bone-shattering sadness when everyone remembered Susan was dying. But no matter what, it was real: no one was pretending to be who they weren't and no one was afraid of each other.

"Hey, buddy," I said and ruffled Garret's hair.

"Hey, Lacey. How's your mom?"

"She's still in ICU, but she's going to be okay if she takes care of herself."

"That's good."

"How long are they keeping her?" Susan asked.

"They think about a week, but they couldn't be specific."

"Lacey's staying with us," Walker said abruptly.

Susan's eyebrow rose as she waited for an explanation.

"Sorry, Mom, that was rude. But she doesn't even have any furniture in her room at home, and it would mean a lot to me if she could stay. Please?"

"Of course she can stay. Lacey and I have already talked about it, but you and I will finish this conversation later," she said as she turned toward me.

Shock registered on my face. I didn't understand Walker's sudden change, especially with Susan. I'd never heard him sound bossy or rude, ever.

"It's okay, Lacey, don't look panicked. You and I already discussed our arrangement, so don't worry. Sometimes we argue just like any other family," she said and smiled gently.

"Okay, I just don't want to cause any problems."

"You're not. Why don't you go put your things in Walker's room and I'll finish talking to him, okay?"

She didn't need to ask twice.

I tossed my duffel bag on the bed and tucked my clothes into the top drawer of Walker's dresser, unwilling to take up much of his space and irritate him any further. After I finished unpacking I stretched out on his bed. Susan's and Walker's muffled voices carried into his room, but I couldn't make out anything they were saying. They weren't yelling, so that was a good sign.

Garrett peeked in the door and smiled. "They're not fighting, so don't stress about it."

"Thanks, Garrett. I just haven't heard Walker talk to your mom like that before."

"He normally doesn't. He's just upset."

"I think it was hard for him to be at the hospital with everything going on with your mom." I sat up on the bed and scooted to the edge.

"How are you doing with everything? I mean, you don't have to talk to me about stuff, but if you want to you can."

"Thanks," he answered and shoved his hands into his pockets. "It sucks."

"I agree, buddy. But I have some good news. Your mom said I could stay with you guys some even while Walker's at boot camp. What do you think?"

"Really? That's way cool!"

"Yeah?" I couldn't hide my smile. "I'll help you with your homework, too. That work for you?"

"I'm good with that. You make it almost fun, but not quite," he said, laughing.

"Good, then you're stuck with me."

"Move, Garrett," Walker said as he pushed past him and closed the door in his face.

"Walker! What the hell?" I asked and jumped off his bed.

"Gotta give him shit as long as I can." He smiled.

"Every time you give him shit I want you to remember that you could've had a sibling like Krissy."

"No thanks. Like I said, she is *all* yours."

"Are you okay?" I asked. "Did you and your mom talk everything out?"

"Yeah, we're okay. I just can't stand the thought of you going back there, Lace. It tears me up inside, and the best thing I can do is keep you here for as long as possible. In the back of my mind, I know you'll go back even if you don't have to, and it pisses me off. I don't want you to go back to that house and that empty bedroom. As soon as we opened the door I could imagine all the shit you've told me about, and I got pissed. I just wanted to grab you and run."

"I have to go back. What if Mama's been sick and it's caused her to act crazy? What if it changed her? If there's a chance to have a good relationship with her, I have to try. I love her no matter what's happened."

He reached for my hand and laced his fingers through mine.

"That's the thing I love so much about you, even though it drives me crazy at the same time. You have an incredible heart. She doesn't deserve you. I love you so much it makes me a little nuts sometimes."

"I love you too. In fact, I want to take you somewhere," I said as I stood and opened his bedroom door.

"Yeah?"

"Give me ten," I said and shut his door behind me.

34

I gathered everything I needed with Susan's help and direction. She thought my plan was a good idea for both of us. I peered out the window as the sun began to lower. My timing was going to be perfect.

I poked my head into his bedroom and smiled.

"Let's go," I said.

Walker laughed at the overstuffed picnic basket and pile of blankets I was trying to balance. I peered over the top and tried not to trip.

"Let me help you," he said as he unloaded my arms.

"Thanks," I said, grinning from ear to ear. The Cheshire Cat had nothing on me at that moment.

"What are you smiling so big about?" he asked as we went outside and I began walking down the path behind the house.

"Nothing, it's just nice to be outside and not in a stuffy hospital."

"You can say that again."

We walked the path in silence until we reached the pond. I put the pile of blankets on the ground and spread out the first one. We sat down and Walker helped me set the food and soda out. I wasn't really hungry, but Walker never failed to have an appetite.

The sun lowered in the sky and the orange-and-pink colors backlit the clouds. Rays of golden light bounced off the pond. It was peaceful —exactly what I'd hoped for.

"It's so quiet here. It reminds me of our first date, watching the sunset at the lake. Obviously, this isn't a lake, but we're still surrounded by trees and water." I smiled as he drew in a deep breath and sighed contentedly.

Everything going on with Mama and I had been hard for him too, but more than that, we didn't have much time together before he left. Also, no one was sure how much longer Susan had to live. Everything in our life was dictated by a calendar. I just wanted to stop time for a moment.

"I love it here. You're right, I think we both just need a break from the shitstorm," Walker said.

The breeze blew across the water and sent a chill through me. I reached for a blanket and wrapped myself in it. We ignored the food; I don't think either one of us was hungry. We just wanted to be alone.

Walker scooted over and slid under the blanket with me and I leaned my head against his shoulder. We snuggled and watched the sun set.

Walker kissed my forehead and stood up.

"Where are you going?" I asked.

"Hang on, I'll be right back."

I shivered under the blanket as the warmth of his body escaped me. Walker gathered rocks and wood and piled it a few feet away from us. I smiled as he meticulously made a circle with the stones and laid the wood inside. In a matter of minutes, a fire roared to life and filled the darkness. It was perfect.

He smiled as he got back under the blanket with me.

"Thank you."

"You're welcome," he said as he wrapped his arms around me. "It's a perfect night, too. I'm glad you thought of this."

"Me too," I said. "Walker?"

"Yeah, Lace?"

"I love you."

Walker tilted my head up and kissed me, his lips warm and soft.

My body didn't take long to respond to him. I'd brought him here for the sole purpose of making love to him; he just didn't know it yet.

His fingers lightly stroked my cheek as our kiss deepened.

"You're the best thing that's ever happened to me," he whispered. "You'll never understand how much I love you."

"Show me," I responded between kisses. "Show me how much you love me." I broke our kiss and pulled off my shirt. Then I released the clasp of my bra and slipped it off. The cold night air brushed across my breasts, my nipples hardening instantly. I studied his face as I stood up, unbuttoned my jeans, and slid them off, leaving me with only my red lace panties on.

The firelight danced across his face. He couldn't have hidden his reaction if he wanted to. His eyes revealed his hunger as I slowly slid my panties down my legs, leaving me completely naked, but this time, I wasn't hiding in his sheets or underneath him. I allowed him to see every inch of me as I stood beside the fire. I'd grown more comfortable with him, and tonight boldness radiated through me. I wanted him to think about this moment when he was alone in bed at boot camp. When he needed me, I wanted the memory of tonight to burn through every part of him.

"You're so beautiful." His voice cracked with emotion.

I closed the gap between us and stood over him. He ran his hands slowly up the inside of my thighs and spread my legs apart. He cupped my ass and brought me closer to him, his tongue finding my wet core.

My fingers threaded through his hair as his tongue fluttered across my clit. I sucked in a sharp breath as he sucked me gently and slipped his finger inside me. I didn't ever want him to stop.

Unable to stand up any longer, I lowered myself to the ground with him. Walker moved with me, never allowing his fingers to stop, while I spread my legs and welcomed his tongue again.

I watched as his tongue licked and sucked my clit. I was so close, and he knew it.

He glanced up, released my clit, and removed his fingers.

"You like that, baby?" he asked, his voice raspy with need.

I nodded and blushed that I'd lost my mind enough to be so bold.

Walker leaned back on his knees and removed his shirt. His muscled chest and stomach were accentuated by the firelight. With a flick of a button, he released himself from his jeans. His blue eyes danced; his muscles were taut. He was ready, and I was ready to take in every inch of him.

He removed his jeans and slid a condom out of his back pocket. He ripped the package open and slipped it on.

"Come here," he said as he lay down on his back. I straddled him as he guided me slowly and I took him inside me.

I gasped as I sat on top of him.

"You okay?"

"Yeah, it's just different."

"Just relax, baby."

Walker gently began moving, giving me time to adjust to our position. It didn't take me long to match his rhythm as he grabbed my hips and moved me up and down the length of him. His strokes pushed deeper inside me, sending waves of pleasure through my body.

"That's it . . . God, you feel so good," Walker said as he buried himself inside me.

His fingers dug into my thighs as I brought myself down harder and faster. His thumb found my clit and he massaged me in gentle circles. The wave built inside me, but I didn't want it to stop. I needed him to stay inside me. My core tightened around him and he moaned in response as he dug his fingers into my ass.

My back arched, allowing him full access as I continued to rock against him.

A moan escaped my lips as I leaned forward, digging my nails into his chest as he rubbed my clit. I couldn't hold out much longer. The combination was too much.

"I . . . oh my God," I panted. "Don't stop, baby. I need you."

Walker arched his hips and thrust deep inside me.

"Come on, baby. I want to feel you come with me."

He quickened his pace as we gasped and moaned. The intense pleasure was too much, and my body tightened around him as I arched my back. I bit my lip so I wouldn't scream as he released with me. The thought of him coming inside me sent me into another spasm. Nothing in the world existed except Walker at that moment.

I collapsed on top of him. He wrapped his arms around me as we took a moment to catch our breath. He remained inside me as we relaxed and relished the moment, the night air playing against our sweaty, naked bodies. My heart filled with emotion and a tear slid down my cheek and landed on his chest.

"Are you okay?" Concern filled his voice as he rubbed my back.

"I love you so much."

"And I love you muches and muches and muches," he whispered as he wrapped his arms around me.

M onday arrived too fast, and even though I had time off work, I still had to go to class. I couldn't hide with Walker forever, no matter how much I wanted to.

I'd called Joss and Emma so we could have lunch together. Not only did I need to catch up with them, but if I was forced to leave my cocoon—I needed my friends.

I entered the crowded student center and found a corner table. Those were often difficult to come by, as they provided the most privacy.

Joss arrived first, followed by Emma. We exchanged hugs and settled in at the table.

"Okay, spill it," Emma said.

"I know, right?" I said. "It feels like I haven't seen either of you in years! So much is going on. Emma, I already told Joss that Mama's in the hospital. I'm leaving after this to go visit her."

"What? What happened and why didn't someone call me?" she asked, exasperated.

"I don't have your number, or I would've called you," Joss said.

"I'm sorry, Emma, I've been so wrapped up in everything and

when I did think about calling you, I was in the car or nowhere near a phone."

"Well, we're gonna take care of that right now while Lacey continues to fill us in." Emma scrambled in her purse for a pen and paper and then wrote her number down for Joss.

"Now there are no excuses—I better hear from somebody when something like this happens," Emma said.

"Yes, ma'am," Joss and I said at the same time. The laughter that followed reminded me that I was surrounded by people who loved me and wanted to hear about what was going on in my life.

I continued to fill them in about Mama's seizure, the hospital visit, and the follow-up with the doctor.

"Lacey, there's no way you could've caused your mom's seizure," Joss said. "I had no idea you even thought that. I would've sent you straight to Emma so she could smack some sense into you."

"I got scared, and when Krissy accused me of causing it, I got *really* scared. You didn't see how pissed Mama got when I told her about Walker."

"I told you I didn't want to be anywhere near that conversation," Emma chimed in.

"Right? But I didn't have a choice after Krissy caught us together in the parking lot after work."

"Leave it to Krissy," Joss muttered. "I thought my brother was a pain in the ass, but Krissy is a piece of work. That girl lives to get you into trouble. The kicker is, you're eighteen!"

"Can't argue with that," Emma said.

"I know. I still haven't talked to Mama after everything that happened, but hopefully I can catch her alone and awake this afternoon. Krissy has already flown out, so it's only Patsy I have to deal with."

"Good! Good riddance," Emma said.

"How are you and Walker?" Joss asked.

"Good." I couldn't hide my grin. My face burned crimson red at the thought of last night.

"Ah hell, you did it," Joss said. "I should've realized it the moment I joined you for lunch, but I was worried about you and your mom!"

"What? What am I missing?" Emma asked.

"How was it?" Joss asked, ignoring Emma's questions.

"It hurt like hell," I said between bites of my salad. "It's gotten a lot better though." I giggled.

"You! Lacey Anne, you're not a virgin anymore!" Emma sputtered.

Joss laughed and shook her head. "He loves her, Emma. It's sweet how protective he is over her. The night after Lacey's mom knocked her out, Walker was at my door discussing the safest place for Lacey to be. He's crazy about her."

Emma sighed and took a drink of her Diet Coke. "I'm so relieved to hear that, but I'm a little miffed I haven't met him yet. I get that you have a lot going on, but I'd really like to meet him. If you two are this serious, then it's important to me. What can we do to make that happen?"

"I have no idea—he's leaving for the military in a few weeks."

"What?" they asked in unison.

I put my fork down.

"Yeah, boot camp in freakin' Texas for six weeks. Susan said I can continue to spend nights and even make trips with them to visit Walker, but he's leaving."

"Well, shit," Joss said. "I guess that calls for a goodbye party then." She smiled. "We can have it at the same place you two met."

My eyes grew wide at the idea. It was perfect.

"Emma, are you okay coming to a party for a little while?" I asked. "Granted, obnoxious drunks aren't your thing, but Walker and I won't be drinking. Joss usually only has a few, and then she herds everyone to the bathroom or out her front door as needed." I laughed.

"You got it, count me in," Emma said. "I'll be fine since you guys aren't really drinking either. I might not stay for hours, but I'd love to be there. Great idea, Joss."

"Well, we gotta do something for Lacey and Walker. What night works, Lacey?"

I grabbed my pocket calendar out of my purse and saw the big X on the day Walker would be leaving. He had family plans with and without me in the few days before he left, which meant that next Saturday night was the only night available.

"Do you think we can pull it off for a week from this Saturday? I'll talk to Susan and get a list of his friends and their numbers to invite them too. Is that okay?"

"Yup, we'll invite them all."

"Okay, I'll just make up some excuse and get Walker there. Too bad we can't hide the cars, but I'm not sure where they could park out of sight."

"Leave it to me," Joss said. "Emma, can you come over early and help me set everything up? We need a going-away cake, I'll take care of the alcohol, but maybe you can get the list of snacks and decorations?"

"On it," Emma said as she scribbled everything down. "You have my number, so call me and we'll plan everything in detail. This is going to be fun!"

"All of it except the part about him leaving," I said, sighing.

"I know, and it sucks, but he'll be home pretty fast. You'll be busy with work and school, and you've got my house and Emma's to go to if it gets crappy at home. We'll have girl's nights and make plans every weekend. We'll be with you," Joss assured me.

"Thank you both—I don't know how I'd get through it all without you."

"Well, you don't have to," Joss said. Emma nodded in agreement.

We wrapped up our lunch and Joss and Emma headed off to class, but I was already finished with my classes for the day. Anxiety prickled through me at the thought of returning to the hospital, but I had to go. At least Krissy was gone; I might get lucky and catch Mama alone.

The hospital was only ten minutes away from campus, and the traffic was light. I paid attention to the parking lot level and entrance since Walker wasn't with me to help find my car this time. Even though I was nervous, it wasn't as bad as the first night I'd come here to see Mama.

I entered the elevator and the numbers lit up as we passed each floor. The doors slid open and I stepped out onto the fifth floor, rounding the corner to Mama's hall cautiously. I didn't see anyone outside her room, so I continued. Her door was closed, so I knocked gently and pushed the door open just enough to stick my head in.

"Mama?"

"Lacey?"

Mama's voice sounded raspy, but she didn't seem mad that I was there. I stepped all the way in and closed the door. My stomach knotted, unsure if Mama even wanted me there. Her color was better even though she was still connected to machines.

"Come in, honey."

"Are you sure, Mama?"

"Yes, there's a chair. How are you? You haven't visited since I got here."

I brought the chair closer to her bed and sat on the edge, holding my bag tight in front of me. At least I could bolt if I needed too.

"I've been here, Mama. The first few days Krissy wanted time with you before she returned to school so I didn't stay long. I'm sorry."

"It's okay, I was just worried about you."

"You were?" I asked and hugged my bag closer to me.

Mama reached out with the hand that didn't have any IVs or needles in it and patted my arm.

"Yes, honey. It was scary for everyone."

Genuine concern filled Mama's face, which I hadn't seen in a long time.

"How are you feeling?" I asked, reaching for her hand and squeezed it.

"Okay. Exhausted, though. They say you're supposed to rest in a hospital, but they make it impossible by waking you up several times a night. They took my blood every few hours. It was a little ridiculous," Mama said as she attempted a smile.

"When are you coming home?"

"They say if I'm still stable tonight I'll get a regular room tomorrow. They think I could go home sometime next week, but it just depends on my progress."

"Okay, that's good. I'll get the house cleaned up so you can come back and rest. Patsy will be tired too, so I'll take care of that."

"That would be wonderful."

"I'm sorry, Mama."

"Sweetie, I'm going to be fine—don't worry, okay? All you need to remember is that I'm coming home soon and I love you very much."

"I love you too." I leaned over and kissed her cheek. "Do you or Patsy need anything?"

"Patsy's at the house now getting some things together for us, but thank you."

"Okay, I'll get the house cleaned before you come home then. I'm staying with Joss and some nights with Emma. I don't want to be alone at the house. I hope that's okay."

"Of course—I don't want you to be alone either. I've got great doctors and nurses taking care of me, so don't worry. I'm doing better every day and the blood pressure medicine is already helping."

"That makes me feel a little better, but I'm still scared. I don't want to lose you, Mama. I want things to be better between us."

"Me too, honey. We can talk about all that later, though, alright?"

I nodded.

The door creaked as Patsy entered.

"Hey, Patsy," I said.

"Hi there, how are you?" she asked.

She still looked tired, but she smiled as she talked to me. I took that as a good sign.

"Okay, you?"

"Better now that your mom has started to improve," she said and smiled at Mama.

It wasn't just any smile, though. For the first time, I saw something between them. Patsy leaned over and kissed Mama on the forehead and sat in the chair on the opposite side of the bed. She took Mama's hand and gently rubbed her arm. I'm not sure why I hadn't recognized it before; why I'd believed Mama when she said they were only roommates. Even though everyone already knew it, I didn't realize it until that moment. As screwed up as their relationship was, they loved each other.

I leaned back in my chair as I pretended to watch TV with them. My gaze shifted between them again as the last several years began to fall into place. The fights, the kisses, Mama controlling Patsy . . . it all made sense now.

I laughed out loud at my naivety.

"What are you laughing at, silly?" Mama asked.

"Oh, I thought they said something funny on TV, Mama. I guess I didn't hear them right," I said and grinned. "I need to go, but I'll come back tomorrow, okay?"

"Okay, thanks for coming by and also for cleaning up the house. I love you, Lacey."

"I love you too, Mama."

36

It sucked that the weeks passed by so fast. My days were filled with classes and Walker filled me every night. Our lovemaking had become more comfortable since the evening at the pond. I wasn't shy or embarrassed with him as we explored each other's bodies and what we liked. The more I was with him, the more I loved him. He gave me a freedom I'd never experienced before.

I fell asleep in his arms every night exhausted and happy.

Mama had taken longer to improve than the doctors had thought, but she was scheduled to come home tomorrow, which meant that I needed to clean the house. I was on my own since Joss and Emma were busy planning Walker's surprise party. He remained clueless unless I'd talked in my sleep, but I didn't think I had. Surely it would've come up in conversation if I were a talker.

Susan and Garrett had written down the names and numbers of Walker's friends for me. Garrett invited the guys that Walker had gone to school with, which helped cut back on the work I had to do. Although I'd met some of Walker's friends, I hadn't realized he was so popular. As the party list grew, I appreciated Joss and Emma even more for all their hard work. I would treat them to a manicure and dinner after Walker left.

Walker offered to help me clean the house, but we both knew that was a bad idea. I promised him I would see him tomorrow. It would be the first night away from him in a while, and although I was happy that Mama was coming home, my heart broke at the idea of not waking up next to him.

I packed my clothes and belongings as Walker sat on the edge of the bed. I wasn't sure who was feeling emptier, him or me.

"Leave a few things, Lace. Just . . . don't take everything. You'll be back before I leave and you're staying some even when I'm gone. So —" his voice faltered. "Please, leave as much as you can."

My heart sank as we both tried to cling to the time we had left, even if it meant leaving some of my clothes in the corner of his dresser drawer. But he was right, I would be back. A faint smile tugged at the corner of my mouth as I unpacked my duffel bag and put my clothes back.

"Walker, we're going to be okay, right?" I asked as I sat on his lap.

He pulled me in for a gentle kiss.

"Don't you doubt it for a second. We're going to be more than okay. The six weeks I'll be away will be hell, but I'll be home as fast as I can. I love you muches and muches and muches."

We took our time and made love. It was slow and gentle, and filled with every emotion we couldn't articulate: fear, desperation, love.

A few hours later, I said goodbye to everyone with promises that I'd return tomorrow; sooner if hell broke loose at home.

I pulled out of Walker's driveway and headed back toward my house. I hated this—I hated leaving. My heart broke every minute I spent without him. My chest ached as I realized this was nothing compared to what it would be like in another week.

It took me the rest of the afternoon to clean the house. At least it would sparkle when Mama and Patsy came home. I hoped Mama liked it and it helped her feel better.

The car pulled into the carport around 6 P.M. and I rushed out the front door to hug Mama and help Patsy bring in her overnight bag. Mama's face held some color, but she still seemed tired. Patsy helped her up the front steps and into the house. Mama got comfortable in her recliner as I started the washing machine. I'd cooked dinner earlier, so Patsy warmed it up in the microwave. I'd followed the meal plan from the doctor and baked chicken breast with fresh green beans. I made a quick salad on the side and served a low-sodium salad dressing.

"This looks fantastic, Lacey! All of it—the house, the dinner. Thank you so much, honey. It means a lot to me," Mama said.

Mama hadn't said such nice things to me for a while, and I couldn't help but be proud of the work I'd done. All I wanted was for her to be proud of me.

"I'm just glad you're okay and at home, Mama. I rented a comedy for us and bought some popcorn if you want to watch it tonight?" I asked.

"What'd you rent?" Patsy asked.

"*Big*, with some guy named Tom Hanks. Have you watched it?"

"No, I don't think we have," Patsy answered.

"Good," I said.

After dinner, I cleared the table and cleaned the kitchen as everyone got settled in the living room for the movie. I wasn't about to let my hard work get messed up already.

The smell of popped popcorn filled the house as we started *Big*. I hadn't spent an evening at home with everyone laughing in a long time. It had turned into an excellent night.

After the movie, I kissed Mama good night, said good night to Patsy, and made my way downstairs. I smiled as I thought about the movie and walked through the family room. My face fell as I reached up and turned the light on to my bedroom. Not only was this the first night away from Walker, but I'd once again forgotten that I still had no furniture. My forehead creased while I realized I would have to shake out my blankets, sleeping bag, and pillow before I even sat down on the floor.

I eyed my phone and decided after I settled in that I'd call Walker. It was after 9 P.M., but unlike Mama, Susan didn't care what time I called.

After I shook out all my bedding and tossed everything into the corner, I went to the family room and grabbed the vacuum cleaner. If I was going to sleep on the floor, then it was going to be clean. The carpet was dark brown and I couldn't see the spiders and tiny scorpions half the time, but I could suck the little bastards up.

Twenty minutes later I had a clean floor and brushed teeth, and I slipped into my sleeping bag. I dialed Walker's number and counted the rings.

"Hello?"

"Hey, Walker."

"Are you okay?"

I could almost imagine him sitting up and grabbing his wallet and shoes in case he needed to come get me.

"Yes, sorry, I didn't mean to startle you. I just miss you, you're not next to me in bed. It sucks."

"Okay good, and yes, it does suck. I've missed you all day. How are you? How did things go tonight?"

"Excellent, actually. I cleaned up and made dinner. Then we watched the movie *Big* with Tom Hanks. I bet your mom would like it."

"Yeah? Things actually went okay?"

"They really did. It was so nice, too. It almost makes me think that maybe Mama being sick made her act crazy and that's what it really was."

"Lace, I want you to be okay and safe, but one night doesn't make everything okay. She hasn't been sick for years and she's treated you like shit since you were thirteen."

"Wow, thanks!" I snapped.

"No, that's not what I meant. If anyone deserves to be treated well, it's you, baby. I'm just worried you're going to let things slide because she got sick. What you need to remember is that she has the choice to get better. She can follow a health program and work with the doctors to get better. So just don't . . . don't."

"I know—you don't have to say anything else. As much as I want things to get better, I realize they might not. Until then, I'll do whatever I can on my part."

Walker sighed.

I didn't want to fight with him, regardless if I agreed with him or not. I would have to deal with Mama on my own after he left, so it was my choice and my decision to make.

"I'm glad you had a good night, but I wish you were here instead."

"Me too. I will be tomorrow night, though."

"You should be here every night until I leave."

"I'll give you as many as I can," I promised.

We made plans for tomorrow and I hung up the phone. The house was quiet as I lay in my sleeping bag and drifted off to sleep.

3 7

I woke up to a peaceful morning, made my way upstairs, and found Mama and Patsy drinking coffee on the back deck. After grabbing the blanket off the rocking chair, I joined them.

The trees behind the house had turned red and yellow. Although the morning air was crisp and almost cold, it was worth it to sit outside and drink coffee.

Everyone was calm. It was almost eerie. As much as I wanted things to get better, I couldn't help but wait for the other shoe to drop.

Patsy left to run errands and grocery shop while Mama rested. I figured it was a perfect time to catch up on my homework before the party tonight. I'd completely forgotten to mention it to Mama, but I wasn't going to wake her up over it. She needed to rest.

I completed my English paper and packed my books for Monday. With it finished, I could relax for the rest of the weekend. I also called work and updated them about Mama. They said another week off was fine. Not only could I be here if Mama needed me, but I could spend more time with Walker before he left next weekend.

My heart sank as I counted the days we had left together. He would leave next weekend. He would walk out of his house and not return for six weeks. His room would be empty, his clothes gone, and his car parked in the driveway. I wasn't sure how I was going to make it without him.

I glanced at the clock and reminded myself that he wasn't gone yet, and tonight we had a party to go to.

I packed my bag for the night and headed for the shower, taking my time getting ready. Since he was leaving, I'd stopped at Victoria's Secret and picked up something special for tonight and next weekend. I was bound and determined that Walker wouldn't be thinking about anyone else while he was at boot camp.

After double checking that I had everything I needed, I ascended the stairs. Mama was in her recliner reading.

"Hi, Mama," I said and kissed her on the cheek.

"You look nice," she said and peered over her reading glasses.

"Thank you," I said and smiled. "I'm off to Joss's house for the night. I was so excited you were coming home I forgot to tell you we're having a going-away party tonight for Walker. He leaves next weekend for boot camp."

"A party? You think you're going to a party, Lacey?" she asked, her voice clipped with anger.

I bit my lip at the thought of how many parties I'd already gone too.

"Mama, don't get upset," I said and sat down on the couch. "Joss's mom will be there. Emma's coming and a few of Walker's friends, that's all."

"You're lying! As soon as I get home you're pulling the same shit! I can't believe it. You're going over there to get drunk and party."

"Mama, take a breath. I'm telling you the truth. You can call Joss's mom if you want to talk to her. She's going to be there."

"I don't give a fuck if she's there or not, you're not going to a party. I don't give a rat's ass who it's for!"

I chewed on my lip as I stood up. Walker was right: it hadn't lasted. Even though Mama had been diagnosed with high blood pressure, there was more to it. She'd been under a doctor's care for a few weeks, her blood pressure was doing better, but she was still tearing me to pieces.

"Mama, I love you very much and I'm not going to argue with you. Your health is important to me, but you need to understand that I love Walker. He's going to be gone for six weeks, and I'm going to spend as much time with him as I can before he leaves. That includes tonight."

I turned away and walked out the front door, leaving Mama fuming alone in her chair.

My knuckles turned white as I gripped the steering wheel and willed my hands to stop shaking, but they shook the entire forty-five minutes I drove to Walker's house. I'd never stood up to Mama like that. I had no idea what to expect when I went home tomorrow either, but I would deal with that then. For the next week, I planned on telling her I was working or at someone's house. I'd also tell her I was with Walker and deal with the aftermath when he was gone.

I knocked on the door as I opened it. Walker was on the phone in the kitchen. Surprise crossed his face when I came in.

I tilted my head and questioned what was going on. He was acting weird.

"Yeah, thanks, bye," he said and hung up the phone.

"What was that all about? You jumped when I walked in the door."

"Nothing, sorry, you just caught me off guard."

"What's going on? Was it another girl?"

Frustration filled me at his secretiveness. As hard as I tried not to, I still worried about him finding someone else. Maybe that was stupid, but he was with Brittany for a long time. Even the list Garrett provided was half girls, and some of them would be there tonight.

"What? No, no, nothing like that. I was just talking to Aunt Linda about some stuff with Mom. I promise there's no one else for me, only you," he said and smiled.

"Promise?"

"Promise," he said and kissed me hello.

"Mmmm, okay," I whispered between kisses as I mentally pushed the fear away. "You smell magnificent. I could take you to your bedroom right now," I said, laughing.

"No dinner first?"

"Yes, so sorry, I'll take you out to eat first and *then* I'll take you to your bedroom."

"That makes me a happy man all the way around," he said and smiled.

I'd told him I was treating him to dinner, but on the way, I planned to make an excuse that I needed to stop by Joss's house first. He had no clue what we were really doing, which made me happy enough to forget my earlier concern about him finding someone else.

We left the house and I mentioned I needed to stop by Joss's house. I almost panicked when I pulled into her driveway. There weren't any cars there except hers and her mom's. Had I gotten the night wrong? I was pretty sure it was tonight. In fact, we'd confirmed everything yesterday at school, so where was everyone?

We got out of the car and I knocked on the door as I opened it, pulling Walker into the dark living room.

"Surprise!" The lights came on, music started blasting, and an entire room of twenty-five people stood there, beaming.

Although I thought I was prepared, I screamed like a little girl. I stepped backward, right onto Walker's foot, and then burst into nervous giggles.

I turned around and hugged him as he acknowledged all his friends. Joss and Emma had done a fantastic job with the "Good Luck," "We'll Miss You," and "Kick Some Ass" banners throughout the living and dining room. Red, yellow, and blue balloons were tied to the lamps and some floated close to the ceiling. The house was already full of people.

Walker got smacked on the back and put into headlocks by all the guys. I rolled my eyes at the girls who hugged him longer than I would've liked, and then made my way to the snacks, where Joss and Emma stood waiting.

"You two are amazing!" I yelled above the music and hugged them both. "Where the hell did everyone park? I thought I'd gotten the wrong night!"

"They're all up the road in the empty pasture," Joss said, laughing.

Arms encircled my waist and a kiss landed on my cheek.

"That had better be Walker or I'm going to punch someone square in the nose," I said.

"Thank you," Walker said.

"You're so welcome, and I'm sorry I stepped on your foot. Are you okay?" I giggled again.

"I'm alright."

Emma cleared her throat and smiled at me.

"I'm sorry, Emma. Walker, you've met Joss, and this is Emma. She's my other best friend who I've told everything. She and her family have let me stay with them on several occasions."

"Thank you, Emma, for being there for Lacey. She'll be okay while I'm gone as long as she has both of you."

"She's gonna be just fine," Joss promised. Her warm smile reassured us all.

More of Walker's friends showed up and pulled him away. The beer started flowing, along with the vodka and rum. I waved at Joss's mom across the room and blew her a kiss. I'd get through all the people eventually and hug her.

People stopped streaming in a few hours later and the house was at full capacity. Walker was having a great time, but every twenty minutes or so he'd come over for a kiss and check if I was doing okay before he got pulled away again. I was perfectly happy hanging out with Joss and Emma. I loved watching him laugh and have fun. Joss always remembered to take pictures, too, which was another reason she was so great. She remembered the important details.

A few couples found some dark corners in the living room and started making out while others started dancing.

Then one of Walker's good friends, James, turned the music off and started chanting, "Speech, speech, speech, speech!" Everyone joined in until Walker stepped up and quieted the room. I joined the others as everyone settled into their seats. I hadn't seen Walker with a large group of people before. The girls stared at him completely mesmerized and the guys settled down the minute Walker asked. Apparently he had the ability to lead, which shouldn't have surprised me, but it did. I just hadn't been around him in high school.

A little more in awe of him, I leaned against the wall. Joss and Emma joined me.

"I can't thank everyone enough for showing up," Walker said, addressing the room. "This has been amazing. I wasn't sure I was going to have the opportunity to say goodbye to a lot of you before I left . . . Joss, Emma, Lacey, thank you for making this happen." He grinned at us.

"Some of you have already heard that I leave next Sunday for boot camp in Texas. I'll be gone for six weeks. My mom and brother will stay here, of course, and I'll come back home as soon as I can. The hope is that I'll get stationed in Little Rock so I'll be close to my family. I won't be far."

He paused for a moment before continuing.

"After I'd already enlisted, something happened. I met someone." He glanced my way.

Everyone sat still as Walker talked, but some of the girls he'd attended high school with whispered and giggled. I'd forgotten how catty it could be.

"I'd like everyone to meet my girlfriend, Lacey," he said as he motioned for me to join him.

My cheeks flamed with heat as everyone stared, and I glanced back at Joss and Emma for support. They met me with broad smiles. My focus returned to Walker and I took a deep breath. I didn't do well in front of large groups. It didn't come as naturally for me as it did him.

"Lacey," he said as he turned to face me.

He reached his hand out to James and took something, but I couldn't tell what it was.

"Lace, I love you. You're beautiful, generous, and caring. You stole my heart in this very living room and I haven't been the same since. You're the strongest person I know other than my mom," he paused as he lowered himself to one knee and flipped open a little box.

"Lacey Anne Beaumont, will you marry me?"

I'm not sure who gasped louder: the girls in the group or me.

I stared at him on one knee as the question sank in. He was asking me to marry him, be his wife, and wear an engagement ring while he was gone.

Holy shit.

"Yes, yes, I'll marry you!" I squealed.

My hands shook as I reached for him. He stood and picked me up in one motion and kissed me in front of everyone.

"I love you muches and muches and muches," he whispered as he put me down. He reached for my hand and the group cheered as he slid the diamond ring onto my finger.

3 8

Shock rippled through me as I stared at the ring on my finger. I had no clue what Walker had been up to. It was beautiful. *Lacey Anne Farren.* I could deal with that. I could totally deal with it.

My heart skipped a beat as I peered at him, grinning from ear to ear. "So, when I walked into your house earlier and you were acting funny, were you talking to James about tonight?"

"Yeah, you almost caught me talking about proposing. James had picked up the ring for me and I was making sure everything was in place."

"Wait! You knew? You knew about the party?"

"Have I told you my brother can't keep a secret?" Walker said, laughing.

"Ohhhh! He's in trouble! He promised he could keep his mouth shut. But, you! I had no clue you had any idea."

"Yeah, I'm much better at keeping secrets," he said as he pulled me close and kissed me. "Mrs. Walker Farren. You're going to wear it well."

"Yes I am," I said, returning his kiss.

We made our way to the other side of the house with Joss and

Emma. Joss hugged me tight and confessed that she'd known the whole time. Emma did as well; they were all in on it. We were supposed to surprise Walker, not me.

Emma needed to leave and I walked her outside. The chill of the night air greeted me as we stepped outside. I rubbed my arms in an attempt to ward it off.

"Are you really going to get married?" Emma asked as we walked to the field and located her car. The flashlight revealed what could have been mistaken for a used car lot. The cars had multiplied like gremlins.

Well, it had started out to be a small party, I thought.

"I love him. He shocked the shit out of me, but I'd marry him in a New York second."

"Promise me you'll wait for a while, though."

"What's the matter? Are you not supporting us?"

I was confused. She'd helped Walker set everything up—didn't that mean she was on board?

"I'm not saying that at all. I think Walker's a great guy, but you both have a lot going on. He's leaving next weekend, his mom is sick, and so is yours. All I'm asking is that you wait to set a date for a while, that's all."

"That's fair. I mean, I understand what you're saying. We won't make any big plans until after boot camp is over and he gets stationed somewhere. We'll know more then, okay? I love you for caring, Emma," I said as I reached out and hugged her. "Thank you so much for helping tonight."

"You're very welcome," she said as she hugged me back.

"Be safe going home," I said and shut the car door behind her.

She pulled out onto the road, and I stood in the cold for a moment. Everything had happened so fast that I hadn't digested it yet. I considered what Emma had said, but we had plenty of time to talk about it. There wasn't any real rush, except Susan. He would want Susan to be there, and so would I.

My stomach flipped at the thought of getting married in a few weeks. It was fast. It scared me, and on top of that, how in the hell would I tell Mama? I didn't have to worry about that tonight, though. Tonight I was with Walker, and we were engaged.

Walker was in the middle of a group of girls who were congratulating him. They didn't have their hands on him, so there wasn't a need to leave a solitaire imprint on their faces. I finally made my way to Joss's mom and hugged her. She fussed over me and my new ring. We made plans to talk about the wedding while Walker was away.

Midnight had arrived fast. Most everyone had left for other parties or gone home. I'd laughed as the girls quickly funneled out the door after the proposal. I was ready to go as well. All the excitement had me anxious to talk to Walker and find out more about where his thoughts were concerning a date.

I made my way into Joss's bedroom and grabbed my purse. We'd spent many nights laughing together and discussing life in this room. Hopefully, I wouldn't lose that when I got married. Nostalgia washed over me as I pulled her bedroom door closed behind me and James walked out of the bathroom.

"Hey," he said.

"Hi, James. Listen, I wanted to say thank you for helping Walker with the ring," I said. "You're a great friend and I appreciate everything you did. It means a lot to me and I hope you and I can become friends."

"He's crazy about you, you know."

"He's the best thing that's ever happened to me," I replied. "Hey, I need to find Walker, but thank you again." I closed the gap between us and attempted to kiss him on the cheek, but he turned his head and our lips brushed.

"Oh my God, I'm so sorry," I stuttered. "I was aiming for your cheek." A flush crept up my cheeks at my clumsiness.

James smiled and moved toward me again. I backed into Joss's door. What was he doing? Why was he so close?

"James?"

"You're just like he said—so beautiful," he whispered as he lowered his mouth to mine.

My eyes widened at the realization of what he was doing.

I pushed against his chest as hard as I could. The door gave me additional leverage, and he stumbled several feet back.

"What the hell was that?" I snapped. "Are you out of your mind? Walker *just* proposed to me. How could you do that to your best friend?" I wiped my mouth.

Anger clouded James's face.

"Stay away from me," I said and hurried away.

I located Walker and we said our goodbyes to Joss and Walker's remaining friends.

We got into my Mustang and I blasted the heat while we waited for it warm up.

"Thank you," he said and reached over to squeeze my hand.

"For what? Your surprise party?" I asked, laughing. Determined to forget the incident with James I decided to focus on what was important.

"For saying yes."

"Were you scared I wouldn't?"

"Hell, yeah! I kept telling James I was screwed if you said no in front of all my friends. I wanted to surprise you, but I put you on the spot, too. So, since it's just us in the car, are you sure you want to marry me?"

I turned in my seat, facing him. His brow furrowed as he waited. I could tell he was worried that I'd said yes just so he wouldn't be embarrassed.

"Yes, Walker, I'll marry you," I whispered.

Relief washed across his face, and he kissed the back of my hand.

"I love you muches and muches and muches, Lacey."

"I love you more than that," I said and smiled.

The car had warmed up and I shifted into drive and pulled onto the dark road.

"Walker?"

"Yeah?"

"You've had more time to think about things than I have. How long do you want to stay engaged?"

"It's difficult to say. I want Mom there."

"So do I."

"I thought we could talk about a date after I got back from boot camp and I could see how Mom's doing. Are you okay getting married after I get home?"

My stomach flipped at the thought of planning a wedding and getting married that soon, but I understood why. We both wanted Susan there. I loved him; I wanted to marry him, there was no doubt in my mind. I just didn't think it would happen so fast.

"Yeah, I'd be good with that, but if she's doing okay can I have a little longer to plan?"

"You can have whatever you want as long as she's doing okay."

We sat in silence for the rest of the way home. I twisted my new ring on my finger. It would take some time to get used to, but I had no doubt that I'd made the right decision. The hardest part would be telling Mama. She would shit a brick, but I was eighteen. She was going to have to face the fact that I was grown. I did, however, realize that it wasn't the right time to tell her yet since she'd just gotten out of the hospital.

Walker's house was dark and quiet when we got home. We slipped into his bedroom and closed the door behind us.

He reached for me, but I held him at arm's length.

"Not yet—I've got something to show you." A mischievous grin eased across my face. I gently pushed him back and he sat on the end of his bed.

I unbuttoned my shirt and dropped it on the floor. My skirt followed. I stood before him in my new black lace bra and G-string I'd bought from Victoria's Secret.

"Wow," he said. "Wow."

I turned around slowly, allowing him to take me in. He licked his lips with anticipation. I'd waited all night for him and by the look on his face, he'd been waiting for me, too.

We didn't wait any longer.

3 9

For most of my life I'd had the nasty habit of being an early riser and waking before anyone else did. I slipped into my clothes and closed Walker's door behind me. I made coffee and snuggled under a blanket on the couch in the living room. It was so quiet and peaceful, with a few rays of sun trickling in through the curtains.

Thoughts of last night flooded my mind, and I leaned my head back on the couch. I was engaged. Never in my life would I have guessed that I could change so much in a few short months. I sure as hell wouldn't have walked out on Mama. It would have been easy to pity Patsy for having to deal with it, but then decided I wouldn't feel sorry for her. I'd pay for my own sins as soon as I got home.

Susan's oxygen tank alerted me to her presence before I saw her. I set my coffee on the table next to me, hurried into the kitchen, and made some for her as well. She entered the living room and I helped her get settled.

"Thank you, Lacey," she said and took the coffee. "How was your night?" she smiled at me over the top of her cup.

"Good," I said. "But you knew that already didn't you?" I glared jokingly.

"He told me he was going to ask you, but I wasn't sure what your response would be."

I held up my hand to show her that I was now her future daughter-in-law.

"Welcome to the family! I couldn't be happier." Susan didn't just smile; she radiated.

"Thank you so much. I'm pleased to be a part of it."

We sipped our coffee and grinned at each other. I felt like we'd just entered the secret club for the cool kids, but we couldn't tell anyone. Any fears that had nagged me melted into the background. I was going to have a real family and a mom who loved me.

Walker appeared at the living-room door and stretched. Thoughts flickered through my mind of taking him right back to bed and leaving his clothes on the floor. A smile tugged at the corner of my mouth.

He lifted my blanket and joined me on the couch.

"Hi, Mom," he said as he stifled a yawn.

"Good morning, Walker. And it *is* a good morning," she said. She still hadn't wiped that silly smile off her face, but neither had I.

"Does Garrett know?" I asked.

"Yup," Walker replied.

"So everyone knew except me? And I was trying to keep the party from you. I guess that didn't work out as planned," I said, frowning.

Walker chuckled and squeezed my hand.

We chatted for a while and just spent time with Susan. She was so happy that I didn't want to break the mood, and neither did Walker.

Garrett joined us and the morning passed us by as Susan shared memories and funny times about Walker and Garrett. I'd spent my first morning with my future family. It was a glimpse of more to come, surrounded by love and laughter. The exact opposite of what I was used to, but I would cherish every moment of it forever.

DREAD TAUNTED me as I pulled into the carport at home, and I slipped off my ring, putting it in my wallet. It would just cause a fight, and I didn't want to argue with Mama any more than necessary. I'd decided on the way home that I would tell her that Walker and I were engaged right before he finished boot camp.

With that decision made, I opened the door and walked into the house. Mama was exactly where I thought she'd be: in her chair.

"Hi, Mama," I said. I didn't want to give her a kiss until I'd figured out what kind of mood she was in.

"Have fun, Lacey?"

Her voice was firm and clipped. She was pissed, but I hadn't expected anything different.

"Yes, we had a good time," I said, sitting down in the rocking chair. "How are you?"

"I've been better, no thanks to you."

"I'm sorry I left like that, but I have one more week with Walker before he leaves. I don't want to fight with you, but I'm hoping we can talk about it. I'm going to spend time with him and then go with his family to Little Rock next Saturday to say goodbye. It would mean a lot to me if you were okay with it."

Mama didn't respond for a few minutes. I couldn't tell if she was planning on what to say next or if she was praying, but the only response I got was the squeak of her chair as she rocked.

"We never talked about the night I went into the hospital," she said.

I didn't answer because she hadn't asked me a question.

"I had a sneaking suspicion you were going behind my back after Walker called the first time, but I believed you when you said you weren't."

"I wasn't dating him then. We had just met," I explained.

"It doesn't matter—you still lied to me when you didn't tell me you were seeing him. You went behind my back and I'm sure you didn't think you'd get caught," she said, smirking.

"Mama, you make it sound like I did something wrong. I went on a few dates and got to know him. How is there anything wrong with that? Can you explain it because I don't understand."

"Of course you wouldn't."

Emma's voice broke my thoughts. *We all know your mama hates men.*

As much as I didn't want to admit it, Emma was right. She'd understood it way before it had sunk into my head. Mama did hate men. I could date anyone, it didn't matter who it was, and she would fight me over it. Finally, I'd realized what had been happening over the last several years. The moments at the hospital, Emma and Joss trying to tell me, but until I met Walker I hadn't recognized the truth.

My mind floated back to my conversation with Aunt Linda as Mama kept talking. I tuned her out as I pieced things together. Even though I wouldn't have known any different, it pissed me off that I'd taken everything Mama said as truth. I wasn't bad or evil. I was in love.

"Lacey!"

"Yes?" I jumped as her tone jolted me out of my thoughts.

"Didn't you hear what I said? You put me in the hospital. You almost killed me!"

My head snapped up as the words traveled from her mouth to my ears. I'd been home less than thirty minutes and she was accusing me of putting her in the hospital. Too bad Krissy was missing it all.

"You're making me sick and I'm going to die if you don't stop your nonsense!"

"Mama," I said, keeping my tone even and calm. "I love you, but I won't stop dating Walker. I hope you can make peace with that."

I got up from my chair, grabbed the banister in an attempt to hide my shaking hands, and went downstairs. In reality, I was safer downstairs. Mama rarely came down; she sent Pasty instead.

My head pounded with fear as I paused in the family room and listened. It was eerily quiet. I might have stood up to her without any violence or major outburst this time, but deep down I figured it wouldn't continue.

And then I heard it. Mama was crying. No, she wasn't crying; she was sobbing. My heart sunk into the pit of my stomach as I listened to her gut-wrenching cries. Patsy would be with her, though, and the only thing I could do now was let it go and keep my distance.

4 0

It amazed me how fast the week flew by. When I wasn't at school, I was with Walker. I spent almost every night with him, telling Mama I was at Joss's or Emma's. I'd kept my distance since standing up to her last weekend.

It was getting easier to leave that world behind and live in the one with Walker and his family. There were even days when I didn't think about Mama at all.

Walker stayed surrounded by family and friends the entire week. The moments we had together were few and far between, but at the end of the day when the moonlight filled his bedroom, that was our time together. We whispered in the dark about future plans and made love. I promised I would take care of Susan and Garrett and write him every day. He promised he would call as often as he could. I tried to hang on to every moment and every touch, but I had no clue of how I was going to get through the next six weeks.

We left for Little Rock that afternoon. Aunt Linda drove and we sat in the back with Garrett. Walker and I stole kisses while Susan and Linda made small talk. Garrett stared out the window. He remained quiet. It was going to be hard for him too.

Walker's cousins and other family members met us for dinner. He introduced me as his fiancée and I was greeted with hugs as they shook Walker's hand and slapped him on the back.

Everyone rehashed stories about Walker's younger years as I listened. Susan's smile was sad, and it no longer reached her eyes. I wasn't sure if she was getting sicker or if she already missed Walker. In the back of everyone's mind, we all wondered if she would make it long enough to hug him again.

As much as I wanted time to stop, it sped by. We said goodbye to his family and left the restaurant. It was time.

The hotel parking lot was full as we searched for a parking space. Walker and I had agreed that he would say goodbye to his family and then I would walk him to his room.

I lost my breath as we stepped into the hotel lobby. It was full of men saying goodbye to loved ones. Tears filled my eyes and I looked down, trying to hide them from Walker. He had enough on his plate already; I had to do what I could to reassure him.

"Last call! Say goodbye and get up to your room!"

I searched for the voice and spotted a man in an air force uniform.

"You do *not* get to take anyone upstairs, so say goodbye right here!" he yelled over the crowd.

"What?" I grabbed Walker's hand.

"Lace, I'm so sorry, I didn't know." He pulled me to him and kissed me.

"I love you, Walker," I said, my voice breaking.

"I love you muches and muches and muches more than that. I'll see you in a couple of weeks when you come down to see me, okay?" His voice sounded strong, but his face couldn't hide his emotions.

I nodded as the man in the air force uniform made his way to our side of the room. He tapped the guys on the back and rounded the last few of them toward the stairs.

Walker kissed me one more time and then walked backward, as though trying to burn the image of us into his mind forever. His eyes searched each of our faces. As hard as he tried to hide it, fear flickered across his face. He was terrified he wouldn't see Susan again. He lifted his hand in an attempted wave as he joined the group of men. Then he mouthed *I love you* and turned his back to us.

Tears spilled down my cheeks as I took Susan's hand. We stood in silence as the group ascended the stairs and out of sight. Walker had just left with my heart.

No one said a word as we walked out of the hotel and got back into the car for the ride home. Unable to stop the tears, I huddled in the backseat. I didn't want to make a scene, but I couldn't stop. When we got back to Walker's house, I went into his bedroom and closed the door. I didn't come out again until the next afternoon.

THE PATTER of rain against Walker's window woke me. My hand reached for him and found his side of the bed cold and empty. I grabbed his pillow and inhaled his scent. The tears returned as I closed my eyes and imagined his strong arms around me, his kisses on my neck, and his hands on my body.

I wiped my tears away and sat on the side of the bed. If there was such a thing as an emotional hangover, I had one. I rubbed my eyes, desperate to eliminate the burn. My stomach flipped at the thought of Walker being hundreds of miles away.

My head throbbed from all the crying as I put my robe on and then entered the empty kitchen. Susan wasn't up yet, so I poured myself a cup of cold coffee left over from earlier in the morning. I heated it in the microwave and wandered into the living room. Settling in under the blanket, I sipped my coffee. I had just snuggled with Walker under this blanket yesterday and now he was gone.

My eyes landed on my ring while I thought about our promises. I couldn't change the fact that Walker had left for the air force, but I'd given him my word that I would take care of Susan and Garrett. I couldn't sit here on the couch and feel sorry for myself. The world was still moving forward and I needed to move with it.

I took another sip of my coffee and placed it on the end table. Then I flung the blanket off and headed for the shower.

The hot water soothed my burning eyes as the steam filled the small bathroom. I stood under the water and made myself focus on the day ahead. This wasn't just about me, and I needed to make sure I was strong for Susan. Plus, I wanted to take Garrett to a movie. Since I had to go back to work in a few days, I wanted to spend some time with him.

Out of everyone, I figured Garrett struggled the most. Not only had his brother gone off to boot camp, but he was left here watching his mom die.

After Susan left us, Garrett would stay with his Aunt Linda, and nothing would ever be the same for him. I understood why Walker did it, but Garrett was only thirteen and he probably couldn't grasp the fact Walker was trying to take care of him.

Thirty minutes later, I was ready to face the world and found Susan in the kitchen. She smiled as I joined her at the table, but her face was paler than normal.

I reached for her hand and squeezed it.

"How are you?" I asked.

"I'm alright," she whispered.

"You don't have to be strong for me, Susan. I realize you're not okay. Hell, I'm not okay," I said, laughing.

"I'm glad you're here, Lacey."

"Me too," I said.

"I . . . I'm afraid I won't see him again," she said as tears spilled down her cheeks.

"We'll visit him in a few weeks. Hang on to that," I said and took her hand.

I sat helplessly as she cried.

"I'm not getting better. No matter what I tell myself, I know I don't have long."

I bit my lip as I lost the battle against my own tears.

"Well, you can't. I haven't had you in my life long enough."

We smiled in an attempt to stop the tears and the fear that ate away at us.

"I know you'll take good care of my sons. And, there's not a doubt in my mind that you and Walker will be okay. I worry about Garrett, though."

"I just assumed Walker had talked to you about everything. He's going to try and get stationed in Little Rock so we can see Garrett several times a month."

"What Walker doesn't understand is he now belongs to the military, and he doesn't get to make those decisions."

"What?" I gasped.

"I couldn't say anything before he left. He's holding onto those hopes of staying close, but there's no guarantee that he'll end up in Little Rock. He has to go wherever they tell him to, and once you're married to him the military will own you too. You'll go where he goes."

I shook my head as she continued to tell me that our plans were no longer our own. Our plans to be near Garrett might not work out. I might not be near my friends anymore, either. I would leave the only place I'd ever lived. I could deal with an hour-long drive, but not another state. I couldn't leave everyone.

"I'm sorry, Lacey. We'll just have to wait to find out what happens. They might work with him, but we won't get that information until after boot camp. I just wanted you to understand there was a chance that plans might change."

"This situation sucks worse every time I turn around."

"It sure does."

I was grateful the rest of my afternoon was filled with an action-packed movie, popcorn, and the arcade with Garrett. Neither one of us brought up Walker or how much we wished he hadn't left. We didn't need to. We both clung to the moments together. Everyone was standing on shifting sand, and we didn't know if it would hold or slide out from under our feet without any notice.

41

Other than attending classes, I stayed close to Susan and Garrett for a few more days. I knew that my excuses of staying with Emma and Joss were wearing thin with Mama and I would have to return home soon, but I wasn't ready to leave.

My time with Susan, Garrett, and Linda was spent at their house where we could answer the phone. We jumped every time it rang in hopes that it might be Walker calling. I had no idea how often he would be able to call, and if he only got one call, I realized it would be to his mom and I would have to wait.

It was also time for me to go back to work. Reality wouldn't allow me to hide from Mama or my life any longer. I hugged Susan and Garrett goodbye and promised I'd be back as soon as I could.

An idea crossed my mind while I stood in the driveway and stared at Walker's car. It had been in the same place since he left.

"Hey, Susan," I said as I stuck my head back in the house. "Do you care if I take Walker's car? I'd like to get a battery for it while he's gone."

"That's a good idea, Lacey. Thank you for taking care of that."

I closed the door behind me and settled myself in his car. My eyes closed and I remembered our first date and the drive to the lake. Walker's cologne filled his car, and for a moment he sat next to me and held my hand.

He had parked the car facing down the hill for the days he needed to let it roll to get it started. I appreciated his planning as I tried to start the car and was met with nothing. I held in the clutch and released the brake. It began moving down the hill, and within seconds I popped the clutch and the car came to life. Shifting into first, I turned on the headlights and pulled out of his driveway.

I shivered and blasted the heat as I drove to the nearest shop and purchased a new battery. Now I wouldn't worry about driving Walker's car and getting stuck somewhere as the weather got colder.

A few hours later, I pulled into the parking lot at work, clocked in, and headed to the children's department. Becky greeted me with a big hug as we chatted across the aisle and caught up on all the gossip that had happened while I'd been gone.

"It looks like you have some juicy news yourself," she said, pointing to my ring. I'd been so wrapped up in my own world that I'd forgotten that no one at work had heard the news.

"Yeah," I smiled. "He proposed the night of his going-away party."

"Have you set a date yet?"

"No, we decided he should get through boot camp and get stationed first." I left out the part about wanting to get married before Susan left us.

"That's a good idea, hon. Life changes a lot when the military enters it."

"I've heard," I said, sighing.

Becky finished her shift and left me alone. I straightened up the clothes racks and changed the sale signs. It was a quiet evening and I kept thinking about Walker and wondering how he was.

I jumped when the phone rang. We had older phones in the store and they bellowed with an obnoxious ring. I made my way through the clothing racks to the register.

"Children's department, this is Lacey."

"I love you and I miss you so fucking bad I can't stand it."

"Walker! Oh my God, I love you too. How are you?"

"Tired and I hurt, but I'm doing okay. I can't say I like Texas much, either. I hope I don't get stationed here."

"Have they told you anything yet about where you're going next?"

"No, I'm not sure when we find out, but I've requested Little Rock and told them that Mom's sick."

"Maybe that'll help if they know what's going on."

"How's Garrett?"

"He's okay. He's really sad. I've been staying at your house since you left, but I'm going home tonight." My voice fell as I finished my sentence.

"Be careful, Lace. I don't trust your mom to not blow up again."

"I can go to Emma or Joss's house if I need to. I'll be fine." I didn't really believe that, but he didn't need to worry about anything else.

"I have to go, baby."

"Already? We just got on the phone!"

"Yeah, I know. I love you. I'll see you soon so let's just focus on that, okay?"

"Okay. I've already got the time off work, too."

"Good, and we can talk about setting a date. I gotta go."

The phone disconnected before I was able to respond. He wasn't kidding when he said he had to go.

My brows knitted together as I replaced the phone in the cradle. He was getting insistent about setting a date. I wanted to wait a while, but we weren't dealing with ordinary circumstances. We were moving fast and I couldn't help but think he wouldn't have proposed at all if Susan wasn't sick and his life wasn't taking a huge turn in a different direction.

I brushed the thought aside as I counted my register and finished work for the evening.

My thoughts stayed with Walker while I drove home. I dismissed the idea that I was heading in the wrong direction and should be driving to his house instead.

Walker's Nissan settled into my regular parking spot and I let myself into a house that wasn't my home anymore.

Mama and Patsy were watching TV. Neither one of them acknowledged me as I went straight to the kitchen and made a sandwich. After all these years of wanting to be invisible, I had accomplished it, at least for tonight. I was okay with that. I grabbed my dinner and purse and headed downstairs without saying a word.

A groan escaped me as I flipped the light switch on. The yellow walls mocked me as I set my purse on the floor. My gaze traveled across the empty room while I finished my sandwich and debated whether to shake my sleeping bag out and vacuum my floor or not. But fear won over. I would continue my bedtime ritual before I joined the creatures of the dark and slept on the floor. After a moment, I realized that I held the power of the vacuum and sucked their lives right down the tube.

I snuggled into my sleeping bag and stared at the phone. The few nights that Walker and I had been apart, we'd talked on the phone before going to sleep. Emptiness settled over me like a wet blanket as I drifted off to sleep.

I woke to Mama's voice the next morning. That was an understatement: she was yelling at the top of her lungs. I hopped out of my sleeping bag, slipped on my shoes, and ran upstairs.

"What? Mama, what's the matter?"

"What the hell is parked in my carport?"

Shit. I'd forgotten to mention that I had Walker's car. I guess I'd enjoyed being invisible more than I should've last night.

"It's Walker's car, Mama. I replaced the car battery for him yesterday."

"You can't just drive his car around, Lacey. It's not yours."

"I know, Mama. I'm taking it back today. I was just trying to help him and Susan was all."

"Damn right you're taking it back today, and I'd better not see it here again. You have a car, one Patsy and I bought you, and I'd better see you driving it next time."

"Okay."

"Get back downstairs, I don't want to see your face," Mama said.

"I have to get ready for work anyway," I muttered.

Mama didn't say another word as I went back downstairs. I hadn't missed her yelling at me or being woken up to her threats.

I would stick it out for a few nights and see if it smoothed things over.

M y old routine embraced me quicker than I thought it would. Between school, work, friends, and Walker's family, I flew under Mama's radar. I stayed with Susan and Garrett as often as I could get away with it. Joss and Emma had covered for me on three different occasions when Mama had called to check up on me.

It was simple enough to make an excuse for me to call her right back; then they would call me at Walker's and I would call Mama. I suspected she knew I wasn't really at their houses. I didn't have any idea why she was checking up on me when God could just tell her Himself. But for whatever reason, God had been quiet lately.

My excuses and plans were dwindling, however, and I was left with going home again. It was only for two days, though. We were scheduled to leave for Texas to visit Walker early Saturday morning. I couldn't wait to kiss him again.

He'd only been able to call me one more time, and the conversation had only lasted five minutes before they made him hang up. Everything he did was dictated to him. I didn't figure he was dealing with that very well, but I'd find out this weekend. First, I just needed to get through tonight.

No one was home when I got there. Mama rarely left the house, but sometimes they'd go for a drive. They were never gone for long, so I cooked dinner and turned on the TV. I shivered as a nagging feeling pulled at me. I ate my dinner, cleaned the kitchen, and waited for them to get home. It was almost 9 P.M. when the car pulled into the carport.

I heard Mama and Patsy laughing as they walked up the stairs. They stopped when they came through the door and saw me there.

"Sounds like you had a good day, Mama. That's great," I said in an awkward attempt to break the silence.

She nodded as she sat down in her chair and Patsy situated herself on the couch.

"How are you feeling?" I asked.

"Good," she said as she grabbed the TV remote and began flipping channels.

"Have you had any more doctor's appointments?"

"Yes, Lacey. What do you want?" she asked. She didn't try to hide the annoyance in her voice.

"I'm just trying to see how you're doing."

"Well, if you ever bothered to come home then maybe you'd find out."

"Mama, I do come home. I return to an empty bedroom and sleep on the floor. It's easier to stay at Joss's or Emma's."

"It's not my fault you don't have any furniture."

I bit my lip. I was too tired to take her bait and I had no intention of spending the rest of the evening defending myself.

"Okay, I'm just here until Saturday morning anyway," I said and turned to go downstairs.

"Why only two days?" Mama asked.

Her voice carried a hint of disappointment. Surprised, I turned back around.

"I'm driving down to Texas to see Walker with Susan and Garrett. We leave tomorrow and I'll be gone all weekend. I just wanted to talk to you before we left."

I didn't wait for her reaction; I hurried down the stairs and got ready for bed.

THE NEXT MORNING greeted me with typical November cloudy skies as I drove to school. I hoped it wasn't going to rain tomorrow while I was driving. This was my first trip to Texas and I didn't want the rain to mess it up.

After classes, I went straight home and managed to avoid Mama for most of the day by staying downstairs and finishing my homework, but the smell of something yummy beckoned me upstairs. I hadn't eaten all day. I was so excited I wasn't sure I was even hungry. My stomach growled in disagreement.

Before I could make a decision, Mama called me.

"Lacey, come eat dinner if you're hungry!"

I didn't need any more of an invitation.

"Wow, Mama. Thank you!" I said, joining her and Patsy at the kitchen table. Mama didn't cook very often, but when she did, she went all out.

I loaded my plate with fried chicken, green beans, and mashed potatoes. Mama filled my glass with tea.

"Are you feeling okay today?" I asked between bites. "You haven't cooked in a while, so I'm hoping this is a good sign that you're getting better."

"I'm not doing too bad. Patsy helped me with dinner." She smiled at me.

"It's excellent."

"Are you excited about seeing Walker tomorrow?" Mama asked.

I wiped my mouth, unsure of where the conversation was going.

"Yeah, I really miss him," I said, laying my fork down on the table, reaching for my tea, and taking a drink.

"I know it's been hard with everything going on, Lacey. But maybe I can meet him when he's finished with boot camp. I figure if he's going to be a part of your life, I should get used to it."

I frowned at Mama's words. She'd been pissed at me ever since Krissy told her I was dating Walker. I couldn't figure out why she was changing her mind.

"Really?"

"Yes, I mean it. Finish eating and then we'll talk more after you get back."

"Okay, I'd like that," I said as I picked up my fork and finished the last bite of my mashed potatoes. I washed everything down with another drink of tea and then it hit me.

My head spun and my stomach lurched. I was going to throw up.

"Mama, I don't feel good."

"What's the matter?" she asked. She didn't bother to get up from her chair.

"I feel sick and everything is blurry," I stammered.

"Well, you didn't really think I was going to let you go down to Texas to see your little boyfriend did you? Stupid girl. I've played along with you long enough. It's time to end this. You will not go to Texas and visit Walker this weekend, or any other weekend for that matter. And another thing—you certainly won't be spending any more time with Susan and Garrett. I'm only going to say this one more time. You've allowed your demons to take you over and now you think you're running off to Texas. Not on my watch."

"Mama, what are you saying?"

I squinted and tried to focus on what she was saying, but my vision blurred and several Mamas sat across the table from me instead of one.

"Patsy?"

"I agree with your Mama. This nonsense has gone on long enough," she said with a smug smile.

I fell out of my chair and onto the floor. Mama's and Patsy's voices continued in the background, but I couldn't understand what they were saying anymore. Walker's face flashed through my mind as I melted into oblivion.

43

The sunlight peered through the curtains and the clock numbers glowed a dark red as I struggled to focus on them. 11 A.M. Wait, 11 A.M.? I blinked and tried to mentally grasp something, anything, but my head remained fuzzy.

What happened? I didn't understand. I'd eaten dinner with Mama and Patsy around 7 P.M. Why was I in Mama's bed?

I reached for the nightstand to balance myself as I sat up, and then it dawned on me. I'd missed the trip with Susan and Garrett, and I wasn't going to see Walker.

Panic filled me as I reached for the phone and picked it up. There was no dial tone. The phone was dead. I sat up and rubbed my eyes. My vision wasn't blurry anymore, but my mouth tasted awful. I reached for the glass of water next to me and drained it.

TIME HAD SLIPPED AWAY from me. I didn't know how long I'd been asleep, but as I lay in Mama's bed and stared into the darkness, I tried to shake off the fog. Tears slipped down my cheeks as I remembered missing the trip to see Walker.

Spotty memories of Mama telling me I wasn't going and I wasn't going to see Susan and Garrett again flashed through my mind. She'd done something to me. Something was really wrong.

Stumbling out of bed, I crawled to Mama's bathroom. I pulled myself up enough to get on the toilet, flipped the light switch on, and peed for what felt like hours.

After I was sure I didn't have any more pee left in me, I grabbed onto the bathroom counter and pulled myself to the sink. I turned the cold water on, washed my hands, and splashed water on my face. I clung to the idea it might help clear the fog from my brain.

My head lifted slowly and I peered at the stranger in the mirror. Makeup streaked my face and my oily hair was matted to the side of my head. My mouth was filled with grit, and I licked my lips in an attempt to eliminate my dry mouth.

I looked like shit. I felt like shit. My head tapped against the mirror, willing this not to be real, but as the harsh reality sunk in I couldn't stop the tears. I had no idea how long Mama had kept me drugged and in her bedroom, but it was long enough to end things with Walker.

Sobs shook my body as I slid to the floor. I cried for Walker, I cried for Susan and Garrett, and I cried for me. Everything I'd worked so hard for had just been ripped out of my hands.

Shaky fingers wrapped around the nozzle and I turned the shower on. I didn't have the strength to stand, so I slid over the side and sat on the bottom. The water washed over me and soaked through my clothes. Every bit of dignity I'd tried to hold on to swirled down the drain with my tears.

My tears turned into a fit of laughter as I realized all the lies I'd told myself. The times I'd patted myself on the back for standing my ground against Mama. What the hell had I been thinking? That I could get away with saying no to her and still walk back in this house unscathed? No one stood up to Mama and got away with it, and neither had I.

I turned off the water and stripped off my wet clothes, grabbing a towel and standing on the carpet while the water ran down my body.

My head was clearer after the shower, but I was still out of it. I sure as hell didn't remember a stack of clean clothes on the bathroom counter.

After I dried off, I dressed in my fresh clothes. I'd gained more control of my legs, and I slowly walked to the bedroom door. I reached for the knob and turned it. It was locked. I jiggled the handle again, but it didn't budge. It was locked from the other side.

What the hell? Mama was keeping me locked in? I glanced around the room and eyed the sliding glass door, but then I realized I would never get past Rex and Ruger without them barking and alerting Mama. I didn't have enough strength to run far, either.

My legs shook as I thought through my possible escapes, but every one of them ended with Mama catching up with me. Weak and exhausted, I crawled back into bed. I was trapped.

Bright sunlight filtered in the bedroom, and I tossed the covers off me with a new energy. This time when I tried the door knob, it opened. I took a few tentative steps outside Mama's bedroom and into the kitchen. I stopped when I realized Mama was in her chair.

"Make yourself something to eat, Lacey."

"How long, Mama?" My voice was raspy and my throat sore.

"Four days," she replied. She'd understood exactly what my question meant.

I gasped. I'd been in a drug-induced stupor for four days? *Oh my God! Oh my God!* I needed to call Susan, but I couldn't with Mama around.

"Don't even think about making a phone call or leaving this house. You can sleep in your room again, but I've taken your phone away."

"Why? Why did you do this? Has Walker called me?"

"No, Walker hasn't called and neither has anyone else. No one is looking for you so don't get any silly ideas in your head. Go eat and then go downstairs. I have to wash your stench off my bedding. If I were you, I would use this next week to spend time with God and rid yourself of your nasty demons once and for all."

"A week? I can't leave for another week? Mama, you can't do that to me. I'm your daughter, not a prisoner, and I'm not demon-possessed! You're fucking crazy!"

She jumped out of her chair, bolted toward me, and pushed me back into her bedroom. I slammed into her bed, unable to recover before the door closed and the lock clicked behind her.

IT TOOK me three more days to earn the door being opened again. I drank water from the bathroom sink and didn't touch any food Mama brought in. I considered attacking her when she opened the door, but she was too strong for me to overpower. Which meant I was going to have to keep my damn mouth closed and play along until an opportunity presented itself.

This time, when I walked out of her bedroom and she told me to make myself something to eat, I didn't argue. I searched the fridge for unopened items. She couldn't have tampered with them if they weren't open. The calendar on the refrigerator door read November 27. I clenched my jaw to avoid the tears. It had been seven days since I was supposed to visit Walker.

I turned away, sat at the table, and stuffed myself until my stomach hurt.

For the next two days, I did everything she told me to. I didn't argue or talk unless I was asked a question. I stayed downstairs except to get food. My strength returned as I began eating regularly again.

I'd just made it to the top of the stairs one afternoon when I heard Mama and Patsy talking. I searched around, but the living room and kitchen were empty. The voices trailed down the hall from their bedroom.

"I get it, Lynn, but she's gonna figure it out at some point."

"I do hear from God. There isn't anything to figure out," Mama snapped.

"Yes, you do, but you also have Krissy and me spy on Lacey so you know what's going on. I was the one who saw her and Walker at the mall. God didn't tell you about it, I did, as well as numerous other times."

"What's your point, Patsy?"

I'd heard enough. I ignored my grumbling stomach and eased back down the stairs.

I closed the door to my bedroom and sunk to the floor. Mama hadn't heard from God about Walker at all. It was Patsy. Patsy spied for her? What the hell! I thought about the times I'd gotten in trouble and couldn't figure out how Mama had found out. She'd convinced everyone that God told her, but God didn't speak to her at all.

As I pieced the puzzle together, I realized there was no way I could tell Mama I'd overheard her and Patsy's conversation. If I wanted out of this house, I was going to have to play it cool.

I stayed in my room for the rest of the night.

T he next day I went upstairs and sat on the couch next to Mama.

"Hi, Mama."

"Hi, Lacey," she said and put her book down.

"I wanted to ask you to forgive me for lying and going behind your back. The last few weeks have shown me you're right. I'm not sure why I thought I could have a healthy relationship with Walker when I'm so messed up. I've spent a lot of time praying and I feel like I didn't love him at all. It wasn't me. It was like I was just walking around in a daze. I didn't have control over anything I did! You were right, I was possessed. I woke up this morning and everything was different. I'm different," I said intently.

Mama shifted in her chair as she leaned forward and stared me right in the eyes.

"Patsy, get in here and help me!"

"Mama, I mean it, I'm not joking. All, this time we've been praying for my deliverance, it finally happened. Look at me! Look me right in the eyes and tell me you don't see the difference!" I leaned toward her and stared back at her.

"I'm different," I whispered. "You saved me, Mama, and I love you. I'm free."

Patsy rounded the corner as I finished. Mama didn't move as we continued to stare at each other.

"Patsy, Lacey's saying she's delivered and the time here in the house did it. We broke her will and the demons left her. Look at her. Does she look different to you?"

I shifted and turned toward Patsy, allowing her to stare at me for herself.

"She does look different, Lynn. There's no hate in her eyes, either. I think it's finally over. I really do!" Patsy said as she clapped her hands and shouted a loud praise to God. Mama and I joined in right behind her.

"Victory to Jesus! Victory to Jesus!" Mama yelled. "My baby has been set free!"

I grabbed hold of Mama and hugged her with everything I had inside me. She pulled me into her lap and rocked me like I was two years old again. We laughed and cried together while Patsy grabbed us all tissues.

Patsy cooked an excellent dinner and we discussed God's grace and goodness while we ate. I wanted to cherish the moment. It was almost like a truth had finally settled inside me. I viewed everything differently, I didn't feel the same, and Mama and Patsy recognized it too.

As the sun set and we cleaned the kitchen together, Mama leaned back in her chair and smiled.

I SPENT the majority of time with Mama after that, and instead of migrating to my bedroom I stayed in the living room, only leaving if she took a nap. If she read a book in her recliner, I read a book on the couch. I cooked our meals, cleaned the kitchen, washed all our laundry, and cleaned the bathrooms. Mama didn't have to ask for anything. I sang softly and smiled often.

Every word she spoke I welcomed with open arms. When she asked how I was doing, I told her. I didn't shut her out or make excuses for my previous years of behavior. I was humble and ready to create a new life for myself, doting on everything Mama said.

I cooked her favorite chicken casserole for dinner and lit a prayer candle while we ate. Patsy talked about her day while Mama and I listened. Not only was I feeling better, but Mama had remained in a good mood. She smiled and laughed as Patsy told the story of her pet snake peeing on the young man in her class who was a troublemaker. Dinnertime had evolved into a time of sharing, listening, and laughing.

Mama finished her dinner and put her fork down. She glanced at me and smiled.

"What? Do I have food on my face?" I asked and giggled.

"No, silly goose. It's finally done. It's over, I can tell. I've observed you all week and you're free, Lacey. You can call work tomorrow and tell them your pneumonia is gone and you can return."

"I still have a job?" I squeaked.

"Yes, I just told them you were sick. Which was true, but they didn't need to find out the extent of your illness. I guess we just had to break you down enough to get those filthy demons out of you."

"Thank you, Mama. Thank you for saving my job, but more than that, thank you for not giving up on me. I love you." I scooted my chair back, walked around the kitchen table, and hugged her.

A few days later I returned to my job.

4 5

My heart fluttered while I pulled into the mall parking lot, pulling my coat tighter and walking to the back entrance. The weather had turned colder during my time with Mama.

Nausea rolled through my stomach at the thought of walking into work. As far as everyone knew, I'd had pneumonia and that was the story I was sticking with.

I went into the store and waved at the ladies at the customer service counter. They all welcomed me back.

It didn't take long for word to travel as I clocked in and reported for work in the children's department. Several people waved and promised they'd be over to visit on their break. I approached the edge of the children's clothes. Becky waited at the corner of the aisle between the petite and children's department. A warm smile filled her face. I walked straight to her and gave her a big, long hug.

"Hey, kid! It's good to see you," she said as she patted my shoulder.

"It's good to be back."

"Well, I prayed for you when we found out you were sick."

"Thank you, the prayers worked," I smiled. "I better get to the register. I'll catch up with you later."

My department was empty, and I made a beeline for the phone. I entered Walker's home number on the keypad. The phone began to ring, but with each ring going unanswered, my hope disappeared. I would call back in a little while.

My next call was to Emma.

"Where have you been? I called you every day, and Joss and I stopped by three times! Your mom said you were sick and that you'd call soon. She started getting nasty with me on the phone, too. I hadn't realized how scary your mom was. I was so worried. Are you all better?" Emma gushed.

"What? You did?" My voice hitched as the tears filled my eyes. Mama had said no one called me.

"I'm okay, but I need your help. Can you meet me tonight after work?"

"Yes, of course. Something bad happened, didn't it? Oh God, Lacey, I'm so sorry."

"It's okay, Emma, I just need help tonight. Can your dad come with you?"

Silence filled the phone for a minute as Emma realized what I'd asked.

"Yes, I'll make sure of it."

Emma and I agreed on a time for them to meet me and I hung up the phone.

I wondered what else Mama had lied to me about over the last eighteen years. Desperation rose inside me. I needed to get in touch with Susan.

I dialed her phone number again, but there was still no answer. Had she tried to call me? Had Walker? Had he been worried, or did he think I'd just not shown up? Gotten cold feet and backed out? We were engaged; he must've realized something was wrong. They had to have known something wasn't right.

For the next few hours I kept myself busy folding clothes and moving sizes around. We reorganized the department every few months, and I'd come back to work just in time for it. I glanced at my watch and realized that my dinner break was in five minutes.

The phone rang and I hurried to the register to answer.

"Children's department, this is Lacey."

"I'm in town for a visit."

"Walker? Oh my God. I'm so glad you called!"

"Are you?"

"Of course, why wouldn't I be?" I asked, confused.

"I'm at the mall, do you have a break coming up?" he asked.

"Yeah, in just a few minutes."

"Okay, I want to see you for a minute. Meet me by the arcade."

I agreed and hung up the phone, thanking God I was here at work when Walker called. He sounded mad, and I didn't blame him, but when I explained what Mama had done, we would be okay. I would see Susan and Garrett again too.

My heart skipped a beat while I hurried to the lunch room, clocked out, and grabbed my purse from my locker. I was finally about to wrap my arms around Walker again. Mama hadn't won after all. Maybe God was looking out for me.

Tears threatened my eyes. I couldn't wait to touch him, to hug and kiss him. He had no idea how much I'd missed him and needed to make things right. Finally, I could explain everything to him.

I hurried out of the store and into the mall. I rounded the corner and as I approached the arcade, I identified his back. He'd filled out from boot camp. He stood lean and strong, his muscles rippling beneath his shirt. The air force had been good to him and I planned on being good to him, too.

"Walker," I said, a bit out of breath from walking fast, but I was too excited to walk at a normal pace.

Walker turned to face me and my smile dropped away. I hadn't paid any attention to who was with him. Walker Farren, my fiancé, was with Brittany, his ex-girlfriend.

I stepped backward. "What's going on?"

"What did you think? That I was going to welcome you with open arms? That everything would be okay when you didn't show up that weekend? You left Mom and Garrett stuck with no one to drive. Aunt Linda had an emergency out of town and Mom can't drive anymore—

you know that. You promised you'd take care of them, but the minute I left, you took off. Thank God Brittany and James brought Mom down. But what was really crazy was when James pulled me aside and told me you kissed him. You have no idea how fucking pissed I was. I could never trust someone who cheated on me, especially with my friend. What the hell, Lacey?"

"What? No! I never—"

"I'm not interested in any more lies. Even after all of that, Mom still tried to call, but you wouldn't even speak to her. She's dying, and you couldn't even find time to talk to her and apologize for the shit you pulled."

I shook my head as Brittany squeezed his arm.

"No, that's not true, you don't understand!"

"I do understand, Lacey. You're not who I thought you were. It's over."

My mouth hung open as Brittany kissed his cheek and flashed her hand with a diamond ring on her ring finger. He thought I'd left him when he needed me the most, but worse than that, he thought I'd come on to his best friend.

Walker and Brittany turned and began to walk away.

"Walker, wait! You don't understand, please let me explain and then if you feel the same way fine, but just listen to me, please. Don't do this!"

He didn't respond. Brittany peered over her shoulder and blew me a kiss. I wanted to wipe that smug grin off her face, but my heart had just been shattered with a sledgehammer and I stood rooted in my place.

They left me standing in a mall full of people, and a piece of me died in that moment. He hadn't let me explain anything. Brittany had waited for an opportunity, and the minute Mama gave it to her, she'd stepped right back into Walker's life.

The sunlight glinted through the front door, and I glanced at Walker as he held it open for Brittany. Our eyes locked for a moment as his shoulders slouched forward. A flicker of sadness slipped across his face as he stepped out of the mall.

Something was wrong. What had happened to him? That wasn't my Walker that had left me standing there.

Tears filled my eyes as I turned away and went back to work. I didn't have the energy to figure it out. I had to focus on taking care of myself first.

46

If anyone had asked, I wasn't really sure what I did the rest of the night. I walked around in more of a fog than when Mama had drugged me, and I couldn't get Walker's angry expression out of my mind.

After everything we'd been through together, he actually thought I'd ditched him and his family. Worse than that, he thought I'd cheated on him. Little did Walker know James had tried to kiss *me*, and how pissed he got when I turned him down.

The announcement that the store was closing came across the intercom system, and I made sure that no customers were left in my department. I counted the money in the register and turned it in as I clocked out.

I welcomed the cold air as I walked outside.

"Lacey!" Emma grabbed me and hugged me. Her father stood behind her.

"Thank you for coming," I said and hugged her back.

"I'm glad I'm not too late. What happened?"

"Let's sit down for a minute. I need to speak to you before we talk to your dad," I said in a hushed tone.

"Okay," Emma said. "Daddy, can you wait in the car for us? We'll be just a few minutes."

He nodded and walked to the car. He was a great dad and a good man. I wasn't sure how I would ever repay him for what I was about to ask.

I took a deep breath as the cold air blew through my coat. "Mama drugged me and kept me locked in the house for ten days, Emma."

Emma covered her mouth as I talked. Tears filled her eyes and she sat there speechless, only able to shake her head.

"I had no idea things had gotten that bad. I'm so sorry." She sniffled and dabbed her eyes.

"At least you tried. You called every day and showed up at the house. I never knew you and Joss came by. Mama never told me." My breath caught in my throat and I struggled to control my emotions. "I thought I was doing well standing up to her, but she was just waiting for me. She's cold and calculating. How the hell do you lock your own kid in the house? How do you drug your own daughter?"

Then I whispered, "It gets worse."

"No, wait, give me a minute," she said, sniffling.

I nodded and waited for her to regain her composure.

"Okay," she said. "Go ahead."

"Walker came to see me."

"That's good, right? Lacey, please tell me that's good."

"No, it wasn't good. He said I tried to sleep with James, his best friend. "

"What? That's the stupidest thing I've ever heard, and how in the world would that happen if you were stuck at your mom's house? What the hell is wrong with him all of the sudden?"

"He was also angry because I didn't show up to visit him that weekend. I practically begged him to let me explain, but he wouldn't listen to anything I tried to say. He's already moved on."

"What do you mean, moved on?"

"He was with Brittany and she was wearing a ring."

"*What?* Are you serious? Oh, honey, he did *not* deserve you. You don't just move on after a few weeks. Nope, it doesn't work that way," she said. "And how in the hell could he have believed a word James said? You would never cheat on him."

"I have no idea, but now he's with Brittany, and he won't let me explain anything."

"Cheating asshole," she muttered.

Her words jarred me.

"He did cheat on me, didn't he?"

"Yes, he did! I realize you're in shock about everything, but he cheated on you. You did *not* cheat on him."

"Emma, something was wrong with Walker. Something happened." My forehead creased in frustration. "I can't think about it right now, though. I have to figure things out. I can't go home and now I can't go to Walker's house like I'd hoped."

We sat in silence for a few minutes and collected our thoughts. Then Emma did what only Emma could've done.

"Lacey, you're in way over your head. Take a step back, breathe, and focus on getting better. You aren't equipped to deal with this on your own, and you need a safe place to heal. You need a break from everything and to find out who you are in all this craziness. Move out, and let's get an apartment together."

Tears spilled over my cheeks and I thanked God for Emma. I swiped at them as I stared into the night, realizing what Emma was saying was true. There was nothing I could do to help Mama anymore, and I'd lost Walker. I had no family left. My heart couldn't hold it all. I was bleeding out right where I sat, and no one suspected a thing—no one except Emma.

"Okay, let's start searching for a place," I smiled sheepishly.

"Daddy and I will go with you tonight. We'll help you move, whatever you need. Mom and Daddy will want you to stay with us while we look for our own place, and you know you want to see Emee every day too," she said, holding up her M&M keychain.

I couldn't help but smile. She'd bought that keychain our sophomore year and had referred to it as Emee ever since.

"Okay. It would be nice to live in our own place, even if it is with your big-ass Elvis clock hanging in the living room."

Emma laughed. "You bought it for me, so don't start gripin' about it. You're gonna be okay. You've got support and people who love you."

"I know. Do you think your dad will be okay going with us?"

"He's gonna be hoppin' mad when we tell him what happened. You realize he might call the cops on her."

"No! No, please, he can't. I just want to get out in one piece tonight."

"Honey, she drugged you and held you captive for weeks. She broke the law."

"I know, but I can't take any more. I can't." I brushed away the tears as they fell.

"Okay, I'll do what I can to talk him out of it. Maybe we shouldn't tell him that part."

"What are we gonna tell him then?"

"Mom and Daddy realize you've had a rough home life. I don't think they'll ask too many questions, at least for a while."

"Well, he'll find out more tonight if Mama gets all crazy. All I need to do is grab my clothes and a few things out the bathroom. Mama sold my furniture so I'll need to shop for more when we get an apartment."

"I'm sorry, she did what?" Emma gasped.

"She sold my bedroom furniture when she thought I'd stayed at Joss's house too many days in a row."

"Who does stuff like that?"

"I don't know. I guess Mama does."

"Let's go." She stood up and waited for me to grab my purse. "I'll talk to Daddy, just follow my lead."

We walked through the parking lot and I was met by a burst of warm air from the car as I eagerly crawled into the backseat.

"I'm sorry we asked you to wait, Daddy," Emma began.

He turned in his seat and faced me. His face seemed grim, and his salt-and-pepper hair added to the grave look on his face.

"Are you okay?" he asked.

I nodded yes. "I need some help, though."

He turned back to Emma. "What's going on?" Jim was a lot of fun, but when he used the Dad voice, everyone listened.

"Daddy, Lacey can't go home. Her mom hurt her and she needs a place to stay. I was hoping you would go with us to get her clothes and a few things. We're gonna start looking for an apartment together so we won't stay at the house long, but right now we need your help. I won't let Lacey go back into her house alone."

Jim sat quietly for a minute as he processed this information.

"Is your mother home, Lacey?" he asked as his forehead wrinkled.

"Yes . . . I think so, anyway. She has no idea that I'm with you and Emma right now."

"Well, she will in a few minutes," he said and started the car. "Let's go get your things then. You'll stay with us and I'll help you girls find an apartment. We'll start looking on Monday."

"Thank you," I whispered.

Even though Jim and Emma were with me, I was scared to death. I was daring to go up against Mama one more time and I didn't know if I was going to survive. Before, I'd had Walker and Susan, but they weren't there anymore. I'd lost the only family I had, and now I was about to lose my biological one, too.

I hadn't even started to process what had happened with Walker or anything else I'd gone through over the last several weeks. I wanted to curl up in a ball and hide.

In a matter of months, I had gone from having the best thing in my life to having nothing. All thanks to Mama. If she hadn't drugged me and I'd shown up to meet Walker, James wouldn't have had the opportunity to lie to him, and we'd be planning our wedding. I wouldn't be sitting in the backseat of Jim's car, terrified to go home.

It wasn't home anymore. Nowhere was home. I didn't belong anywhere.

JIM PULLED into the driveway and we were greeted by the dogs. Emma reached down to pet them.

"It's gonna be weird not coming here anymore," she said.

"I know, but I can never come back."

"Let's go, girls," Jim said and motioned us forward.

I walked up the stairs in front of them and went into the house.

"Hi, Mama," I said as I let Emma and Jim in behind me. Jim walked around the other side of me, and his presence filled the room as he stood tall.

"Well hi, Emma. It's so nice to see you. Lacey didn't tell me you were coming over. Did you have car problems, Lacey? Why is Emma's dad with you?"

"No, Mama. I came by to get my things. I'm moving out," I said as my voice cracked with emotion.

"What? Lacey, you can't do that. You don't have anywhere to go."

"She'll stay with us for now," Jim said. "You two go get Lacey's stuff together."

I grabbed a few garbage bags and Emma and I headed downstairs. My heart was heavy as I realized this was the last time I'd be walking down these stairs. Things could've been so different. It didn't have to end this way.

"I'll grab everything from your bathroom," Emma said.

I nodded as I made my way through the family room, gathered what I needed, and continued to my bedroom, throwing my clothes into bags.

The bra and panty set I'd bought before Walker had left caught my eye, and I picked it up. I stood there and stared at it as I thought about the last time I saw him. He'd cheated on me. No matter what happened, that was the bottom line, but the thing that hurt the most was that he didn't have anyone come look for me.

Why hadn't he asked Aunt Linda to come over with social workers and search the house? They would've found me. He knew Mama was crazy. Why had he left me? I tossed my bra and panties in the bag, along with all my pain, as I thought about James and what a sneaky bastard he was. Walker had no clue who had really lied to him.

"Hey," Emma said as she approached me. "I know you feel like you're broken into a million pieces, but we're going to get through this. Just hang on until we get to my house—then you can lose your shit in my room. I'll give you some time to cry, okay?"

"Yeah, okay," I said as I blinked the tears out of my eyes.

"What else do you need?"

I pointed at the few piles on the floor and grabbed my pillow and sleeping bag. I shook them out to make sure I wasn't transporting dangerous cargo, rolled them up, and searched the room again.

"You haven't been here since I've been sleeping on the floor," I said. "I wouldn't have anyone over anyway. Except Walker," I choked on my words as I remembered the only time he'd been here.

"I can see why. If I'd seen this, I would've kidnapped you instead." She frowned as the words left her mouth. "Sorry, I didn't mean to say it like that."

"It's okay." I took one last look around. "That's it. Did you get everything out of my bathroom?"

"I did. There's nothing left."

"Let's go."

Emma walked in front of me and I turned around and said goodbye to my prison one last time as I turned off the light.

Emma and I climbed the steep stairs and reached Jim. Emma handed him some of our bags.

"You lied to me," Mama said. "You're not okay. You've given over to those demons after all!"

"Mama, that's not true. I'm very different, but it was because of what you did. If you don't like what's happening right now, then you should've done something about it a long time ago. You should've gotten help, Mama. You're sick. Our family isn't healthy. We're extremely fucked up. It's not okay to hit people and tell them they're possessed just because you don't want them to leave you. I stayed to try and help you, but you weren't interested. My biggest mistake? I should've left you a long time ago, but it's hard when you love someone so much."

"Don't you walk out that door, Lacey! You won't get to come crawling back when everything falls apart."

"It already has, Mama. I don't have anything else left to lose. I love you, but you won't ever hurt me again. Do us all a favor and get some help."

I walked out of the house and down the stairs for the last time. Her screams echoed through the house and out the door. I heard her call me a bitch as Jim helped me load my stuff into the trunk. I bit my lip to stop the tears. I was tired of crying. I just wanted to walk away.

"Goodbye, Mama," I whispered as I slipped into the backseat and Jim backed the car out of the driveway. Mama stood on the porch, still screaming. I'm sure the neighbors were getting a helluva show tonight.

47

J im helped us unload the car when we got to Emma's house. I said hi to Emma's mom and we headed to Emma's room. I stacked my stuff in the corner so we wouldn't trip over it.

"I'm glad your dad was there tonight. Thank you so much . . . for everything."

"Well, just don't go back. Nothing she could say or do will ever make up for what she did. Not only did she hold you captive, she broke you and Walker up. He would've never gone back to Brittany if your mom had just stayed out of it."

"If that's supposed to help me feel better, it's not."

"I'm sorry. He's still a cheating jerk, though. But I'm going to give you some space like I promised. You can hang out here by yourself or join us for a movie. It's up to you. No pressure—you do what you need to do."

"Okay." I said, and she closed the door behind her.

Burying my head in my hands, I sat on the floor with my bags of clothes. I would never be the same after losing Walker. I would never kiss him again or have a water fight when we washed the dishes. I hadn't been able to say goodbye to Susan or Garrett, either. As fast as

I'd gained a family that I loved more than my own, I'd lost them. How would I ever get over that?

My mind replayed the breakup and Brittany's smirk. I'd agreed to marry him, but he had tossed it away within a few weeks and proposed to her. They deserved each other.

Either I'd meant nothing to him, or Walker had broken inside just like me. Maybe leaving his mom was too much for him to take. I wasn't sure, and now I would never have the chance to ask him.

He should've sent someone over to my house, called the police, or *something*, but he didn't. He'd left me trapped and held against my will. He'd left me in every way possible, but I still loved him.

I cried over losing Walker and I cried over losing his family. I cried about Mama locking me up and hating me so much she would hurt me the way she did. I cried because no one came for me and I cried because I stayed as long as I did.

I cried until I couldn't cry any more.

TIME PASSED and I buried myself in work and school to make up for the weeks I'd missed thanks to Mama. I'd lost my editorial column at school, but I didn't have it in me to write anymore anyway. I went through the days with a smile plastered on my face, but I was empty and broken.

Jim had helped Emma and I find a good apartment close to campus. We were scheduled to move this weekend. I couldn't wait to have my own room again. I loved Emma, but I needed some space to crawl into bed and cry all day if I needed too. She'd tried to give me space to grieve, but being in a house full of people made it difficult.

On the days I couldn't take anymore, I drove out to Walker's. His car sat in the driveway, unmoved. I never stopped by or called Susan and Garrett again. I was afraid someone might spot me, but it didn't keep me from going back. Unfortunately, I hadn't figured out how to hurt any less than a few weeks ago. I didn't think it was possible to heal this betrayal after I'd given Walker every part of me, and I went back and forth from loving him to hating him for going back to Brittany.

In the end, though, it didn't matter. He'd moved on without me.

Saturday arrived and once again I packed my things in a car. Emma and I'd gathered some furniture for our new place and stored it in the garage. I owned a bed and dresser again; they were both snow white. Maybe I was attempting a fresh start. I didn't really care; I was just trying to get through the days.

I swore under my breath as we moved the furniture up two flights of stairs and into our new apartment. We'd agreed we would feel safer on the top floor. I regretted our decision by the third trip.

Jim and a few of his friends helped us move the heavy stuff. After we'd set a few things up, we ordered pizza and fed everyone. We sat at the table and kitchen counter of our new apartment, exhausted but relieved it was over.

Emma stared at me as I ate my pizza.

"What?" I asked.

"I was just curious what you were thinking."

"That I don't ever want to move again," I said, laughing.

"I won't disagree with you there," she said and raised her Diet Coke.

We finished eating and Jim hugged us goodbye, making us promise that we'd call him if we needed anything. Emma closed the door behind everyone and locked it.

"Well, here's to our first night in our new apartment. I'm excited."

"Me too. And thank you for everything," I said. "You're pretty awesome."

"I don't feel awesome. I let you down. I wasn't there when you needed me the most."

"Let it go—neither was Walker, and we were engaged. It's over. You've been here helping me get my shit together."

"Is it working? Am I helping at all?"

"Yeah, you are."

I stood and stretched. My muscles screamed as I tossed the paper plates into our new trash can.

"I'm gonna hit the shower and crash out," I said.

"Wait, I have something else for the apartment," Emma said as she raced out of the kitchen and into her bedroom.

"Okay, come into the living room," she yelled.

I walked into our living room and Emma smiled from ear to ear. She held a framed collage of pictures that included our times at high school and more recent ones too.

"I love it," I said, smiling. "It's perfect."

I hugged Emma and then went to my new bedroom and closed the door behind me. Emma and I agreed I'd take the larger bedroom with the bathroom and pay a little more rent than she did. She thought I'd more than earned my space and privacy. She recognized I needed time to heal.

I turned on the shower and filled up the tiny bathroom with steam. I hurt everywhere, and I looked forward to my shower and a new bed.

Half an hour later, I crawled into my own bed, turned the lamp off, and fell asleep.

4 8

I woke to Emma singing Elvis and making breakfast.

"Good morning!"

"Morning," I said and grabbed a cup of coffee. "You're seriously chipper for so early in the morning."

"I know, I can't help it," she said and smiled as she flipped a piece of French toast over.

"Your French toast kicks ass," I said as I sipped my steaming-hot coffee.

I settled in at the table and grabbed the Sunday newspaper. Emma flew out of the kitchen and placed my plate right on top of the paper.

"Hey, what—I was going to read that."

"Oh, sorry," she said as she turned back to the stove.

I stared at her as I finally woke up enough and realized that her energy wasn't from the excitement. She was nervous, and when Emma got nervous she got flighty. She would flit around the house and clean, bake, or whatever she needed to do to calm down.

"Emma, what's going on?" I asked between bites.

"Nothing, I just wanted to make breakfast for us, is all. Is it good? Do you want some more?"

"I'm good, thank you."

I held up my plate and grabbed the paper before she could take it away. There was something she didn't want me to see, which meant that I needed to see it.

Shaking the pages open, I scanned for anything that might be of interest. I had no idea what she was freaking out over.

Then I turned the page.

How any paper could have weddings and obituaries listed on the same page was beyond me, but there I was, greeted by both. My breath shot out of me like someone had punched me in the stomach. In the upper left-hand corner was a picture announcing Walker and Brittany's marriage. I scanned the announcement and read that they'd gotten married the weekend before Emma and I had moved.

My eyes continued down the page. On the bottom, in the opposite corner, was Susan's obituary and funeral announcement.

"Nooo! Oh my God!" I cried out, instantly breaking into tears.

"Oh, honey, I'm so sorry."

"When?" I asked, handing her the paper to read.

Emma opened the paper back up.

"A few days ago. I'm so sorry."

"When's the funeral?"

"Today," she whispered.

"What time and where?"

"Lacey, you can't go! Walker and Brittany will be there too. You can't put yourself through that."

"When and where, Emma?" I stood up from the kitchen table.

"It's at three o'clock today at the Westside Church," she said and folded the paper up nicely. She had the foresight to realize I would want to keep it.

I glanced at my watch. I had enough time. I grabbed the paper off the kitchen counter and ran to my bedroom. I wasn't going to miss Susan's funeral too.

THE CHURCH WAS PACKED with cars. A lot of people loved Susan, including me. I hoped she now knew that I hadn't left her alone, that I'd wanted to be a part of her life. She'd been the closest thing I'd had to a real mom, and I would forever love her for it. She'd given me the strength to stand up to Mama and follow my heart. I just wish it had turned out differently.

I wore a black dress and borrowed one of Emma's mom's hats, which had a veil that hid my face. My intentions weren't to cause any problems, I just wanted to attend the funeral.

The front door opened, and someone slipped out as I entered the church. I stood toward the back and waited to find out where Walker and Brittany were before I chose my seat. I realized they would sit at the front of the church, but I couldn't take a chance of being spotted before they were settled.

My eyes scanned the group for any familiar faces, and I finally located Garrett. He sat on the second pew alone, looking at the floor. My chest ached with the urge to grab him and hug him. I needed him to know that I hadn't left him and I hadn't broken my promises to him or to his mom.

I stepped forward, determined I was going to speak to him, when Walker and Brittany entered through a side door. My feet rooted themselves to the floor. Walker seemed different. I'd never seen him in a suit before, but that wasn't it.

His jaw clenched and unclenched as he sat next to Brittany. She snuggled up to him, but he didn't put his arm around her. He stared straight ahead and didn't speak to anyone. I couldn't blame him; he'd just lost his mother.

I chose a seat toward the back and hoped I'd be able to grab Garrett after the funeral.

The service was beautiful. A picture of Susan was displayed at the front of the church and her casket was beside it. Aunt Linda spoke for a few minutes and then Walker's father stepped up to the podium. I'd never met him before. I frowned and wondered why, after years of not spending time with his sons, he would come to Susan's funeral.

Then I realized he was most likely here for Garrett. He was still his legal parent, regardless of their actual relationship.

He spoke fondly of Susan and their years together. I wouldn't have expected anything less. Susan had a heart of gold, even when she was sick. Anyone who said differently needed their head examined. She had opened her arms and life to me and had taken me in.

A few other people I didn't recognize took the podium. Music played as everyone lined up to say goodbye to Susan. Walker and Brittany stood next to the casket, which meant I wasn't going to make it. I wasn't going to get to see her one last time before they lowered her into the ground.

As people said their final words, I sat quietly in my pew. Garrett still sat in his seat, but I still couldn't reach him. I just wanted everyone to leave.

I wasn't sure if God heard me or if I'd finally sat there long enough for everyone to clear out. But it looked like I had my chance. As I hurried down the aisle, I prayed no one would catch me. I stopped short when I reached the coffin.

I gasped. Susan's lifeless body lay in the coffin and she was so thin and pale. She'd lost more weight before she died.

"I'm so sorry I wasn't there. I love you," I whispered.

"Lacey?"

I froze. Hadn't I waited long enough to not get caught? I turned slowly, afraid to see who'd called my name. Relief flooded me as Garrett stood in front of me.

"Garrett," I whispered. "Please don't tell Walker and Brittany I'm here. I just wanted to see you and say goodbye to Susan. I'm sorry. I'll go now."

"No, wait. Don't go yet," he said. He stuffed his hands in his pockets as his eyes pleaded with me.

"What? Are you sure?" I asked, unable to hide the surprise in my voice.

"Yeah, I want to talk to you."

"Okay, but we need to go somewhere we won't be spotted. I'm not here to cause trouble."

He nodded and followed me out the front door of the church and to my car. I took off my hat as I unlocked the doors and we slipped into my car. I turned it on to provide some heat as we talked.

"Will anyone be looking for you, Garrett?"

"No, they're busy in the kitchen. I don't understand why they have food at a funeral."

"Me either, buddy." I paused for a moment. "I—I'm so sorry. I'm sorry for everything. I'm sorry for not being there for you, I'm sorry I broke my promise to Walker, and I'm sorry I let your mom down."

"What happened? Why didn't you come back?" He turned away and stared out the window. I realized he was trying not to cry in front of me, so I looked away and gave him a moment.

"I *was* coming back. I was packed and ready to go with you to Texas. I was supposed to drive, remember?"

"Yeah, which is why it was so weird when you didn't show up. Mom got really upset and called Brittany to drive us down there, and James came too. She wanted to visit Walker and didn't care who drove. She realized her time was short."

"My mom stopped me from going. I can't tell you any more, but I was on my way, and I had no intention of leaving you or Walker. I was going to marry him and you were going to be my little brother. You were the family I'd always wanted. Please, you have to believe me."

"You've never lied to me before, so I think I believe you. I tried to call, but your phone line was busy. Since we couldn't get in touch with you, Mom had me call Aunt Linda's hotel in Missouri, and then she called the cops. Lacey, did you know they showed up at your house?"

"What?" My eyes widened as shock and nausea rolled in my stomach. Help had arrived, and I had no idea.

"Yeah. They said your mom let them in and you were sleeping. They saw you and said everything was fine."

"It wasn't fine, Garrett," I hiccupped. "Not even close. Mama never said anything, either." I stopped myself before I said too much to him. She most likely hid the information from me so I wouldn't think I could escape.

"After everything with the police, we thought you just didn't show up. But it didn't seem like you, and I didn't know what to think."

"I wouldn't have known what to think either, Garrett. Thank you. Thank you for trying."

"Yeah, Mom didn't give up, either. Even though she was in the hospital, she asked me to try and call you one more time, but your mom said you weren't home. She realized Brittany was getting her nasty-ass claws back into Walker. She was upset you didn't show, but she didn't want Brittany back in Walker's life. He's different when she's around, Lacey, and I don't mean in a good way."

I nodded, not sure what to say. At least it explained the difference I noticed in Walker during the service, but I didn't want to discuss it with Garrett. He had enough on his mind.

"I heard your dad talk up there," I said.

"Yeah, he's in town for a little while. He's trying to patch things up with Walker and me."

"Are you okay with that?"

"I don't have much of a choice—I'm only thirteen. I live where the court tells me to live."

"Wait? Are you moving?"

"Yeah, I think so. I think they said I'll leave in a few days and move to Missouri."

"I thought you were going to stay with Linda!" I gasped.

"I can't, Dad said no."

"Shit! You're moving?"

He nodded.

"Can't someone do something? I mean, why make you move on top of everything else?" I asked.

"He's my dad. I don't have a choice," Garrett said and shrugged his shoulders.

It was tearing Garrett apart, and I couldn't do anything to stop it. I grabbed my purse and wrote down my new phone number and mailing address.

"You better stay in touch, Garrett. I mean it," I said, folding the paper and placing it in his hand. "I get that this is weird, but you're like my little brother and I love you. I miss you really bad." I couldn't stop the tears anymore.

"Yeah, I might like you a lot too," he said. "I need to go before someone starts looking for me. I'm glad you came. I'm glad Walker met you, because whether he knows it yet or not, you're the best thing that's ever happened to him. He was a good guy when you were with him. You made us all better people."

I squeezed his hand as he opened the car door and glanced at me before he closed it.

He seemed taller as he walked away from me for the last time.

My body doubled over in my seat while I cried. I was grateful for the time Garrett and I had together, but hearing that he was leaving the state made me feel helpless and alone. I guess, in the back of my mind, I'd hoped I would somehow still get to see him, but that had changed. We'd just said our last goodbyes.

I sat in my car for another hour before I could see through the tears well enough to drive home.

EMMA WAS SITTING on the couch when I walked through the front door. I kicked my heels off in the corner and joined her on the sofa.

"I won't ask how it was," she said softly.

"I talked to Garrett and I said goodbye to Susan." My voice cracked as I told her about Garrett finding me at Susan's coffin and how we'd snuck out to my car and talked. She held my hand as I told her about the funeral and seeing Walker and Brittany together, and how my heart broke when I realized how different Walker was with her, and how Garrett had confirmed it. She listened until I no longer had anything else to say.

She hugged me and reminded me that she was there for me no matter what.

I went to my room, changed my clothes, and cried myself to sleep.

49

onths came and went and before I realized it: spring was here. The trees bloomed with bright pink-and-white blossoms and the South had come back to life, but I hadn't. They say not to make any new decisions when you're emotional, but I'd lost too much too fast and I needed something back.

I'd skipped my last class of the day and was driving toward my old house. Emma would be pissed if she found out, but I missed Mama. It sounded crazy, but she was my Mama, and you don't just walk away from a parent and remain whole. Maybe we could try again.

I reached the top of the hill above Mama's house and pulled over. Being there made me remember what she'd done, the decisions she'd made to break up Walker and me, the lies, the abuse.

What was I doing? Was I hurting so much that I was willing to return to the abusive relationship that had almost destroyed me?

The leaves rustled, and I turned my radio off and listened. I thought Mama was in the window, but I couldn't tell for sure. A heavy sigh escaped, and I leaned my head back. I'd made a mistake. I was better off without her, no matter how much it hurt. It hurt worse being in her life than it did being out of it.

I started my car again and drove down the hill, but instead of turning right to go to Mama's, I turned left and drove away, glancing up to see the house grow smaller and smaller in my rearview mirror.

It was Emma's late day of classes, and I arrived at the apartment before her, which gave me some time alone. I went into my bedroom, closed the door in case she came home early, and reached under my bed, pulling out a Victoria's Secret box. I opened the lid and rifled through the contents. The box held Susan's obituary, Walker's marriage announcement, and pictures of Walker and me together. The picture of him on his knee proposing was on the top. The shock had just registered on my face right before the photo was taken. I remembered every detail of that night. It was painted on my heart in vivid colors.

Each memory imprinted on my heart as I stared at the pictures. I held them to my chest as I dug a little further into the box, reaching for a sealed envelope and pulling it out. I replaced everything else except the letter.

I'd received it earlier that week, but I hadn't opened it, afraid of what the letter might say. I was scared I would have another heart-break in my life, and I couldn't deal with any more bad news. The envelope peeled opened easily, and I carefully pulled out a white piece of paper. The University of Oregon logo was at the top of the page. I paused and held my breath as I unfolded the rest of the letter.

Dear Lacey Beaumont:

WE ARE happy to extend you a full scholarship to the University of Oregon. We welcome you to Oregon and our university as you study communications.

There was no need to read the rest. I'd done it. I'd reapplied in January and had been accepted with a full scholarship beginning in the fall and this time, I was going. Mama had said no the first time, but I wasn't asking anyone's permission anymore. There was more than enough in my savings account to make the trip and survive until I found work on campus.

It was time to start over. It was time to follow my heart to where I'd always wanted to go: Oregon.

I pushed the box under my bed and laid the letter on my nightstand. I would tell Emma when she got home. We'd still have the summer together, and she'd have plenty of time to find another roommate. I wished she'd go with me, but it was my path to follow. Emma's path was here in Arkansas, becoming a nurse and being close to her family. I didn't have anything or anyone tying me down.

No matter how hard I tried, I couldn't heal while the memories and pain still suffocated me. Everywhere I looked, something reminded me of Walker or the weeks of hell spent with Mama. Emma was doing her best and Joss remained supportive too, but it wasn't enough. I couldn't keep treading water. I needed to leave—it was my turn to find out who I was and live my life.

I picked up the letter again, and hope rose inside me. I was going to Oregon.

THANK you so much for reading TORN! This story ends with Lacey and Walker no longer together, but it's not over yet. Continue Lacey's journey in Captured and Freed available in the Torn Series boxset. Universal link: https://readerlinks.com/l/1336177 or Click here!

TURN the page and enjoy a sneak peek of Captured, Book 2 in The Torn Series Available Now.

Enjoy giveaways, the inside scoop about J.A. Owenby, and never miss a new release again!

Sign up today at https://www.authorjaowenby.com/newsletter.

50

CAPTURED, BOOK 2 SNEAK PEEK

My blood-curdling scream ripped through the night and jolted me from my sleep.

"—Lacey! Lacey! It's me, Emma."

"Wh-what?" I asked, peering into the darkness. As my eyes adjusted, I could see Emma standing in the doorway.

"It's okay, you're safe," she said as she turned on the light and approached me.

Tossing my covers off, I sat up in bed, wrapping my arms around myself in an effort to still the violent tremors that traveled through my body. Sweat trickled down my spine as a wave of nausea washed over me. I hopped out of bed and made it to my tiny bathroom in time for my stomach to empty its contents from the night before.

"Oh gosh, are you okay?" Emma asked.

"Yeah." I flushed the toilet and splashed my face with cold water. "Dammit!" I said, slapping my hand down on the bathroom sink. "Please tell me that did not just happen."

"I think it did happen."

Emma joined me in the bathroom, her house shoes flopping with each step she took. She lowered the toilet seat and sat down. Concern spread across her face.

I tucked a piece of long, blond hair behind my ear and sat on the side of the white bathtub.

"I'm so sorry. I—"

"—Don't apologize. I'm just worried about you."

My chest filled with a deep breath, and I tried to focus on the way the tile felt under my bare feet, the warmth of the night air on my skin, the hardness of the tub, anything to bring me back from that horrible place.

"The dream—I was trapped at Mama's." My voice barely hovered above a whisper. "But this time, she locked me underneath the house. There was only dirt and spiders. . ."

"Jiminy Christmas," Emma replied softly.

"Sorry I scared you. I didn't even know it was me screaming until I woke up and you were in my bedroom."

"Well, I know you're leaving tomorrow for Oregon, but I think you should reconsider your career choice."

"What do you mean?"

"Personally, I think you missed your calling. Those scream queens in the movies have nothing on you," she said.

A smile eased across my face. "You would know, you love those stupid movies," I said and stood up.

My body had calmed down some and I wasn't shaking uncontrollably anymore. Exhausted, I made my way back to my bed. I glanced at the clock; it blared 3:00 A.M.

"Ugh," I said and plunked down on my bed. "I'm tired but wide awake now."

"Yup, me too, so scoot your skinny butt over. We're having a slumber party."

I laughed and made room next to me for Emma.

A heavy sigh escaped me as I realized this was my last morning not sharing a room with someone. Emma and I had decorated it together, and I'd grown fond of it. I'd picked out a black-and-pink bedspread, which provided some much-needed contrast to my all-white furniture and the white apartment walls. I would leave my furniture with Emma, though; it wouldn't fit in my dorm room.

"I'm excited and scared at the same time about leaving tomorrow," I said. "What if I have nightmares like this while I'm there?" A long thread hanging off my bedsheet gained my attention and I pulled at it.

"Well, this is the only major one you've had lately. I think you're worried about the move—it's a lot to handle, but you've come so far in the last six months."

"Yeah, you're probably right. The nightmare just really scared me is all."

"Try not to think about it anymore. You have so many good things to look forward to. This time tomorrow, you'll be in Eugene! And I'm so excited to hear what your new college is like."

Turning, I looked at Emma. I knew she didn't want me to leave. She would be my only reason to stay, but it wasn't enough—we both knew it. The last few months had been torture.

We hung out and laughed about all the silly things we'd done while living together. We talked about what we would miss, and we made plans to visit each other a few times a year. I wanted her to visit me on campus and see what life was like outside of Arkansas, and I agreed to visit her the moment my schedule allowed me to.

As the first rays of sunshine spilled through my bedroom curtains, we made coffee, moved out onto the deck, and watched my last sunrise in Hot Springs, Arkansas.

I CHECKED my watch and glanced around the crowded Western Sizzlin'. It was Sunday, and everyone and their mother went to this place to eat after church. This afternoon was no exception. I scanned the entryway and the crowded front section of the restaurant for Emma's parents while she parked the car, which was loaded up with my luggage. I bit my lip as tears threatened my eyes at the thought of saying goodbye to them.

As if losing Walker weren't enough, I also hadn't spoken to Mama since the horrible night I moved out. If it hadn't been for Emma and her family, I wouldn't have had the strength to follow through with it.

Jim and Linda had supported me through an awful time in my life, and I loved them like they were my real parents.

When I finally shared everything with them—Mama's abuse, the imaginary demon possession, Walker leaving me, and the weeks I'd spent locked in Mama's house—I thought I'd lose them. I figured I'd come home one afternoon and find all my belongings on the apartment patio. But it never happened. They loved me and supported me while I healed enough to take a step out on my own.

Emma walked through the front door of the restaurant. "There they are," she said and waved at her parents.

I followed her through the crowded restaurant, scanning faces as I walked. Even though I hadn't seen Walker in months, I still looked for him. When you loved someone that deeply, they didn't just disappear overnight. Moving to Oregon would hopefully help me let go and move on.

"Hi!" I said as I hugged Jim and Linda.

"Are you ready?" Linda asked and grinned from ear to ear. "You know we're going to miss you, but this is an excellent step for you." Her manicured red nails flashed as she clapped her hands together. She'd recently colored her hair a soft brown which now matched her eyes.

"I am, and apparently, it's only eighty degrees there right now, too. Can you imagine the end of August in the eighties? Good riddance to the hundred-and-two-degree, muggy weather. And how is it possible I use half a can of Aqua Net and the minute I step outside, all my hard work collapses?" I asked, giggling.

"It sounds like you'll have a few months to settle in before the rain comes," Jim said as he stroked his salt-and-pepper beard.

"I love the rain, so hopefully it won't bother me at all," I replied, scanning the menu.

We focused on choosing our food and resumed our conversation after the waitress took our order. I promised Jim and Linda I'd visit as soon as I could. Emma mentioned planning a trip to Oregon. We chatted while we ate, and the butterflies began to flutter in my stomach the closer we got to leaving for the airport.

The waitress cleared our plates and filled our cups with coffee.

"Here, we wanted to give you something," Jim said as he placed a package on top of the table.

"Aww, you didn't have to get me anything," I said. "You've already done so much. I don't know how I'll ever repay you."

"It's not about repaying anything," Linda said. "It's about family."

I frowned and stared at the large present. It was wrapped in bright-blue paper with a white bow.

"Go on, open it," Emma said as she motioned for me to hurry up.

"Okay," I said and tore the paper open. My mouth dropped as I stared at a brand-new phone and answering machine.

"It's for your dorm room. You can call us anytime to say hello or if you need anything. You're family now, which means you're stuck with us," Linda said, laughing. "I couldn't stand the thought of you thousands of miles away, not being able to call us anytime you wanted to. You've come so far in the last few months. We're so proud of you."

Jim nodded in agreement as Emma leaned over and hugged me.

"I'm not sure what to say," I whispered. "Thank you—this means the world to me." Standing, I hugged Jim and Linda, wiping away the tears that were running down my cheeks.

Part of me didn't ever want to let them go, but I knew it was time. I'd worked hard for this.

"No crying," Linda said as she dabbed her eyes.

"Are you talking to yourself or Lacey?" Jim said, chuckling.

"I'm gonna use the ladies' room before we leave," Emma said as she pushed her chair away from the table and stood up. "Be right back."

As I turned to ask Linda a question, something caught my eye. Emma was talking to someone. When I saw who it was, my hand jerked and I knocked over my coffee cup. I jumped back in my seat and grabbed napkins to mop up the mess.

I searched for Emma again, but she was gone.

So was Walker.

"Are you okay?" Linda asked.

"Yeah, guess I'm just a little nervous about the move," I said and attempted a smile.

Linda and Jim helped me clean up the spilled coffee, my eyes darting nervously around the restaurant. I didn't see him.

Maybe I hadn't really seen him at all. But I knew better, and I'd recognize him anywhere.

"We'd better get going—we still have an hour-long drive to the airport," Emma said as she returned to our table.

Her cheeks were flushed, which confirmed what I'd seen. Walker was here, and I was about to leave and fly two thousand miles away. I'd managed not to run into him for nine months, and the day I was scheduled to leave, there he was.

I nodded, gathered my belongings, and said goodbye to Jim and Linda one last time as we all exited the restaurant and located our cars. Regrouping my thoughts, I tried to focus on the journey in front of me. It was over with Walker, and I was moving on.

"It sucked saying goodbye to your parents," I said, sliding into the passenger seat of Emma's car. "I don't wanna ugly cry all the way to the airport, so it's your job to make me laugh."

"Are you kidding? I'm trying not to cry too. If I do, I'll have to pull over on the side of the road, and you'll miss your plane."

"Oh Lord, let's not. I'm scared, but that doesn't mean I wanna miss my flight."

"Haha, I know, right?" Emma asked. "I'm so proud of you, but this sucks monkey toes. Never in a million years would I have thought my best friend would move so far away. I know you're gonna do great, but I'm gonna miss you so bad. Promise me you'll call me a few times a month. In fact, call me and then I'll call you right back so you don't have to pay for it."

"Emma, I can't."

"You will if it means I won't get to talk to you otherwise! I'm serious—it's not about you, it's about me."

I covered my mouth and tried not to giggle, but it escaped anyway. She glanced at me and giggled as well.

"I'm serious, now. This isn't all about you," Emma said, which made me laugh harder.

"Oh my God, stop!" I said, gasping for air. "I'll call, I promise. Just don't wreck the car."

"Lacey Anne, I swear, no one else makes me giggle over such stupid stuff."

"Same here."

My pulse quickened while I looked out the window and tried to decide if I should say anything about Walker. The painful reminder of him and Brittany at Susan's funeral resurfaced.

"Walker—I saw you talking to him," I whispered.

"Crap! You did? Jeez, he just had to show up when you were almost out the door. I wanted to give him a good pop in the arm."

"What did he say?"

"Do I really need to tell you? I mean, you're leaving. What good will it do?"

"Please, I just need to know."

"He saw me going to the bathroom and said hi," she said. Her grip on the steering wheel had tightened; her knuckles were turning white. There was something she didn't want to tell me.

"What else?"

"Don't make me tell you," Emma pleaded.

"Emma, now," I said firmly.

"He asked about you," she muttered.

"What? I don't think I heard you right."

She sighed and flexed her fingers, allowing the blood flow to return.

"He asked about you. I told him it wasn't okay—he doesn't get to ask about you after what he did."

"Oh, no. You didn't." Exasperation filled my voice. "He had no idea what happened with . . . he never heard the truth."

"I know, and he doesn't just get to saunter up to me and act like nothing happened. He asked if you were there and I told him he'd better stay away from you or I'd crack him upside the head."

I was too upset to laugh, even though the thought of Emma actually hitting Walker was funny.

"Oh my God, you did not say that!" I said.

"Of course I did. Why wouldn't I? He needs it if he's still married to Brittany."

"What?"

"Nothing," Emma said.

"What do you know?" I asked, narrowing my gaze.

Emma tapped her fingernails on the steering wheel.

"Look. I'm leaving, and nothing will make me stay," I said. "Just tell me so I can move on."

"I ran into him about a month ago while I was at the grocery store. He and Brittany were having problems. He asked about you then, but I told him to leave you alone and let you move on."

"Holy shit," I muttered.

"You can't stay here for him. They're still together as far as I know. He's married, you're not, and you're moving away."

"I wish it were that simple," I said.

"Go meet a nice, good-lookin' Oregon boy and move on."

I bit my lip and stared out the window. Walker had asked about me twice in the last month, and I was leaving. Emma and I rode the rest of the way to the airport in silence.

WANT MORE? Continue Lacey's journey in Captured and Freed available in the Torn Series boxset. Universal link: https://readerlinks.com/l/1336177 or Click here!

Edited by Molly McCowan

Cover Art by Book Cover Luv

Second Edition

ISBN-13: 978-1-7321510-8-6

ISBN-10: 1-7321510-8-3

Click here to gain access to previews of J.A. Owenby's novels before they're released and to take part in exclusive giveaways.

❀ Created with Vellum

ACKNOWLEDGMENTS

To my husband, you made this book possible. You are my forever, and I love you muches, and muches, and muches more than that.

To my kids, no matter what, I love you always.

Mom, thank you for sharing your gift. I miss you.

Molly McCowan, my kickass editor, you're stuck with me now. Thank you for your support, encouragement, and all the tears you made me cry as my story and dream came to life. It's been a beautiful thing.

Sheri Kaye Hoff, I couldn't have done it without you. Thank you for believing in me and helping me believe in myself. You have value beyond words, and I'm blessed to have you in my life. Here's to Vegas!

To the real Emma and Joss, you've stayed in my heart no matter where my path led. Thank you for never giving up on me.

To my wonderful and crazy friends who have supported me through all the stages of this book. I love you all: Jeannie and Dale Kemper, Aubrey and Sundance Minear, Jason and Jessica Pavelka, Ed Julian, Gabe Jones, Tina Mattern, Jenny Cornwell, Angie Fowler, Sissy Plummer, and Kara Long.

Xena the Warrior Princess, I know I've driven you a bit crazy at times, but thanks for being such an amazing friend. I'm not sure I could have done it without you making me laugh and pouring wine down my throat.

To the Lake Hamilton High School class of '88, you're awesome! Thank you for the wonderful memories that stayed with me, and for all of your support.

I hate spiders and scorpions. Hate them. Hate . . .

ALSO BY J.A. OWENBY

Bestselling New Adult Romance

The Love & Ruin Series

Love & Ruin

Love & Deception

Love & Redemption

Love & Consequences, a standalone novel

Love & Corruption, a standalone novel

Love & Revelations, a Valentine's Day novella

Love & Seduction, a standalone novel

Love & Vengeance, COMING 2021!

Love & Retaliation, COMING 2021!

Romantic Thrillers

The Wicked Intentions Series

Dark Intentions, Coming January 2021

Fractured Intentions, Coming February 2021

Standalone Novels

Where I'll Find You

Coming of Age

The Torn Series, Inspired by True Events

Fading into Her, a prequel novella

Torn

Captured

Freed

ABOUT THE AUTHOR

J.A. Owenby lives in the beautiful Pacific Northwest with her husband and cat.

She's a published author of six short stories, and she is currently working on her second full-length novel. She also runs her own business as a professional resume writer and interview coach—she helps people find jobs they love.

J.A. is an avid reader of thrillers, romance, new adult, and young adult novels. She loves music, movies, and good wine. And call her crazy, but she loves the rainy Pacific Northwest; she gets her best story ideas while listening to the rain pattering against the windows in front of the fireplace.

You can follow the progress of her upcoming novel on Facebook at Author J.A. Owenby and on Twitter @jaowenby.

Sign up for J.A. Owenby's Newsletter:
BookHip.com/CTZMWZ

Like J.A. Owenby's Facebook:
https://www.facebook.com/JAOwenby

J.A Owenby's One Page At A Time reader group:
https://www.facebook.com/groups/JAOwenby

BOOK PLAYLIST

Parson James: "Stole the Show"
    Halsey: "Hold Me Down," "Drive," "Haunting"
    Ruelle: "Take It All," "Oh My My"
    X Ambassadors: "Renegades," "Unsteady"
    Echosmith: "Cool Kids"
    Banks: "Beggin' for Thread"
    Nick Jonas: "I Want You," "Nothing Would Be Better," "Push"
    Adam Lambert: "Underground"
    Ella Henderson: "Yours," "Ghost"
    Jessie Ware: "Say You Love Me"
    Jason Derulo: "Trade Hearts"
    Mumford & Sons: "Believe"
    Florence + The Machine: "Long & Lost"

Use Spotify? Check out the full playlist here.